Quilt or Innocence

A SOUTHERN QUILTING MYSTERY

Elizabeth Craig

AN OBSIDIAN MYSTERY

OBSIDIAN
Published by New American Library, a division of
Penguin Group (USA) Inc., 375 Hudson Street,
New York, New York 10014, USA
Penguin Group (Canada), 90 Eglinton Avenue East, Suite 700, Toronto,
Ontario M4P 2Y3, Canada (a division of Pearson Penguin Canada Inc.)
Penguin Books Ltd., 80 Strand, London WC2R 0RL, England
Penguin Ireland, 25 St. Stephen's Green, Dublin 2,
Ireland (a division of Penguin Books Ltd.)
Penguin Group (Australia), 250 Camberwell Road, Camberwell, Victoria 3124,
Australia (a division of Pearson Australia Group Pty. Ltd.)
Penguin Books India Pvt. Ltd., 11 Community Centre, Panchsheel Park,
New Delhi - 110 017, India
Penguin Group (NZ), 67 Apollo Drive, Rosedale, Auckland 0632,
New Zealand (a division of Pearson New Zealand Ltd.)
Penguin Books (South Africa) (Pty.) Ltd., 24 Sturdee Avenue,
Rosebank, Johannesburg 2196, South Africa

Penguin Books Ltd., Registered Offices:
80 Strand, London WC2R 0RL, England

First published by Obsidian, an imprint of New American Library,
a division of Penguin Group (USA) Inc.

First Printing, June 2012
10 9 8 7 6 5 4 3 2 1

PUBLISHER'S NOTE
This is a work of fiction. Names, characters, places, and incidents either are the
product of the author's imagination or are used fictitiously, and any resemblance to actual persons, living or dead, business establishments, events, or
locales is entirely coincidental.

The recipes contained in this book are to be followed exactly as written. The
publisher is not responsible for your specific health or allergy needs that may
require medical supervision. The publisher is not responsible for any adverse
reactions to the recipes contained in this book.

The publisher does not have any control over and does not assume any responsibility for author or third-party Web sites or their content.

"Beatrice?" said Posy with a smile. "It's such a pleasure discovering other early-morning walkers. Maybe we can make this a regular date!" She reached down to stroke Noo-noo's head, and the corgi eagerly flopped over for a tummy rub.

The two women chatted as they strolled into the park. Posy's beagle soon interrupted their small talk, though, lunging against her leash and giving an insistent, baying bark. Noo-noo joined in, figuring something must have been wrong even if she couldn't suss out what it was.

Posy frowned as the dog persistently pulled at the leash. She knelt down next to the dog and put a comforting hand on her. "Duchess! What's going on, girl?"

Now the beagle whimpered. Noo-noo's fur stood up on her back and she growled, as if suddenly realizing the source of the beagle's concern.

"Beatrice, there's something lying on the ground over there. Near that group of trees," Posy said in a quiet voice.

Beatrice handed Posy Noo-noo's leash and walked cautiously up to the object, forcing her suddenly weak limbs to move forward. She saw Judith, splayed unnaturally on her back, blood pooling behind her head and eyes staring blindly into the trees.

For Riley, Elizabeth Ruth, and Coleman

ACKNOWLEDGMENTS

My heartfelt thanks to my editor, Sandra Harding, for her expertise and encouragement. To my agent, Ellen Pepus, for her support and advice. To Debby Stone, with thanks for her insights into the wonderful world of quilting. (Any inaccuracies here are my own.) My mother, Beth Spann, for being a talented first reader. My family for their support. And to Coleman, Riley, and Elizabeth Ruth for making life and writing fun.

Chapter 1

"I've come to rescue you," said the wild-looking woman at Beatrice's front door.

Beatrice, a recently retired art museum curator, gaped at the woman, completely flabbergasted. She certainly didn't need rescuing. In fact, she'd just brewed a relaxing cup of herbal tea to celebrate the fact that there were only ten more moving boxes to unpack in her new cottage.

Besides, who'd want to be rescued by this woman, even if rescuing were in order? She looked like she needed rescuing herself . . . with her brightly colored, mismatched clothes and disorganized gray braid hanging to her waist. Beatrice made up her mind to briskly and firmly shut the door and try out the new bolts and chains and the alarm system . . . but then the woman held out her hand.

"I'm Meadow. Your next-door neighbor. Welcome to Dappled Hills!"

Beatrice managed a smile and a handshake. She'd

wondered who lived in the odd converted barn next to her country cottage. Beatrice's daughter, Piper, who lived right down the street, had warned her that her neighbor was a little *different*, and she saw exactly what Piper meant.

Now Meadow clutched her arm and pulled her outside. "Come on, Beatrice. You'll miss it!"

Beatrice pulled back. Wasn't this how kidnappings happened? How could she possibly be abducted in tiny Dappled Hills, North Carolina, when she'd been safe for so many years in Atlanta?

"I'm sorry, Meadow," she said with dignity. (She would *not* be a victim!) "But I'm going to have to insist that I stay at home. I just brewed some chamomile tea and need to put my feet up after all the rigorous unpacking I've accomplished . . ."

But her words were completely wasted on Meadow, and Beatrice found herself being propelled with surprising strength toward the bright red barn on the spacious property next door. And Meadow wasn't letting her slide a word in edgewise.

"We're all practically here," she said inexplicably. "The unpacking is exactly what I'm rescuing you from. And everything is set out. I have tea, too, but it's sweet."

With great relief, Beatrice saw a police car pulling into Meadow's driveway. Well, at least Dappled Hills had a very responsive police unit. She waved her free arm in what she hoped was an alarmed, help-seeking fashion.

A short, balding man climbed out of the patrol car. He had a tired stoop to his shoulders and a stomach that had seen its share of heavy Southern cooking. "Is there a problem here, ma'am?"

Beatrice blinked as Meadow leaned over and gave the policeman a peck on the lips. "No problem, Ramsay. Except remember that I told you the guild is meeting here this afternoon. So don't devour our snacks, please. I put some pretzels in a Baggie for you."

He shook his head wearily. "I was asking if the *other* lady had a problem. Ma'am? Everything all right? Meadow, for pity's sake! Could you let her go for a minute? You've scared her half to death. Is this our new neighbor?"

Beatrice nodded, and the policeman held out his hand. "Ramsay Downey. I'm Dappled Hills' police chief. Welcome to town. My job is to keep the citizens safe . . . from people like my wife, Meadow." He gave Meadow a dour look.

Meadow was so singularly focused on propelling Beatrice inside her house—or barn—that she overlooked his jab. "There's also a sandwich in the fridge for you, Ramsay, besides the pretzels. And I picked some berries today and sugared them—they're in the fridge, too." And again she hurried toward the barn, turning around and gesturing at Beatrice. "Come on!"

Beatrice looked helplessly at the policeman. "It's no use resisting," he said in a resigned voice. "It's how we ended up marrying all those years ago. You might as well just follow her. She's not quite as crazy as she looks," he added kindly. "And you'll learn a lot about quilting."

Beatrice realized she must have seemed completely baffled when he chuckled and said, "She didn't mention the quilting? She's even more scattered than usual, then! The quilting guild is meeting this afternoon and she probably wants to introduce you to everyone— that's all. And maybe give you a kit to complete a block, too, knowing her."

With growing trepidation, Beatrice approached the barn. There was nothing like having your peaceful afternoon hijacked by a quilting nut. And she had no intention of doing any quilting. She knew a lot about the artistic *merits* of quilts, she could appraise one, and she could tell some of the likely history that went into a particular quilt, but she was happily ignorant of the precise methods of constructing them.

And then all her thoughts left her as she entered the light-filled space of the converted barn. She'd thought it would be dark inside, but skylights scattered through the top of the roof and sides of the barn cheerily illuminated the space. What must have previously been a hayloft now looked like a sleeping loft and sitting area. And the high ceiling—Beatrice stopped and tilted her head back. It soared up like a cathedral, with impressive exposed rafters and posts. There were vibrant-colored quilts, mostly with asymmetrical designs, hanging on the walls and the backs of chairs and any other available surface.

"It's beautiful," she breathed.

Meadow's face creased in a smile. "I love it, too." She then shoved a tall glass of what looked like iced tea into Beatrice's hands and continued urging her along. Ramsay had pulled his lunch from the fridge and found his little Baggie of pretzels and disappeared. Now Beatrice saw that there were two women across the big, open room. The kitchen, dining room, and living room were all one big area—but it looked like there was a door that might lead to an attached master suite.

On closer inspection, Beatrice realized the women were twins, although they looked a bit like a before-and-after photo. They were probably in their early thirties, but one of the sisters seemed a lot older. She had a beaky nose and stiff militarylike comportment, and wore a long-sleeved floral dress, her thin hair drawn up in a bun. The other sister wore a pretty floral dress and had a much softer look. Fabric and scissors surrounded them, and baskets beside them were filled with quilting supplies and tools.

The softer one spoke to her, beaming. "It's an amazing house, isn't it? Except it's a barn!"

Her sister frowned. "But with no animals," she said, in the tone of one who demands perfect accuracy.

Meadow put her hands on her generous hips with mock indignation. "No animals, Savannah? What's Boris, then—chopped liver?"

At the sound of his name, a massive creature bounded up from behind the kitchen counter and bolted across the room. It galloped up and Beatrice flinched as it charged right at them. The quilters non-chalantly continued sewing their blocks. The dog jumped onto Meadow, putting its tremendous paws on both her shoulders. Meadow hugged it, crooning to it softly, then gently pushed him back down.

"What breed *is* Boris, exactly?" asked Beatrice.

Meadow said in a considering voice, "Well, Ramsay and I think he might be part Great Dane, part New-foundland, and part corgi."

The minuscule part that was a corgi, thought corgi-owner Beatrice, was clearly cowed by the other genetic components.

Beatrice started as Meadow gave her an impulsive hug. "We're *thrilled* you could quilt with us this after-noon. More tea?" Meadow automatically refilled Bea-trice's glass without waiting for a reply. Although, thought Beatrice with some irritation, she hadn't even taken a sip yet.

Meadow's eyes twinkled at Beatrice from behind her red-framed glasses. "Savannah and I were just saying the other day—Savannah, you remember my saying this, don't you?—that we really needed another mem-ber in the Village Quilters guild."

Savannah gave a jerking nod as she expertly stitched an appliqué with darting movements.

"And the very next thing I know, you've moved in next door, Beatrice! It's divine intervention." Meadow beamed at her again as she absently continued filling the others' glasses with tea . . . even though, thought Beatrice as she squinted across the room, it appeared they'd been drinking water. The other two women didn't make a peep to stop her.

Beatrice cleared her throat. Really, it was too much. Meeting new people in a new town, being expected to suddenly take up quilting . . . it was all a tremendous adjustment. But she had to admit that the people of Dappled Hills were nothing if not friendly.

Meadow chuckled. "Mercy, but you do look confused. Introductions are in order! Good thing we only have a few members here today. Fewer to boggle your brain with. Although it looks like your brain might not be the boggling type. Of course, you already know me—I'm Meadow Downey, your next-door neighbor and new best friend." She bowed at Beatrice, eyes glittering.

The plain woman with the stiff comportment gestured a needle at the pretty woman beside her. "We're the Potter sisters. I'm Savannah and she's Georgia." Savannah continued steadily stitching beautiful needlework with her bony fingers.

"Savannah, Georgia," murmured Beatrice weakly.

"Our mama just adored the city," said Georgia. "It was all moonlight and magnolias to her."

"Mama," repeated Savannah gruffly, and both women's eyes grew misty.

Meadow, apparently accustomed to these emotional displays, pulled tissues from a nearby box and dropped them neatly in the sisters' laps as the doorbell rang. "This'll be Posy Beck," she said. "And she's the final quilter I'm expecting today."

The door opened to reveal a tiny, bespectacled, older woman with wide blue eyes and a gentle smile who greeted the other ladies warmly. She settled on the sofa next to Georgia and pulled strips of cloth from her tote bag. "You're Piper's mama?" she asked with a smile as she pulled on a fluffy cardigan, despite the warmth of the room. Beatrice nodded, and Posy said, "I absolutely love your daughter. She didn't mention you were a quilter. I own Posy's Patchwork Cottage right in the middle of town. I'd love for you to pop by to visit."

Beatrice shifted uneasily. "No, actually. I'm really *not* a quilter, Posy. That is, I worked on a group quilt once about twenty years ago." She winced at memories of stabbing herself with the needle, her crooked stitches, and the huge knots she'd left on the back of the quilt. "I've *researched* quilts. I've set up quilt *exhibits*. I've even appraised some quilts. But actual quilting?" She shook her head.

Meadow snapped her fingers. "That's right! Piper told me you were a museum curator in Atlanta. We've got a Southern folk art expert right here in our midst, ladies! And don't worry. It won't take you *any* time to get into quilting again. It's just like riding a horse. Or a bike," she said with an absentminded frown, as if she knew she was mixing that up somehow. She poured a tall glass of tea for Posy, who smiled fondly at her.

"What I'm actually a *lot* more interested in is what you're all working on," she said.

Georgia beamed at her. "Savannah and I are making

a quilt together since we've already finished our blocks for the bee tomorrow. What do you think?"

Beatrice moved closer. The rich, earthy colors of fall made up the quilt—and she saw it was actually autumn themed . . . with a medallion of apples and pumpkins and black cats appliquéd onto the center of the vibrant plaid background. "Beautiful," she proclaimed, softly. "Absolutely beautiful. It looks like a quilt to curl up in on a cold night. With a mug of hot chocolate."

Savannah's sharp features turned a mottled red at her praise. She continued briskly stitching. "We do work well together. Don't we, Georgia?" she said in a voice that brooked no argument. "Although I usually favor geometric patterns, Georgia had her heart set on doing this one as soon as she saw the pattern. And it was her turn to pick."

Georgia tittered. "We do work well together, despite our different approaches. Poor Savannah is struggling to adjust to living with me—still. And it's been almost a year now since I've invaded her kingdom."

"Georgia is divorced," said Meadow in a stage whisper that Beatrice supposed Meadow thought quiet.

Georgia continued, "Savannah is ultraorganized and I'm an organizational disaster, so our living together has been like *The Odd Couple*. She's got a thread organizer with thread divided by color. Then she has this huge plastic wall unit with drawers of fabric organized by manufacturer or season. And my stuff is pretty much a ragbag of fabrics and threads. I've got blocks and tops and fabrics scattered everywhere. But when we make a quilt, we're in perfect harmony."

"I can tell," said Beatrice, still studying the quilt. Then she glimpsed a notebook at Savannah's feet.

Savannah saw Beatrice looking at the notebook and said, "I'll admit that organization has its advantages. I put together this quilting bag and everyone has copied it. Except for Georgia, of course. She takes a more loosey-goosey approach to quilting supplies." She bobbed her head at Beatrice to pick up (and, Beatrice guessed, admire) the notebook. It *is* very cleverly arranged, thought Beatrice as she flipped through the plastic sleeves. A spot for notions of every kind. Each plastic pouch was attached to the notebook by Velcro so you could just carry the tools you needed. Ingenious. "What are these?" asked Beatrice, holding up a pouch of what looked like pizza cutters.

"A most marvelous invention for quilters: rotary cutters. I don't think I can even remember life without them—I've blocked it all out! It's revolutionized cutting fabric," said Posy. "Beatrice, you just put your ruler where you want to cut and then the rotary cutter slices right through it."

The women settled into small talk about their families and neighbors. There was an air of camaraderie in the room that felt very genuine. This feeling of *belonging* wasn't something that Beatrice had come across very often, aside from her work at the museum. Even there she'd frequently worked alone, just her and the art. She hid a smile as Savannah suddenly dispelled the harmony by hissing, "Georgia! Watch your stitches!"

Georgia frowned ferociously at her appliqué as if to scold it into submission.

Beatrice said, "Posy, your quilt is gorgeous. Of course, I wouldn't expect anything less from a quilt-shop owner." Her quilt was a celestial riot of whimsical suns and moons and stars scattered on an inky background.

Savannah stopped stitching at the mention of the quilt shop. "Posy, tell us what you've found out about the shop. Did Judith back off on raising the rent?" She reached over and rescued a pricey-looking pair of scissors that Georgia had absently picked up, and stowed them safely back beside her.

Posy shook her head, looking down at her quilt. "No, she's planning to go ahead with it. I honestly don't know what I'm going to do. I just never imagined that Judith would try to force me out of the Patchwork Cottage."

Beatrice frowned. "Your landlady? Surely that doesn't make sense. She'd have to find another tenant for the space."

"Miss Judith has *plans*," Meadow said with a sniff. Her indignant tone made Boris growl menacingly at the unknown threat. "She's got some fancy women's-boutique idea in her head, and apparently there's someone interested in the space. Judith is adamant she can get more rent." She snorted.

Georgia's face clouded over. "But she's a quilter, too! Why would she want the Patchwork Cottage to close?

Where would we get all our supplies? Where would she get hers?" Her voice was tight with worry. "I don't want to have to worry over getting supplies online—it's just not the same as running the fabric through my fingers and seeing all the colors in person."

"Everything will work out fine," Savannah said, fiercely stabbing her needle into her fabric. "Judith is temporarily insane—that's all. She'll soon come to her senses and realize that Dappled Hills isn't the right place for a designer boutique. It's the *perfect* place for a quilt shop."

"Judith is a sister quilter, but she makes me mad enough to spit sometimes," Meadow said. "She's forever making little digs at me. And I don't think she likes Boris," she added in a scandalized tone, reaching out to give the dog a sympathetic rub.

Beatrice strained to hear Georgia's quiet voice. "She's only making digs at you because she wanted to be the beekeeper."

Meadow explained to Beatrice, "That's what we call the president of the quilting bee."

Savannah frowned. "She's sniped at Georgia, and me, too. Although I guess that anyone who loves quilting as much as Judith does can't be all bad, right?'

"No one is *all* bad," Posy said with certainty. "When I have a chance to sit down and really talk to her about the shop and what I think it means to all of us, I'm positive she'll reconsider raising the rent."

Savannah looked cross. "We're quilting, ladies. This is our time to relax. Let's move on to a nicer subject."

"Yes! Let's move on," Meadow said enthusiastically. "And we all should be eating! I knew there was something I was forgetting. Snacks make everything in life better." In a flash, Meadow was back with a huge platter full of food. "Pimento cheese–stuffed celery, sweet Vidalia onion dip and spicy fried pickles." She beamed at the happy murmur from the quilters. Beatrice wasn't sure what to make of the offerings. It was the kind of food that could either be very good or very bad.

But, apparently, it was all good. Posy leaned over and said in a confiding way, "Meadow is the most fantastic cook. Everything on that platter is to die for! But make sure you try her pimento cheese. It's creamy-looking, but has a real kick to it with the jalapenos. I think she has a little cream cheese in there, and I'm completely nuts over creamy cheese. And now, Beatrice, tell us a little about you. I want to learn more about our new quilting friend." Her eyes twinkled at Beatrice as she filled a small plate with fried pickles and celery.

Beatrice fiddled with her napkin and cleared her throat. "Well, let's see." She thought for a moment. "Actually, there's nothing really interesting to share." They stared at her in disbelief. "There really isn't." It was sad, but true. Her life in recent years had revolved around work.

"Except that she just moved in yesterday and she's already a member of the Village Quilters!" bubbled Meadow. "I've waited for someone to move into that cottage next to me for ages. Ages! It's sat empty, and I

kept thinking it was going to become a crack house or
something else really dire."

Posy gave a tinkling laugh. "A crack house? In Dappled Hills? It was more likely to be turned into an art
gallery or a church or a charming coffee shop." Posy
was practically consumed by the huge polka-dotted
pillows on Meadow's sofa and hard to see.

"Or something. Or maybe the house would get
rented out to a college student who'd have wild keg
parties and stagger drunkenly through my yard. Instead, I'm *blessed* with a lovely older lady who quilts.
What could be better?"

Beatrice opened her mouth to refute her quilting
(and possibly her loveliness), but decided it was futile.

Posy said, "Shouldn't you amend the *older lady*,
Meadow? If *she's* older, and she must only be in her
early sixties, then what am I?"

"Simply sensational, Posy. Didn't you know seventy
is the new sixty? As for Beatrice, I'm going to try desperately to get over the fact that she has pretty hair that
apparently doesn't even have to be dyed!" Meadow
peered closely at Beatrice's chin-length soft bob, and
Beatrice resisted the urge to put a protective hand on it.
"That light blond, almost silver, sort of platinum color
is way too natural-looking to come from a bottle. Life
sure isn't always fair, is it?" Meadow sadly lifted her
own gray braid and stared reproachfully at it.

"I do have some highlights put in," said Beatrice,
feeling almost guilty.

"It's the perfect hairstyle for your heart-shaped

face," said Posy with a sweet smile. "I bet it's a low-fuss style, too. I have to go to the beauty parlor to get my wash and set every week."

"It's pretty easy to take care of. I didn't have a lot of time when I was working to worry over my hair, so I chose something simple," said Beatrice.

The prettier sister, Georgia, said timidly, "Savannah, Beatrice's hair is the style I was thinking would look good on you. You have a heart-shaped face, too."

Anything would look a lot better than the severe bun that Savannah sported. Savannah's heavy brows lifted. "You know perfectly well that I'm not preoccupied with my appearance, Georgia. Although I think Beatrice looks very nice. I'm sure Beatrice was used to attending exciting events in Atlanta, where it was important for her to look stylish."

"I hope Dappled Hills won't be too boring for you, Beatrice," said Georgia shyly. "There's not nearly as much going on. But sometimes there's an amateur night at the theater—that's usually a lot of fun. Well, the *singing* isn't as much fun, but I love some of the skits, and the local barber does a stand-up routine that's always hilarious. So there *are* things to do here."

"Sometimes," said Savannah in a repressive voice.

Looking more cheerful, Meadow added, "Oh, and since Beatrice just happens to be a folk-art expert, she'll have to give a talk at one of our programs. That'll take care of one of them, anyway. I have the dickens of a time trying to plan and schedule those."

This was territory Beatrice felt a little more comfortable with. "I'm sure I could manage that, Meadow. Folk art wasn't my *only* focus, but I did get to arrange some wonderful exhibits at the museum."

"And so you left a big career behind to come to Dappled Hills?" Savannah asked. "And look after Piper, I guess." Her voice implied that looking after people was the most understandable motive of all.

"Oh, Piper does fine on her own, I think. She's always been such an independent child. I was simply ready to retire. I'd been thinking about slowing down for a while. And I thought it would be a nice change to move to a small town—and be near Piper, of course. I didn't realize I'd be directly across the street from her, but it was the perfect cottage. I fell in love with it as soon as I saw it."

Meadow pursed her lips and gave Beatrice a considering look. "I've had a brilliant idea. My son Ash is here from California, visiting me this week. He's absolutely gorgeous," she said, completely seriously, "and a real *gentleman*. I'll introduce Piper to Ash at the quilting bee—which is tomorrow! Let me call him. He was working on his laptop when I left. Oh, shoot! No, I remember . . . he's gone to lunch with an old friend from high school. But I'll bring him to the bee for sure. And you'll need to come with Piper, Beatrice. Being independent is *fine*, of course, but it's even better to have a soul mate. Tomorrow is the first day of the rest of her life!"

Beatrice was beginning to long for her little stone cottage and the soft gingham sofa in her tiny living room. She could read her new book, *Whispers of Summer*, to the dulcet sounds of her corgi snoring. Somehow she'd pictured her retirement in quieter terms than quilting guilds and bees and quirky neighbors pulling her into a swarm of social activity.

There was a knock at the door and Meadow popped up again like a jack-in-the-box, bouncing toward the front door, Boris dutifully giving a guard-dog-bark in a deep, growling, hellhound way.

Posy smiled. "Dear Meadow and darling Boris. So much energy!"

Beatrice's daughter, Piper, was at the door, looking pretty as always with her dark hair in a pixie cut, her cute figure, and her gray eyes that matched Beatrice's. Piper hugged Meadow. "When I saw Mama wasn't home, I guessed you might have invited her over. Thanks for taking care of her for me. Did you know that if people don't drag Mama out of the house, then she'd happily spend hours poring over dusty antiquities or tomes on Early American furniture?" She gave Beatrice an unrepentant grin and a fleeting kiss on the cheek.

"We'll have to set Mama up with some quilting supplies," said Piper to Posy. "Or she can do some blocks for the bee. I finished mine, so I'm all set for tomorrow."

"Oh!" said Meadow with a start. "That reminds me that I need to get us set for our next project." She attempted to look official and businesslike, but the effect was somewhat ruined by the fact that she had picked up the water pitcher to refill Beatrice's tea and was now gesturing so much that the tea sloshed over the sides. "Y'all, this time I want us each to do a very personal quilt. Not one from a pattern book. I'd like each of us to come up with a block that shows something particularly meaningful for us and incorporate it in symbols on our blocks. Everyone in the group will create a 12.5-inch-by-2.5-inch block so that it will finish to 12-inch-by-12-inch when sewn together. I'll get in touch with the ladies who didn't make it today. I've got the background for the blocks, to unify the look and show we're working on a theme."

Frowning, Savannah said, "And we'll auction it off? Who is going to want something that's so personal, Meadow? It doesn't seem like it would be an interesting quilt for anybody but us."

"They'll *love* it, Savannah! They'll absolutely love it because it'll be the coolest quilt around." Savannah still looked unhappy. "You just need to give it a go. I know you're practically married to your geometric designs. But life isn't just about Dutchman's Puzzles or Pieced Stars. You need to color outside the lines a little bit."

"Some of us need to color a little *inside* the lines," said Savannah, with a cross nod at the crazy quilts scattered through Meadow's house.

Meadow either didn't hear Savannah or chose to ignore her. "I've already officially invited your mama to the bee tomorrow," said Meadow to Piper. She turned and gave Beatrice an exaggerated wink to show she still had matchmaking on the brain. "Beatrice, it'll be the best way for you to get up to speed with what's going on with quilting today."

Beatrice stood up to leave. She was having visions of a fully booked calendar, courtesy of Meadow, if she didn't escape. "Thanks so much for the tea and sandwiches. Really lovely to meet all of you. Of course we'll come to the bee tomorrow."

She heard Meadow calling after her and chortling as she left. "Be there or be *square*! Get it? Square!"

Chapter 2

The next day, the cottage was very, very quiet. Perfect, Beatrice reminded herself, for reading a book. But try as she might to relax, enjoy her tea and focus on the poetically descriptive passages of *Whispers of Summer*, she had the niggling sensation that she should be doing something else.

She shifted back and forth on the sofa before getting up to put a small load of laundry in the compact washing machine. She hand-washed the china coffee cup, although it could just as well have gone into the dishwasher. Finally, she decided to check her mailbox. Was her mail getting forwarded from Atlanta like it was supposed to? Rats . . . it was empty. What time was the mail supposed to come in Dappled Hills? Hadn't it come yesterday *morning*? And here it was, almost two o'clock in the afternoon and there was no mail to be seen.

Piper would know. She'd just give her a quick call.

"Mama? What's up?" Piper sounded distracted.

"I was wondering about the mail. Shouldn't it already have come by now? Do you think I simply didn't get any mail today? That seems very unlikely. Usually I'll have a catalog or some other junk mail. Do you think it's not all getting forwarded from my old address?"

There was a pause on the phone and then Piper's voice sounded more alert—and a little ornery, thought Beatrice with surprise. "You're worried about the mail service," she said flatly.

"Not *worried* about it. Just curious why the mail hasn't arrived. And what its usual arrival time is."

"Mama," said Piper, and there was distinct exasperation in her voice now, "you need something to do."

"Oh, I have things to do. I'm reading *Whispers of Summer*."

"No, you need more things to do than that. But Dappled Hills won't offer the same kind of entertainment as Atlanta. Actually, it does have the same entertainment as Atlanta. The selection is just a little different. So we have amateur night at the Plaza Theater instead of a performance of *Les Misérables*. And you might not be able to grab a gourmet meal in downtown Dappled Hills, but you can get one of Bertha's blue-plate specials at her diner. We need to keep you busy—with the quilters."

"Piper, quilts make stunning artwork, but I just don't feel compelled to make one myself."

"There's no better way to meet people in this town than being part of the quilting guilds. You could even act as sort of an artistic director—help generate ideas for the community quilts we do and keep us on track and organized. I bet Meadow would love to have you help her out."

"I guess," said Beatrice, unconvinced. Meadow certainly didn't seem like the most organized person on the planet.

"I'll walk over with you tonight to the church for the quilting bee. We've got to get mail delivery off your mind. Next thing you know, you'll be obsessing over the garbage pickup."

Beatrice pinched her lips shut. The garbage-pickup schedule was going to be her next question.

"Tell you what. Why don't I come over for a short visit before we head out for the bee? I can help you unpack the rest of your boxes. Once you're settled, I bet you won't feel like you're at loose ends anymore."

"Where are all your boxes of food?" asked Piper, peeking into a couple of boxes and finding only books.

"You're making a pretty big assumption," said Beatrice. She pulled out some of the books, smoothing the covers and sliding them into the bookcase.

"An assumption about *food*?"

"An assumption that I cook." Beatrice tried to keep a defensive tone from creeping into her voice.

"You *used* to cook, Mama. All the time. We had chicken casseroles and pot roast and hams!"

"And then your father passed away and I went back to work. And then *you* moved away. I made the amazing discovery that the grocery stores had heat-and-eat meals right there in the deli section. Why had no one mentioned this to me before? Some nights I'd pick up a salad or a meatloaf plate. Or maybe a pasta dish or a small gourmet pizza. There was plenty of variety."

"Uh oh. You might be in trouble then, Mama. Bub's doesn't have ready-to-eat."

"Bub's? That's the name of the store?" Beatrice felt her head start to throb. Bub's sounded like the kind of store that might also sell live bait.

"It's been around for at least a hundred years. Rumor has it that the original owner was so devilish that the townsfolk called him Bub, short for Beelzebub. The sign is very faded and no one can really make it out. Everyone has called it Bub's for as long as the oldest residents remember. And I think you and Bub's are going to have to get acquainted with each other pretty soon, unless you're planning on eating out every meal."

"There are good restaurants here?" This, at least, was promising.

"Well . . . yes. But they have funny hours unless the leaves are changing," said Piper in a careless voice as if what she was saying made perfect sense.

"What in heaven's name have leaves got to do with restaurant hours?" asked Beatrice.

"It's prime tourist season when the leaves are changing," said Piper. "But otherwise it's hard to find a restaurant that's open in the evenings. Easy to find a place for lunch, though."

"It's all right," said Beatrice, holding her head high and dignified. "I used to cook once. I'll just start cooking again—that's all."

"Well, my original plan was that I'd help you cook a quick supper before we headed over to the bee. But now I'm thinking that we might better head on over there. Meadow will be sure to have brought food, and she's a great cook."

Beatrice grunted, still annoyed over the food-and-cooking part of it all. "Are we walking over?"

"Might as well," said Piper. "It's a nice evening and a short walk to the church."

Noo-noo cocked her head to the side, hopeful. "Not this time, girl," said Beatrice, reaching down to pet the corgi. "We'll have a walk next time, I promise." She found her pocketbook and followed Piper out the door, locking it behind her.

"What did you think of everyone at the guild meeting? Weren't they fantastic?" asked Piper as she and Beatrice strolled down the driveway to the street. "Meadow especially. She's *wonderful*. She's friendly with my school's principal, who asked her to help me find a place to rent when I first came to town for my teaching job. It just happened to be on the same street as hers, so we've become good friends."

Beatrice's heart warmed a little toward the impossible Meadow. "Yes, Meadow seems . . . um . . . really nice."

Piper cut her eyes sideways at her mother. "I know that tone, Mama. Is she too quirky for you?"

"She seemed a teensy bit manic—in the nicest way," said Beatrice hurriedly as Piper knit her brows. "She kept refilling my glass to the brim and filled Savannah and Georgia's with tea, even though they were drinking water! I felt like Alice at the Mad Hatter's tea party. I was waiting for Meadow to ask me why a raven was like a writing desk, and for all the quilters to switch places with each other."

Piper laughed. "You'll really see Meadow in action at the quilting bee. She wanders around, cramming food on your plate. You won't even know how much you've eaten because she'll keep piling on the food whenever she sees an open spot on your plate. She cracks me up! And Ramsay—that's her husband—is great, too, if you ever get a chance to meet him. He's the Dappled Hills police chief and is always on the go."

Probably, thought Beatrice, to escape his eccentric wife. "Actually, I've already met him. I flagged him down, as a matter of fact, when I thought Meadow was kidnapping me. She wasn't very clear on the fact she was just encouraging me to go to a quilting guild meeting with her. Unfortunately, Meadow seems to have gotten the impression that I'm desperate to stay busy. Now she's assigned this group quilt project and seems like she's expecting me to take part in it, too. Any ideas on how to extricate myself from a bunch of invitations and just be left alone?"

"I think you might be out of luck, Mama. It's just not possible to be aloof here like you could be in Atlanta."

"I don't want to be *aloof*. I just want some quality reading time in my hammock. Quality reading time with a mint julep."

Piper shook her head. "You're going to want to become friends with these women, Mama. Take Savannah and Georgia. They might seem peculiar, but they're the most loyal friends you'll ever meet and they *live* for quilting. Georgia's really sweet and absolutely crazy about animals. She has a little online business making cat and dog clothes. She went through a terrible divorce . . . such a sad story. Sometimes I think I never want to get married."

Beatrice chose to ignore that last remark. "Georgia seems nice, I think, but that Savannah is bossy and imposing. And they live together?" she asked.

"They do. I think that's how Savannah keeps Georgia in line. She's *so* organized. You'll have to see the quilting library she's got in their house. It's all alphabetized by author. I dropped by to borrow a book and Savannah checked it out like it was the public library. She carefully inserted a little dated card in the back of the book and everything. I don't think Savannah's *bossy*, just one of those people who likes fixing things. So when Georgia's marriage fell apart about a year ago, Savannah insisted that Georgia move in with her so she could keep an eye on her. She's so overprotective of Georgia that you'd think she was her baby sister instead of her twin."

Beatrice thought of Savannah's tightly buttoned-up blouse, tight bun and domineering manner and wondered how much Georgia really enjoyed being kept in line. Savannah seemed to have such a grip on Georgia that it was amazing Georgia had ever been able to pull away enough to marry.

"And Posy, the lady who owns the quilting shop? Her husband, Cork, owns a wine shop in town. We sometimes get together for food and wine—we had a tomato pie full of mozzarella and Parmesan a couple of weeks ago. It was the perfect refreshing supper. The tomatoes came right from their garden, and Cork brought a new wine for me to try. They never had children, so Posy treats their little beagle like a child— she'll put her in outfits, and she talks to her like the beagle's going to talk back. We sat out in their garden, laughing and talking, and hummingbirds darted around us all through supper."

"Cork! That's an interesting name."

"Isn't it? It was inevitable, though. He owns a wine shop and he even *looks* like a cork."

"Bald?"

"I'm afraid so," said Piper with a smile.

"Well, I can see the advantages of befriending some-one whose husband owns a wine shop," said Beatrice. "Clever girl. And Posy did seem really sweet. It wasn't a very big group at the guild meeting, though. Who else is in the guild that might be going to the bee?"

"You'll be meeting the wicked Judith, I'm sure. Did everyone talk about her yesterday, since she wasn't at the meeting?"

"Of course they did. I hear she's threatening to close

Posy's quilt shop and makes jabs at Meadow because *she* wanted to be the beekeeper. Is she as evil as everyone is making out? Or just misunderstood?"

"That's for you to decide. She sure does have a lot of people mad at her, though. So, Judith will be there tonight at the bee, for sure—she never misses an opportunity to irritate large numbers of people at once."

"Who else will probably come to the bee?"

"There's another mother-daughter quilting team who'll be there." Beatrice rolled her eyes, and Piper chuckled. "Now, Mama. We're on our way to a quilting bee . . . It's safe to call ourselves quilters. Anyway, Felicity is the mom and Amber is another teacher."

"Is she your age?" asked Beatrice.

"She's a few years older, but she's a lot of fun. And she's my best friend here."

"Did she grow up here?"

"She did, but I think she's ready to move on to a bigger town. Y'all should have simply switched towns and houses. Daisy mentioned to me the other day that she was trying to help Amber find a teaching position in Atlanta."

"Daisy?"

"Don't worry. I'll help you remember who everyone is. Daisy is married to the local doctor and belongs to nearly every organization in town. She does *lots* of volunteering. And she knows *everybody*. She'd actually be a great person to introduce you to Dappled Hills and get you involved."

Involved? She was going to have to stay on her toes

to keep from being *too* involved in this town. The residents seemed almost a little *too* friendly.

Piper suddenly swung around and looked behind them. "Look out!"

She shoved Beatrice into someone's yard and jumped neatly out of the way herself as a boatlike, aging Lincoln ran up onto the sidewalk before roaring back onto the road and away. The driver raised a skinny arm and brandished a fist at them as the car pulled diagonally into a parking spot at the church.

Beatrice was breathless and shaking, but Piper had started walking again. "For the love of Pete! Piper! Someone tried to *kill* us!"

Piper chuckled. "That's Dappled Hills, North Carolina's famous Miss Sissy. She's . . . interesting."

"She drives on sidewalks!"

"Miss Sissy just has a creative interpretation of the word *road*. Plus, I guarantee you that she's going to complain that *you* ran *her* off the road."

"That *I* did?" Beatrice was incredulous.

"Didn't you see her shaking a fist at you? She's going to tell you off for being a road hog."

"We were on the sidewalk!"

"Not in Miss Sissy's opinion," said Piper.

Despite feeling stomach butterflies at meeting more people—and at trying to remember more names and anything she might once have known about quilting—Beatrice felt immediately at home as they walked up to the beautiful old church, its stone walls blending naturally into the lushness of the surrounding trees and flowering bushes.

Piper recognized every vehicle in the parking lot. She nodded at a lavender Cadillac. "I see Felicity is here. She used to sell gobs of cosmetics for the Eula May company. Her husband died when Amber was just a teenager, so Felicity had to suddenly go back to work—like you did, Mama. Apparently she was a born salesperson. Felicity ended up being a top seller and built up a Eula May sales team and managed their sales. They ended up giving her a lavender Caddy." She grinned. "And Savannah and Georgia are here—I see their bikes."

Beatrice was alarmed. "They ride motorcycles?" The mental image of straitlaced Savannah on a Harley popped unbidden into Beatrice's head. She could picture it: cigarette dangling from her thin lips, skull and crossbones barely visible on her thin shoulder. Beatrice shuddered.

"No, just regular bicycles. They ride them almost everywhere. Sometimes they scare me to death on those curving mountain roads. I'll be driving around a curve and suddenly there's Savannah, sitting straight up and pedaling furiously, and I have to swerve out of the way. She seems to think she's on the same footing as cars. Honestly, I'm not even sure Savannah knows *how* to drive a car; I only ever see her on her bike. Georgia drives herself to school sometimes, though, if she has a lot of supplies to carry in."

"How remarkable," said Beatrice drily.

A handsome older man with twinkling eyes and silvery-streaked hair greeted everyone as they came through the door. "A male quilter?" Beatrice murmured.

Piper gave a soft laugh. "He's the minister." At her mother's look of disappointment, she added quickly, "He doesn't thump Bibles, Mama, I promise. He's a perfectly lovely man. I'll introduce you."

Piper introduced Beatrice to the minister, Wyatt. He gave her a kind smile, and Beatrice felt her crabbiness at nearly having been run over melt away a little.

"Welcome to Dappled Hills. Piper was so excited you were moving here."

Beatrice felt a little tongue-tied. "Mmm. Yes." She reached up a hand to smooth some wayward strands of hair from her face, then worried she might have lipstick on her teeth.

Piper shot her an amused look. "Mama's had a whirlwind of activity since she's moved here. Meadow kidnapped her yesterday afternoon and made her go to the guild meeting."

Wyatt's eyes crinkled in a smile. "A trial by fire, then."

"S-sort of," she stammered, before Piper pulled her into the church's dining hall, where a dozen or more women were gathered, chatting and busily organizing supplies. Sewing machines lined one wall, and bags of batting and half-finished quilts lay everywhere. Irons and ironing boards were set up along another wall. Several tables had been pushed together to form a large surface holding cutting boards, rulers, and rotary cutters.

Piper told Beatrice, "I want to introduce you to Amber. She was one of my first friends in Dappled Hills. She loves going out at night or going on road trips over the weekend. I keep telling her I've got papers to grade, and she practically yanks me out the door." Piper laughed.

Amber didn't sound like the best influence in the world.

Beatrice squinted at a figure across the room. "I'm guessing the woman over there must be the infamous Judith," she said in a low voice, pointing to a woman in a bright pink pantsuit with bright red hair.

"Is it?" Piper peered doubtfully at the woman. "Wow, it *is* her. What's she done to her hair? It was a perfectly normal shade of basic brown yesterday. Her hair is even redder than Daisy's." She knit her brows at Beatrice. "How'd you know it was her? Especially since her back is to us."

"Just a hunch. Those women standing around her all have their hands on their hips or arms crossed and they're looking pretty tense."

"I'm sure we'll be hearing what *that* was all about later. Oh, here comes Daisy. Remember, she was the one I said would be able to help introduce you to the town."

A plump, redheaded, middle-aged woman wearing a very short skirt, heels, and a silky shirt with a plunging neckline came toward them, beaming.

"Piper, I see your precious cargo arrived safe and

sound in Dappled Hills," said Daisy with a smile in her voice. She held out a hand, with several diamond rings on it, to clasp Beatrice's. "I can tell you're Piper's mother—you look so much alike. I'm Daisy Butler. Welcome to Dappled Hills!"

Actually, she and Piper didn't look very much alike at all, although they did have the same eyes. Maybe that's what Daisy was referring to. Piper was smiling at both of them delightedly, as if she were sure they were going to be the best of friends. "Nice to meet you, Daisy."

"Mama arrived in town only two days ago, but Meadow's already signed her up for the quilting guild," said Piper.

Daisy nodded. "Wonderful! That will be a great introduction to Dappled Hills for your mother. The Village Quilters guild is the finest and oldest organization in town. Quilting is part of the mountain heritage, you know. There are quilters here who are fourth and fifth generation. I sort of fell into quilting myself. My family is from Charleston and quilting doesn't figure into the culture there quite as much." Daisy tilted her head and looked thoughtfully at Beatrice. "Maybe you'd be a good candidate for the Women's Auxiliary, too. It's a lovely group of women and does a lot of good in the community."

"Maybe after I settle in a little," said Beatrice, as Daisy walked off to join Savannah. Dappled Hills might be a slower pace, but it looked like she could really keep busy if she wanted to. Not that she did. She was planning on spending her retirement buried in books in her backyard hammock. With the relaxing mint julep.

Piper said, "Here's Amber and her mom, Mama."

Amber was small, slim, and very blond, with a wide grin and a devilish look in her eye. "Mrs. Coleman? I've heard so much about you! All good stuff, of course," she said with a grin, as Beatrice raised her eyebrows at Piper. "You're amazing to retire and move here from Atlanta to be near Piper. Piper is really lucky to have you for a mom."

Piper stuck her hands on her hips. "You're not exactly unlucky yourself in the mom department!" she said as an older version of Amber joined them.

"True. And I'm not just saying that because she's standing right behind me," said Amber.

Piper introduced Beatrice to a very well-maintained lady who must have been in her early seventies—although she might not own up to it. She looked fantastic and wore a good deal of artfully applied makeup.

"Well, of course you're Piper's mama," Felicity said, giving Beatrice a quick appraisal. Beatrice wasn't sure how to take Felicity until she finally grinned and said, "She's as cute as a button and you look just like her. You're a quilter, too?"

Beatrice shook her head. "No, my quilting abilities have been vastly exaggerated, Felicity. In fact"— Beatrice lowered her voice and looked to make sure that Piper was safely engrossed in conversation with Felicity's daughter—"I'm dying to escape. Messing up my own quilt is one thing, but messing up a *group* quilt is something else entirely."

Felicity waved her well-manicured hand. "Pish! Who cares? The folks who get these quilts will be thrilled to bits and sure won't be inspecting the stitching. If you don't *want* to stitch, you could find something else to do, though. Different quilts are in different stages. Some are still in the piecing stage, some of the quilt tops need to be sewn together, and others just need batting and backing."

"Maybe I can just be on pressing duty," said Beatrice, looking at the row of irons. "I shouldn't be able to destroy any quilts by ironing." But she felt uneasy about doing even that. "Is there anything special to remember about pressing?"

Felicity said, "The only thing to mention about pressing is that it is pressing. We press the blocks instead of ironing back and forth. But I don't want you to think that you have to do something boring like pressing, Beatrice. Besides, we picked one pattern to accommodate beginners—dark thread on dark fabric. And what a fabric it is!" She gestured eagerly over to the table. "Go ahead! Take a gander at it."

So Beatrice did. And she was instantly smitten with the patterns and fabrics.

"These are wall-hanging quilts and they'll go up for auction at the art festival. The money raised there will benefit the children's hospital," explained Felicity. She gave Beatrice a knowing smile. "What do you think of them?"

The quilts' complexity and beauty were determined by the individual quilters in each group. Beatrice felt especially drawn to a couple of patterns. One quilt top had cheerful butterflies dancing around a flowered bush—the butterflies themselves looked appliquéd from a retro-looking fabric and really popped off the quilt.

The other was a medallion pattern of a graceful wreath of Southern flowers—magnolia, yellow jasmine and azalea with a hummingbird hovering at a blossom.

"They're gorgeous," said Beatrice without hesitation. She felt like she was back in the art museum. She reached out to run her hand over the soft fabric.

There were nearly thirty people in the dining hall now. Beatrice asked Amber, "Is this group all from the Village Quilters? There are so many women here!" She thought about her miniature living room with the gingham sofa and single chair. How would she ever be able to host this group? And how had Piper hosted it in the tiny duplex she rented?

"Actually," said Amber, "we've got two guilds in town. The Village Quilters has been around the longest, but there's also the Cut-Ups guild. Not everyone comes to every meeting, of course. And when we have a meeting, usually we're doing lap quilting, so it's not like the monthly bee where we have a bunch of sewing machines out and are assembling the blocks and batting. We might be hand-piecing or working on appliqués. Or we could even be embellishing a quilt with beads, buttons or ribbons."

"How did you ever get interested in quilting, Amber? I'm guessing it's not something that a lot of your friends were doing." She remembered what Piper said about Amber's longing for big-city life.

"Oh, Mother got me into it, of course," said Amber with a low chuckle. "She figured it would be a good way to keep an eye on me and keep me out of trouble. It's a plan that's met with limited success. But Mother can be very determined when she wants to be. I've enjoyed it more than I thought I would, though. Plus, Meadow's been giving me tips, which is fun."

Beatrice saw, with some trepidation, Miss Sissy hobbling over to the table, hunched over her wooden cane but still seeming surprisingly spry, considering her age. Her face was deeply creviced with wrinkles, and her hair, ostensibly in a bun, had so many wiry strands sticking out of it that she looked like she'd just rolled out of bed. Piper noticed Miss Sissy's approach and hurried over to her mother, as if to run interference.

Miss Sissy, eyes set deep into hollows, looked directly at Beatrice. She shook an arthritic fist. "Road hog!" she bellowed.

Beatrice jumped, but Piper seemed very calm. "Miss Sissy, this is my mom, Beatrice. She moved here from Atlanta the day before yesterday."

"Wickedness!"

"Miss Sissy," continued Piper to her mother, as if nothing untoward had happened at all, "is one of the best quilters in the Southeast. She's been quilting for— how many years, Miss Sissy? Sixty?"

"Seventy!"

"How amazing," said Beatrice. She hazarded a smile at the cronelike woman, but it was returned with a fierce frown. Amber rolled her eyes at Beatrice to show her feelings about Miss Sissy. Beatrice actually found herself relieved at the sight of Meadow approaching their group, pulling a man in his early thirties along behind her.

"I went to school with Ash. I remember when he was just a ponytail-pulling kid who couldn't color in the lines to save his own soul," murmured Amber. "He sure has changed."

Meadow bounced up, her arm around the man, and said proudly, "Hi, y'all! This is Ash. He's officially the world's best son for coming all the way from California to visit his mama."

Ash leaned over and shook Beatrice and Piper's hands, grinning. "I think I'm a *better* son for coming along with my mother to a quilting bee. I mean, who *does* that?"

Piper gave a gasping laugh as she took in with admiring eyes Ash's tall figure and dark features. Now it was Beatrice's turn to snicker at Piper, who finally found her tongue to say, "You should stick around and learn a little about your mom's favorite hobby."

Ash said, "I think I might pass for tonight. But I'll admit I did have an ulterior motive for coming to the quilting bee. After Mother sang your praises to me, Piper, I wanted to ask you out for dinner tomorrow night, if you're free."

Piper flushed. "Sure, I'd love to."

Meadow was hopping from foot to foot in her excitement.

"Great! Pick you up around six, then?" With that settled, Ash headed back out again into the gathering darkness.

Meadow looked smug. "I told you he was something special."

"You did," admitted Piper. "You'll forgive me for thinking you might be slightly biased—being his mother and everything. But you were absolutely speaking the truth."

Beatrice sadly looked on as Meadow gave more Ash propaganda to Piper. Yes, he was all that Meadow had said he was. But he lived on the other side of the country. Talk about a long-distance relationship!

"Someone new? In Dappled Hills?" said a dry voice behind Beatrice. It was the woman Piper had pointed out as Judith. In some ways, she looked very similar to Daisy, without the provocative clothing. She was middle-aged and on the heavy side, with bright red hair. Beatrice introduced herself and struggled to think of something to say. Judith didn't seem to be much of a conversationalist. In fact, she kept looking around the room as if she'd prefer to talk to anyone else but Beatrice. Beatrice said, "It's nice of the church to loan the guilds the space, isn't it? It's really a nice, large room."

Judith raised her carefully arched eyebrows. "The church relies on us," she said with a sniff. "Considering the fact that several improvements were made to the property as a direct result of the quilts and other crafts we sell at bazaars. Loaning us a room to craft quilts for charity is the very least they can do."

Beatrice, relieved that at least there was a topic of conversation, was eagerly addressing this line of thought when Judith gave an exasperated sigh and briskly walked away, muttering, "Someone's about to screw up a perfectly good quilt." The unlucky recipient of Judith's advice (or criticism) certainly didn't look very grateful.

Savannah squinted at the wall clock, then shooed the ladies into their seats as beekeeper Meadow started the bee by talking about a past project and what they were doing for the children's hospital. Several members showed off some completed quilts. Meadow mentioned a caravan they were planning to a nearby town for a quilt show. Then they started quilting. Beatrice held back for the first fifteen minutes, watching Piper and the other ladies make neat stitches as they connected their blocks and chatted.

"Mama," said Piper, "don't you want to go ahead and get started? You'll be fine."

"You really can't mess up," said Meadow, reaching over to pat Beatrice on the hand. "Even if you *do*, there are a dozen women here who can fix whatever you've done."

So Beatrice threaded her needle, knotting the end in a quilter's knot, which she'd looked up on the Internet before she'd left with Piper for the bee. She slowly slid the needle into the beautiful fabric—and stopped cold.

Piper's perfectly good block stared at her. Beatrice didn't want to do anything to mess it up.

"You know, I think I'm just going to sit this one out. I'd rather practice at home on my own quilt instead of someone else's."

Meadow and Piper both made protesting noises, but Beatrice stood firm. This wasn't the venue for picking up quilting. She'd end up stabbing herself with the needle and bleeding all over the block or making crooked stitches.

She sat back in her chair, pretending to watch Piper's stitches, but really feeling very cross. Was being an art curator the only thing she knew how to do? It wasn't the kind of thing that was actually *useful*. Now that life had slowed down to a crawl (although not for long, if the good ladies of Dappled Hills had any say), she was realizing that all of her basic life skills had gotten extremely rusty.

But after a few minutes, she forgot her irritation and found she was enjoying watching the quilting. The women sitting knee to knee, talking over familiar problems as they rhythmically stitched through the quilts, the irons steaming at the sides of the tables, the gentle hum of the sewing machines in the background, and the soft batting and fabrics on the tables all lent a relaxed, comforting feel to the dining hall. And the art—and it really was art—they were creating was truly breathtaking. The patterns coming together created a visual field trip.

Beatrice found that she was able to jump in and help

out with other parts of the quilt assembly. She carefully ironed the quilts after they'd had their tops and borders sewn on. She tracked down and removed any forgotten pins. She helped layer the top, batting, and backing for the quilt on the floor, gently stretching out the backing to prevent wrinkles, in preparation for the quilters who basted the layers together.

Meadow helped her straighten the quilt layers. "You'd be the perfect adviser for the Village Quilters, Beatrice. With all your art-world experience, you're exactly what we need. We're wanting to enter more of our quilts into juried competitions . . . but some of us are better at coming up with original designs than others. I know you'd be great at quilt design."

"Piper had mentioned something to me about possibly playing another role in the guild. I've just never done anything like that before. But I do love to draw. Would I draw a scaled template?"

Meadow nodded. "You could put together a four-patch quilt block or a nine-patch block pattern and sketch it out on graph paper. Easy peasy! And then cut it out and write the pattern name on the back of the template in case someone wants to use it again. We need fresh ideas! And I could use some help putting kits together for the quilters—cutting out all the pieces for the blocks and sticking them in zipper bags. And I need a quilting herder, too," said Meadow, hooting with laughter. "Somebody to make sure they hand their blocks in on time for any group quilts we do."

"Well . . . I'm not so sure about my cutting abilities. I'd have to practice or else you'd end up with a lot more scraps for crazy quilts than you'd planned on. But designing quilts sounds more up my alley than the quilting," said Beatrice. She felt a quickening of interest at the thought of designing patterns. She definitely knew her way around a piece of graph paper.

"Great! Then you can help us out before our next bee," said Meadow, beaming. "I'll be sure to give you lots of notice."

Savannah snickered. "Georgia *should* be able to come up with some ideas for our group quilt. She's got five or six quilting-magazine subscriptions."

Georgia looked reproachfully at her sister. "But there's never more than one or two patterns that I want to make. So I almost *have* to subscribe to that many to get enough ideas."

The quilting bee eventually broke up for the evening. More members came up at the end, introduced themselves and welcomed her to Dappled Hills. Felicity and Amber chatted with them for a few minutes, too.

Piper pointed at the paper shopping bag Amber held. "Is that the quilt you were telling me about yesterday? Can I see it?"

Amber placed the bag down on the hardwood floor and bent to pull the quilt out. "Well, sure. We're glad to find a home for it, honestly. With Mother getting ready to move to a retirement home, we're trying to get her downsized. And I don't have room in my place for even my own stuff, much less Mother's." She unfolded the quilt halfway and showed it to the ladies.

Savannah and Georgia hurried up, Savannah puffing in her haste to see the quilt. "Is that the quilt that you're giving Judith?" she asked.

"It's beautiful," said Georgia, reaching out and smoothing her hand over a few of the squares.

"Is it?" asked Felicity, squinting at the quilt doubtfully. "What I think it *actually* is, is very old and hogging space in my linen closet."

"Mama's house is jam-packed with quilts," said Amber.

"You know, it used to pain me to even *think* about giving up my quilts. They've been around so long that they're practically members of the family! But there are just so *many* of them that it's not fair to Amber to unload them all on her. The women in my family have quilted for so many generations—and my mother didn't help matters by collecting quilts from flea markets and yard sales. I'm not even completely sure which of the quilts were made by family members and which were made by strangers." Felicity sighed. "When Judith visited me last week and offered to take this one off my hands, I can't tell you how relieved I was. I cannot *wait* to move into a smaller place. Trying to keep up with a yard, dusting those empty rooms and cooking for one is absolutely killing me." Felicity laid a blue-veined hand dramatically on her heart and winked, broadly, at Beatrice.

There was a flash of pink from the corner of her eye,

and she turned. Judith was standing there staring at the quilt with quick interest.

"Is that my quilt?" she asked, reaching out and pulling it out of Felicity's grasp. "Thanks for bringing it. I'll hang it in a place of honor." She gave a sort of phony smile.

Beatrice asked, "May I see it?" in a tone that allowed no disagreement. She pulled it gently from Judith's grasp, into her arms and over to the group of long tables they'd spread the quilts over. Beatrice studied the quilt for a minute, then carefully but tenderly ran a hand over the closely woven, silky fabric. It was a double nine-patch quilt of white and crimson on an umber background. She gave Felicity and Amber a tight smile. "I know Judith is getting the quilt for free. But it's very old."

"It's old, all right. I feel bad dumping it on Judith, but she's kind enough to take it on. It's true she's not paying anything for the quilt. Maybe I should be paying *her* for taking it off my hands."

Beatrice shook her head. "No. I mean, we all know it's old . . . The stitching is raised because the batting has shifted. I'm sure the batting is cotton or wool—not polyester. The appliqués and piecework have clearly been hand stitched, and there's no sheen at all to the quilt. One striking thing is the handiwork—this stitching is quite decorative, which is a little unusual for older quilts, which were ordinarily meant for a utilitarian purpose. It's old. But it's not *just* old. It's antique. If I had to guess, I'd say this quilt dates back to the Civil

War period. And it's in amazing shape—there's no fraying on the binding at all. It must have been carefully stored."

Felicity and Amber could only stare at her.

"Um . . . did I mention that Mama was an art curator?" asked Piper in the silence.

Felicity frowned. "I thought it was just *plain* old. *Regular* old. So you're saying, Beatrice, that it's *valuable* old?" She gave the quilt an appraising look. "If it's valuable, Judith, I'm going to have to rethink this. You know how I'm trying to build up my savings for the retirement home."

Judith moved with lightning speed to snatch up the quilt, but Beatrice smoothly blocked her, carefully rolling the quilt and putting it back in the bag. She handed the bag to Felicity, who held it tightly against her. "The only thing to do," said Beatrice briskly, "is to have Felicity reconsider the arrangement now that she knows the quilt's value."

Judith's face was white with fury. "I'm sure you're wrong about the quilt's value. This is a reproduction of an antique quilt that's cluttering up Felicity's house. She's trying to downsize and I'm doing her a tremendous favor by taking it off her hands . . . She told me so herself."

Beatrice said, "If it's not valuable, then you won't mind if she thinks it over for a few days. Don't kid yourself that you were trying to help Felicity unclutter her house. A real friend wouldn't have been so quick to grab the quilt. I think you know exactly how valuable that quilt is—and were hoping Felicity and Amber wouldn't realize it. No, you were *counting on* the fact that they wouldn't."

Amber glared at Judith through narrowed eyes. "So you were going to cheat Mother out of her quilt. I was wondering why you'd suddenly do something nice. It was completely out of character for you to actually act human. What were you planning on doing with the quilt? Selling it to the highest bidder on eBay? Or did you already have an interested buyer?"

Judith smirked. "What do you *mean*, what *was* I planning to do with the quilt? I've *still* got plans for the quilt. After all, it's mine. It's gorgeous and historic and was given to me, fair and square, by the owner herself."

"But it's not in your possession," said Amber with a short laugh. "And I hear that possession is nine-tenths of the law."

Judith said, "I'm sure the quilt will end up with me, though. Your mother isn't someone to go back on her word, is she?"

"No," said Felicity in a firm voice, standing stiffly. "No, I'm not. But I won't be taken advantage of, Judith. I'll sleep on it and then we'll work out what to do with the quilt tomorrow. I didn't know its value and I can use the extra money."

Judith looked scornfully at Felicity. "I should have known you'd go back on your word. And stop acting like a hard-luck case by moaning about needing money. The reason you don't have any money right now is because you don't have any money sense at *all*. I know you lost all your money to some con artist with a pyramid scheme."

Posy said quietly, "There's no point in getting ugly about it, Judith. It's a gorgeous quilt, but I'm sure you don't want it under these circumstances."

Judith snorted. "Posy, you're stirring up trouble because you're upset at losing your shop."

Beatrice heard a startled cry of consternation from the quilters. Posy's face turned white. "Judith, you said we'd talk about it."

Judith raised her hand peremptorily. "I'm all done talking. I'm a businesswoman, Posy, and I've got to think about my business instead of giving friends charity. I've got a tenant who is interested in moving into the space and is willing to pay me more rent for it. It's time for you to start looking for a new location for the shop."

Daisy, the doctor's wife, said tightly, "So it's all about *money* and *greed*, isn't it, Judith? When it comes down to money, friendship gets tossed aside every time."

"I think it's all about *money* and *greed* for you! Daisy Butler isn't everything she seems to be," said Judith with a short laugh. "And what you *are* is soon to change, too."

Daisy's face flushed to match her hair. She looked like she was trying to string words together but could only stutter like an old car engine trying to turn over on a cold morning.

Georgia jumped in. "Posy's Patchwork Cottage is a second home to Savannah and me. We *rely* on it. All the quilters do." Her low voice quavered and she seemed to be steeling herself, fists clenched to handle confrontation.

"You and Savannah rely on the shop to get supplies?" Judith said, sneering. "Well, maybe you do, Georgia. But I know how *Savannah* gets supplies." She gave a sly smile.

Georgia gave a strangled cry, and Savannah stepped protectively in front of her. Her smile was icy, but her fierce expression indicated that she was at a boiling point. Beatrice made a mental note not to ever get on her bad side. "Don't talk to Georgia like that, Judith. Or you'll be sorry."

Judith snorted. "Shoot, I'm already sorry. Sorry I wasted my time here tonight. And sorry I took Felicity at her word to give me the quilt. She looks like such a sweet little old lady." The well-preserved Felicity flinched.

"Pride!" bellowed Miss Sissy from the back of the group. "Wicked pridefulness." Beatrice wasn't sure if that non sequitur meant Miss Sissy was on Judith's side or Felicity's.

Meadow's expression was thunderous and she displayed a temper that seemed quite at odds with her usual peaceful air. "A quilting bee," she said in a sonorous voice, "promotes harmony of thought and purpose. You've destroyed that harmony, Judith—and you need to leave."

Judith shrugged. "Sorry you feel that way, Meadow," she said in a cutting voice. "But you don't have to kick me out, because I wanted to leave, anyway. I'm going to change into walking clothes, head out to the park, and take a walk—I need some fresh air after all this childishness. Thanks for nothing, Felicity," she said, her lips twisting. She disappeared into the darkness outside the door.

There was a moment of silence—and not the reverent kind—after Judith stormed out.

Daisy's face was still mottled with anger. "Well, I certainly hope I don't run into Judith again tonight. I was planning on taking a stroll tonight myself, since Harrison has got ER duty. I guess if I see Judith on a walk, I'll head off in another direction."

Amber trembled with fury. "At least we have the quilt back. She was scheming to cheat you, Mother, I'm sure of it. She knew exactly how much that quilt is worth. Now she's saying you don't live up to your word. She's nasty."

"This is really the final straw. It's past time for Judith to be expelled from our group," said Meadow, arms crossed. "She managed to insult half the people at the bee—and this is supposed to be a charity event! She's stirred up trouble once again, and it's time to put a stop to it. I'm going to talk with her tomorrow." Meadow rubbed her eyes. "Tonight has positively exhausted me, y'all. It really has. And it makes me feel so dispirited."

The quilters murmured in concern. Meadow said, "I'd like to make some big plans for the guild, you know? More shows, different kinds of quilts. But on nights like tonight, I feel like I'm swimming against the current. What does any of it matter if we can't even get along with each other?"

Beatrice noticed that Piper was looking at her pointedly. Then she remembered that Piper had wanted her to help Meadow with some of the administrative side of things—and some of the brainstorming. She cleared her throat. "Meadow, I'm not up to par yet with the quilting, but I'm happy to help you out with planning a direction for the group. It sounds like you want to maybe change course and start doing more shows. Maybe after I get settled in a little I can help you with that."

Piper beamed at her as Meadow nearly squeezed the life out of Beatrice with a bear-sized hug. As Meadow started excitedly babbling about possibilities for the guild, Beatrice was already regretting that she'd spoken up.

The next morning when Beatrice got up to get her paper, there was a glass Nehi Orange Soda bottle on her front porch. She stooped, frowning, to pick it up. Stuck in the bottle was a message in a very careful, up-and-down, uniform print: *Don't push it!*

She looked around but there was no sign of anyone anywhere around. Don't push. . . what? Beatrice stomped back inside in irritation and tossed the bottle in the recycling bin. What wasn't she supposed to push? Was the note referring to the way she'd brought up the whole antique-quilt issue? The fact she'd volunteered to help spearhead the effort to change the direction and purpose of the guild? Or did the anonymous person mean something else entirely? Beatrice shivered. She couldn't tell if the note had been left with malicious intent, or as a friendly warning. And, really, were *any* warnings friendly?

She looked down at her corgi, Noo-noo, who was lying on her back, sound asleep. "Some guard dog you are," she scolded. Noo-noo opened her eyes halfway before drifting back to sleep.

The incident last night at the bee, compounded with the anonymous note this morning, left Beatrice more shaken up than she wanted to admit. She tried reading the tiny local newspaper before giving up completely. The *Dappled Hills Dispatch* was full of names she didn't know going to places and events she hadn't heard of. She blinked in amazement at stories written about a seven-year-old girl's birthday party, a family reunion, and extensive and somewhat rambling coverage on the winning streak of a Dappled Hills Little League team. There was also an odd column where residents could trade unwanted goods with each other. She had a sudden and intense longing for the *Atlanta Journal-Constitution*.

A walk was what she needed. She'd clear her head a little and get some feeling of control over her day. She needed it and she had a feeling her tubby corgi did, too. She quickly dressed in her usual uniform of khaki capris and a button-down shirt and ran a brush through her platinum hair. "Where's your leash?" she asked

Noo-noo, and watched as the dog exploded into action, scrambling to get off her back as Beatrice found the leash and collar for their walk.

The morning mountain air was crisp, and Beatrice pulled her light jacket up around her neck as a breeze blew by. Noo-noo, whose regular walks had been disrupted by the moving and unpacking, pulled eagerly at her leash. Clouds of misty fog covered the ground in patches as Beatrice and the corgi headed briskly toward the park.

A tiny figure approached them, walking an equally small dog. As they walked closer, she recognized Posy, the quilt-shop owner, with a beagle trotting ahead of her. Noo-noo joyfully jogged toward the dog to greet it.

"Beatrice?" said Posy with a smile. "It's such a pleasure discovering other early-morning walkers. Maybe we can make this a regular date!" She reached down to stroke Noo-noo's head, and the corgi eagerly flopped over for a tummy rub.

The two women chatted as they strolled into the park. The beagle soon interrupted their small talk, though, lunging against her leash and giving an insistent, baying bark. Noo-noo joined in, figuring something must have been wrong, even if she couldn't suss out what it was.

Posy frowned as the dog persistently pulled at the leash. She knelt down next to the dog and put a comforting hand on her. "Duchess! What's going on, girl?" She looked into the beagle's eyes, as if waiting patiently for her to tell her what was upsetting her.

Now the beagle whimpered. Noo-noo's fur stood up on her back and she growled, as if suddenly realizing the source of the beagle's concern.

"Beatrice, there's something lying on the ground over there. Near that group of trees," Posy said in a quiet voice.

Beatrice handed Posy Noo-noo's leash and walked cautiously up to the object, forcing her suddenly weak limbs to move forward. She saw Judith splayed unnaturally on her back, with blood pooled behind her head and her eyes staring blindly into the trees.

She croaked, "Oh, my Lord, Posy, it's Judith. We need to call the police."

"Not an ambulance?" asked Posy.

"I don't think so."

With some difficulty, Posy pulled the still-barking dogs over to a bench as, with shaking hands, Beatrice fumbled with her phone to dial 911.

[hapter 3

A police car soon drove up and Ramsay Downey stepped out, looking grim. He strode quickly to the figure on the ground, then back to Beatrice and Posy. "Are you ladies all right?" he asked. "This must have scared the life out of you." They nodded, and he sighed. "I don't know what to say, Beatrice. I promise you that violent crime is a most unusual occurrence in Dappled Hills. In fact, I can't ever recall us having a murder here." He rubbed his head. "The very lack of crime is the whole reason I chose to do police work here to begin with!"

He looked wearily toward Judith's body. "I'll call the state police and get a forensics crew. Let me check the scene and make sure it's secure, and then I'll let y'all go as soon as I can."

Minutes later, the women explained how they'd discovered Judith's body, while Ramsay, wearing a pair of reading glasses that looked circa 1950, took notes in a messy scrawl. Ramsay's gaze narrowed. "Meadow mentioned to me yesterday that y'all had a quilting bee last night. Right?" He winced, as if thinking of all the different women he'd need to talk to about Judith's last few hours.

Beatrice cleared her throat, and Ramsay raised his eyebrows at her. "I was just wondering what happened to Judith, Ramsay. It looked like she'd been hit over the head with something really heavy or hard," said Beatrice. She pinched her lips shut, realizing that Ramsay probably couldn't talk about it.

But Ramsay seemed to have no problems talking about the case. "Looks like blunt-force trauma to me," he said thoughtfully. "A hammer or a crowbar or something heavy like that."

Beatrice shivered despite the fact that the early-morning crispness of the mountain air had turned warmer.

The black coffee Piper handed her didn't help a *lot*, but it sure didn't hurt. Beatrice stirred in extra sugar. They were in Beatrice's kitchen, but Piper had efficiently located both the coffeemaker and the Ziploc bag of coffee that Beatrice hadn't yet unpacked, and made a pot.

"I'm so glad you didn't find Judith's body all by yourself," said Piper. "Although I'm not really sure what you and Noo-noo were doing out so early in the morning. I know you're used to getting up early to get ready for work, but I kind of thought you might have already made the adjustment to retirement time."

"Actually, there was a reason behind the walk." She

explained about the anonymous note she'd found on her front porch that morning.

Piper's gray eyes widened. "Anonymous letters? You've been in Dappled Hills for three days and you've already made enemies?"

Beatrice gave Piper a quelling look. "I think it has less to do with me and more to do with whoever left it for me. Maybe it was Judith. If I messed with anyone's plans, it was hers. Felicity and Amber would never have known that quilt was so valuable if I hadn't said something. Judith could have dropped off the note before she was murdered in the park. Maybe she wanted to spook me a little as punishment for ruining the deal she'd made with Felicity."

There was a jaunty series of raps on the door, and Piper peeked out. "It's Meadow," she said with a sigh of relief, as if instead there might have been a crazed, note-leaving killer lurking on the porch.

Meadow wore a rainbow-colored housecoat over purple-and-yellow plaid pajama bottoms, and her eyes were huge behind her red glasses. "What's happening? I heard sirens a little while ago and then I saw Piper walking over. Kinda early for a visit, isn't it? Is something wrong? Ramsay was patrolling all night, but I was expecting him home for an early breakfast. When he didn't show up, I phoned him, and he said he had a new case to work."

Beatrice was proud of herself for not pointing out that Meadow herself was out visiting at seven a.m. Instead she and Piper filled Meadow in on the recent events. Meadow alternately gasped and cried out in dismay throughout the retelling.

"It's karma," she said, sitting back in her chair and waving her hands around in the air to simulate cosmic order, or perhaps disorder. "What goes around comes around. Judith's wickedness finally caught up with her. But it's still so hard to take in since she was just as alive and mean as anything mere hours ago. So we were all arguing heatedly with her one minute at the quilting bee, and then a few hours later she's dead as a doornail. Could it have been some sort of an accident? Maybe Judith just fell and knocked her head. Or maybe she had some kind of medical problem and keeled over."

Beatrice thought of Judith's unusual sprawl, her lifeless eyes and the blood covering the ground around her. "There wouldn't have been that much head trauma from a mere fall. It looked to me like she'd been struck hard by a heavy object." She shook her head. There was no way Judith's death could have been natural. "I'm sure Ramsay will be talking to some of the quilting group from last night," she said. "Considering we were probably the last people to see her alive—and were arguing with her."

Meadow looked concerned. "Especially Amber." She shifted uneasily in her chair. "And I was the one who wanted to throw Judith out for being disruptive. Oh, and then she was ugly to Savannah and Georgia, making some sort of nasty inference about Savannah. And Posy! She was threatening to close the Patchwork

Cottage. Oh, heavens. Posy and Amber will look the most suspicious, for sure."

Piper mused, "This will be really rough on them."

Meadow was thoughtful. "Daisy has never gotten along with Judith, for that matter. They squabbled all the time. And Judith was trying to insinuate something ugly about Daisy, too, as I recall. Something about Daisy not being what she seemed." She turned to Beatrice. "Did you meet Daisy last night? She's the doctor's wife. She and Judith always butt heads because Daisy has really put a lot of time into her quilting and is making the rounds to all the regional shows. Judith was always really jealous of Daisy's talent and all her blue ribbons. Judith always wanted to be the best at *everything*. Maybe Daisy murdered Judith before Judith could murder *her*."

Meadow suddenly looked even more uncomfortable, then saw Beatrice staring at her and plastered on a fake smile. Beatrice's eyes narrowed a little. "Meadow, was there something else that you've thought of?"

Meadow made a noise like a balloon deflating. She shrugged. "You mentioned a hard object. It just made me remember something. I saw Posy." Meadow opened her mouth again, then snapped it shut.

"*Posy?* What was she doing?"

"I don't really remember," said Meadow slowly. When Beatrice made a scoffing noise, Meadow raised her eyebrows and said, "No, I really *don't* remember. The main thing was that she was returning Boris to me. You know how my sweet Boris loves going on adventures. He had run off and Posy had found him while she was out and was bringing him back to me. I know she said something about the reason she was out—maybe about the shop—and I thought perhaps she was heading over there because she'd forgotten to lock up. At the time it wasn't really important, since I didn't know anything about the murder."

"Did Posy seem like her usual self?"

Meadow nodded. "Pretty much. There was only one kind of funny thing. She had a shovel up in the front seat of her car."

"A _shovel_?"

"She'd pulled way up in my driveway so that she could lug Boris to my door without him running off again. I saw the shovel up there in the passenger seat when I opened the door. But Posy is a huge gardener, you know," said Meadow quickly. "If she's not piecing a quilt then she's out in her yard, filling the birdfeeders and planting flower beds or weeding. It's really not that weird that she had a shovel in her car."

Maybe it wasn't weird, but it made things complicated that Posy, who had much to gain from Judith's death, was out the night of the murder with a heavy object.

Meadow suddenly leaped out of her chair, startling Beatrice. "This is horrible. Horrible! Sitting around, thinking the worst of our friends. So we should go shopping . . . immediately. Quilt-shop therapy time." She squinted over at the clock. "Or maybe in three hours, since it's only seven a.m. and the stores aren't open yet."

Beatrice felt a little torn. She hadn't planned on going shopping for quilting supplies yet—she hadn't even decided what she was going to quilt. But she did want to find out a little more information, and Posy's shop sounded like it might be a hub for Dappled Hills gossip.

"I guess I could come along," she said slowly. "But, Meadow, I'm not feeling confident about submitting a block for the group quilt. I think I'm going to play around with making my own quilt first. Probably something that I'll burn after it's done," she said with a short laugh. "But I'm happy to help with figuring out a strategy or a new direction for your group, or to help organize the guild."

Meadow's plan was apparently to ignore any mention of Beatrice not participating in the guild's group project. "Beatrice, you'll feel much more comfortable with quilting when you have a chance to practice with your own tools. We'll make a shopping list for you. I'll do that after I get back home. We'll go to the Patchwork Cottage and get templates, patterns, rulers, fabric, cutting mats . . . the works!"

Piper shrugged helplessly at Beatrice. Meadow seemed to be an unstoppable force.

Meadow continued, "Besides, we should check in on poor Posy. I hope Ramsay and the state police haven't been too hard on her. He gets so grouchy when he hasn't had any sleep. Or food, I guess, since he didn't make it home for breakfast. He was grumpy, anyway, because I forgot to tape *Wheel of Fortune* last night. He's probably trying to behave himself, though, since it's Posy. So, let's go ahead and get ready and then we'll shop! And maybe I can squeeze some information out of Ramsay." She looked doubtful. "If he comes home."

Piper said, "By the way, Meadow, I enjoyed meeting Ash last night." She flushed a little. Beatrice felt that slight sinking feeling again. She wanted Piper to be with someone who made her happy. But did it have to be someone who lived clear on the other side of the country?

Meadow beamed. "He's the smartest, nicest, hand-somest man. You're still planning on going out tonight, aren't you?" she asked in a concerned voice. "I know there's been a . . . well, a tragic event . . . but life must go on! Besides, he'll only be here for the week. There's not much time." She answered her own question. "Of course you are. When I get back to the house, I'll tell him dinner is still on. If he's awake. It's still super early! Okay, chop-chop! Let's get ready!" And she was gone.

Beatrice passed through the door and into the Patch-work Cottage, a quilter's paradise. Soft, up-tempo music played, comfy chairs and sofas invited you to sit and visit for a spell, and there were bolts of colorful cloth and more supplies than you could possibly imagine.

Beatrice saw quilting hoops, quilting books, specialty threads, buttons, rotary cutters and selections of different-sized needles. Posy draped quilts for display over antique washstands and an old sewing machine in the corner. There were quilts on every available spot on the walls and even the ceilings. The shop looked to have all kinds of nooks and crannies to it, including a consignment corner where quilters could sell their quilts. The whole shop had a welcoming, homey feel. There were even rocking chairs at the front of the porch with *Field & Stream* beside them, to occupy husbands while their wives shopped. No wonder the quilters had been so adamant about keeping the shop open.

Posy didn't look nearly as serene as the atmosphere in her shop. Daisy Butler, wearing a very tight lavender track suit with a cleavage-revealing V-neck, was trying to console her. Daisy shook her head at Meadow and Piper as if to say that Posy wasn't in great shape.

Posy greeted Beatrice with a hug, tears glistening in her bright eyes. "I'm so glad you were with me this morning. I know that's an awful thing for me to say. I'm really so sorry you had to find Judith, but thank goodness I wasn't alone. I think poor Duchess took some comfort in having Noo-noo there, too."

Beatrice nodded. "I feel the same way. It's been a rough morning, hasn't it?"

There were shadows of exhaustion around Posy's eyes. "Oh, y'all. Ramsay thinks I murdered Judith."

"What?" asked Meadow in outrage. "Stuff and nonsense. Ramsay thinks no such thing, Posy. You're our friend." Meadow's thunderous expression didn't bode well for Ramsay's off-duty hours. She clearly thought she was going to force him to cross Posy's name off his list of suspects.

Posy smiled gently. "You're a wonderful friend, Meadow, but this has nothing to do with friendship. Ramsay is just doing his job."

Daisy said quickly, "Clearly, though, Judith's death is a mugging gone horribly wrong." Her words rang hollow, though, as if she knew better.

Posy shook her head sadly. "That's not what the police think, Meadow. They think someone followed Judith to the park and murdered her. Or lured her out there to kill her. And I'm the one who had so much to gain from her death, after all. She told me last night that she was going to force me out because she'd found another tenant who'd pay more rent. I was going to lose my shop, which is so much more to me than simply a business. And now?" She held out her hands helplessly. "Problem solved. In the worst way possible."

Daisy knit her brows. "Is it really solved, though? Wouldn't Judith have left the shop to someone in her will?"

Piper said, "Judith has a daughter who's a little younger than I am. She doesn't live in Dappled Hills, though. I met her the last time she came to town to visit Judith."

Meadow made a shooing motion. "Judith's daughter won't want to bother with selling or tampering with real estate! Especially not from a long distance. I'm positive she'll be delighted to get a rent check in the mail every month."

"Besides," Daisy said, smoothing down her track pants with a plump hand, "gobs of people wanted Judith dead. Yes, Posy had a motive. But I never saw Posy seem *mad* at Judith. She never got all that angry. And, really, can we imagine mild-mannered Posy clubbing anybody over the head and killing them?"

Meadow put her hands on her hips. "Well, who *do* you see clubbing Judith on the head? I'm the one who was so furious with her last night, if you're going to limit suspects to people who were angry."

Daisy said quietly, "I was mad at Judith, too. Plenty of times. We all were. But why would we kill her? What possible motive could we have?"

Beatrice saw Meadow color and wondered if there was something Meadow might have said if Daisy hadn't continued talking. "No, I think the murder has more to do with that antique quilt. Or *quilting* itself. No one likes being taken advantage of like Felicity was. It must be the lowest feeling ever."

Beatrice said, "But, Daisy, Felicity was perfectly reasonable last night. She stated very calmly that she needed time to think the deal over."

"But *Amber* wasn't reasonable," Daisy said with emphasis. "Amber was upset that Judith was trying to cheat her mother. As I recall, Judith was putting down her mother because she'd lost her money in a pyramid scheme."

Meadow jumped in. "As Amber's friend—and mentor—I cannot let you blame her for murder, Daisy! There's simply no way she'd kill somebody over strips of cloth and some batting. *Or* because of some inane put-down Judith made about her mom."

Beatrice hid a smile at the thought of the scattered, excitable Meadow being someone's mentor.

Daisy said quickly, "I wouldn't dream of accusing Amber of murder. I'm simply pointing out that people act out of character sometimes—especially in the heat of the moment. Or when they've had too much to drink."

Meadow was about to hotly contest this fact, but then pressed her lips together tightly.

"I'm not saying it definitely *was* Amber who killed Judith," said Daisy. "Think about Savannah or Georgia. Judith has picked on Georgia for ages, and it clearly makes Savannah very defensive and upset. I can easily picture Savannah killing someone if she thought her sister was being hurt."

Meadow was indignant. "Daisy, I can't believe you! Savannah and Georgia and Amber are our friends!"

Daisy said, "Well, *somebody* we know is a killer. That's a fact, ladies. The sooner we get to the bottom of it, the quicker we'll stop gossiping about which of our friends is a murderer."

Beatrice said, "Do any of us have an alibi for last night? The murder must have happened sometime after the quilting bee and before dawn. Posy and I were in the park really early this morning, and I could tell

that Judith must have been lying there for a while."
Beatrice tried to forget the sight of Judith's stiff limbs.

There was silence for a moment, and Beatrice felt as
though there were some undercurrents in the room that
she couldn't quite figure out. "After the bee, everyone
went home," said Piper finally. "At least they seemed
to be heading that way. Since I'm by myself, there's no
one to vouch for me."

"I was alone," said Beatrice.

"Me, too," said Meadow, still with that faint color
staining her cheeks. "Ramsay was out working all
night."

Daisy said, "I was at home with my husband some
of the evening, but he had ER duty most of the night at
the county hospital."

Posy said quietly, "My husband was at home, but
Cork was snoring away when I came in and still sleeping when I left to take Duchess for her walk. Long day
at the wine shop, I guess. Besides, nothing seems to
wake Cork up—he sleeps like a baby."

"Posy, you shouldn't say things like that," said
Meadow, eyes large. "Did you tell Ramsay that?"

"But, Meadow, it's the truth."

"You should've just told them that Cork was home.
That was the truth, too. And that he's a very light
sleeper and would have woken up immediately if
you'd left the house to nip out and murder Judith."

Posy's brow creased with worry.

The shop bell chimed and wizened Miss Sissy, back
bent in a bow, thumped in with her wooden cane. She

scowled at the group. "What's wrong?" she barked. "Somebody die?"

Back home and ready for a rest, Beatrice pulled her wrought-iron table over next to the hammock in her backyard and brought out a small pitcher of fresh lemonade and a glass filled with ice. She lay down gently in the hammock, put on a pair of reading glasses and happily opened her book, *Whispers of Summer*. Noo-noo lay on the ground next to her, making little snorting snores. The yard was dappled with sunlight, and a soft breeze wafted through the air. *This* had been her vision of retirement. She gave a sigh of satisfaction.

After only ten minutes of reading, though, she felt restless. Shouldn't she be doing something? Emptying the dishwasher? Mailing bill payments? She probably should have gone by the store to pick up something for supper. She wasn't *used* to relaxing, she told herself. It was probably something she'd have to work up to.

Her mind kept drifting away from her book and back to Judith's death. In an ordinary day at the museum, she'd always been engaged in *some* kind of mental exercise—researching a new exhibit or studying various aspects of the folk art she was appraising. Every bit of art in the museum told a story, and she'd felt like a detective investigating the story behind each piece of art. There must be a story behind Judith's death, too. She hoped Piper's best friend wouldn't be at the heart of the story. Piper had seemed very concerned about Amber when they'd talked yesterday. The police were sure to be interested in talking with Amber, especially after they learned about her heated argument with Judith over the quilt last night. Could the girl really be a cold-blooded killer, though? It was hard to picture. Maybe, if she poked around a little, she could find a way to clear Amber's name.

Beatrice shifted in the hammock. Too bad the quilting hadn't been quite the relaxing activity that Piper and Meadow had assured her it would be. Meadow, true to her word, had made an exacting list of supplies for Beatrice, and Posy, despite her anxiety, had gently and skillfully found some fabrics that she thought Beatrice would enjoy working with. It all seemed effortless for Posy, as if she automatically knew beautiful color and texture combinations. Beatrice felt like she had to turn her creativity on and off like a faucet. Back at home, she'd watched a short beginner-quilter video on her computer, but the forty-five minutes she'd used to apply the techniques to her own quilt had been disastrous.

Piper thought quilting would prove a great way to get Beatrice's mind off discovering Judith's body. And it had done that—only because the experience had been so frustrating. It had taken ten minutes just to thread the needle. Then she'd tried some basic hand-piecing—sewing a couple of scraps together by hand. It should have been simple to sew a triangle of light fabric to a triangle of dark fabric, but the back of it was a catastrophe and the front hadn't been much better. She knew that quilting was a big way to connect to the other women in the community, but she was becoming more convinced that her role should be that of an adviser or organizer or even designer rather than a hands-on creator.

Beatrice jumped, heart pounding, as Noo-noo exploded into barking and bolted toward the back door, looking back at Beatrice as if telling her she needed to follow. But by the time Beatrice had extricated herself from the hammock and found a spot to put down her book, Posy was already unhitching the back gate.

"Beatrice, I'm so sorry! You're trying to relax and you certainly need to after such an unsettling morning."

"No, actually, I was thinking how horrible I am at relaxing. And this refreshing lemonade isn't nearly as refreshing as the mint julep I keep thinking about. Especially after this extraordinarily long day. How about if I make us both one?"

Posy took her up on her offer, and in a few minutes Beatrice was back outside with a small tray of drinks and napkins.

"I think," said Posy thoughtfully, "that relaxation is a acquired skill. It must be really difficult for you to make the adjustment from being a busy curator to being a retired lady in a hammock."

"I'll have to put in some practice, I guess. I had no idea that I was going to be so bad at the art of relaxation." They both took healthy sips from their glasses. "Posy, I'm so glad you came over." To her surprise, Beatrice found it was true.

Posy had settled into a wicker chair, and Noo-noo had apparently developed instant devotion, and lay her head on Posy's leg. Posy bent to talk to Noo-noo. "Your hearing is amazing!" she said to the dog in an earnest voice. "Absolutely amazing. You could hear me knocking at your front door and you weren't even in the house! Good thing I could hear *you* in the backyard, or I'd still be knocking." She beamed at the corgi.

Noo-noo flopped over on her back and watched her with glowing eyes. Posy seemed to have that effect on animals.

Finally Posy sat back, glanced around the backyard, and said to Beatrice with a smile, "I brought you a little something from one of the downtown stores. I was worried you might already have one, but I don't think you do."

Beatrice now noticed that Posy had placed a canvas bag on the ground beside her. Posy opened it up and pulled out a bright red hummingbird feeder, and handed it to Beatrice with a smile. "Posy, that's so sweet of you. No, I *don't* have a hummingbird feeder. I lived in a condominium in Atlanta and there was no place to put one."

Posy said, "Oh, good! I was a little worried you might already have one, but then I just figured that you could have two. I hope you'll have a good time with the hummingbirds. They're such wonderful little birds, but really so ferocious! You'll have hummingbird battles in your yard at all times."

"I can't wait. I've always wanted a hummingbird

feeder. Such a thoughtful housewarming gift, Posy. Thank you."

"A housewarming present, but also a thank-you for being such a good friend this morning," said Posy seriously. "Could you tell that I was absolutely terrified after we found poor Judith? Such an awful scene ... finding her body, our unhappy little dogs, the fog everywhere. You were so cool and matter-of-fact that you calmed me right down. I'm still worried, of course—I know that I've got to be a main suspect. But I'm so grateful that you were there and were so competent in such a stressful moment."

"It was frightening for both of us—and for Duchess and Noo-noo, too, I'm sure. But I'd only just met Judith, and my first impression obviously wasn't wonderful. It was really startling to discover her that way, but I don't think I'll have too many nightmares over it. You've had a much longer relationship with her, and I'm sure it was a huge shock for you to see her that way."

A shadow flitted across Posy's placid features, so Beatrice quickly moved on, not wanting to make Posy think about their discovery of the body. "As far as being a main suspect, I wouldn't be surprised if all of us will fall under suspicion. Don't worry too much about being singled out—everyone was arguing with Judith last night."

Posy looked sadly at Noo-noo, who seemed so in tune with Posy's feelings that her brown eyes were also mournful. "I can't imagine any of them murdering Judith. Having an argument is one thing, but killing someone in cold blood? I simply can't see it. I've known most of those ladies my whole life."

"That's the thing about murder, though, Posy—I think *anyone* could be capable of it, depending on the circumstances. We all have our triggers. If we feel threatened or angry or belittled, who knows what could happen when we're at our worst? Judith was pushing everyone's buttons last night. She made ugly accusations and insinuations and tried to take advantage of an older lady who thought of her as a friend. Then she plainly stated her intentions of taking a solitary walk in the park to clear her mind." Beatrice shrugged. "We all heard her. We were all angry with her. It could be anyone."

Posy sighed. "Judith *was* acting especially unpleasant last night. It's a shame you didn't have a chance to meet her when she was behaving better. She was a gifted quilter and a great booster for our guild. Judith was very supportive of the Village Quilters and proud of the progress our group had made and the ribbons we'd won."

"But I've also heard she was extremely competitive and was unhappy when fellow quilters won awards or got chosen as beekeeper," said Beatrice.

"We all have our faults, I suppose." If it was a reproof, it was a very gentle one.

Beatrice took a deep breath and then jumped right in. "There was something I wanted to ask you about, Posy. Meadow dropped by this morning. She admitted, although she hadn't wanted to, that she'd seen you out last night. With a shovel in your car."

Posy made a soft gasp and gave a little jump. She said quietly, "I *was* out that night. And I *did* have a shovel in the car with me. But I didn't murder Judith."

"What were you doing?"

"It was probably the strangest night ever, followed by the strangest *morning* ever. I was getting ready for bed when we got an automated call from the alarm company that the shop was being broken into."

"The Patchwork Cottage?"

"Actually, no. Cork's wine shop. But those calls are starting to be a regular occurrence, because the alarm is malfunctioning somehow. Once or twice, though, Cork *has* had someone break in, so we have to take it seriously."

"But *you're* the one who went out to check on the shop?" That didn't seem very chivalrous of Cork.

"No, Cork went—but he had a real bee in his bonnet about it. He'd actually been sound asleep and snoring when I came home from Judith's house, so the call woke him up. He decided to stay in his pajamas and drive over real quick to see if he saw anything. He wouldn't even call Ramsay and let him know—he was that convinced it was going to be a false alarm."

"So how did you end up driving around with a shovel?" asked Beatrice.

Posy said sadly, "I told Cork to take some kind of weapon with him, in case there *was* somebody breaking into the shop. But he was so crabby and stubborn that he took off in the car. I decided to pull some clothes on and follow him. I grabbed the shovel, which was the first big thing in the garage that I could get my hands on. I'd just finished preparing a flower bed for planting, so it was really convenient." Posy swallowed. "I know it sounds horrible, especially since I had a problem with Judith and I was so close to the scene of the crime."

"Did you catch up with Cork?"

"I did, but by the time I got over to the shop, Cork was already stomping out, saying that there was nobody there. So, really, I was no help at all."

Posy looked so miserable that Beatrice almost hated to prompt her. She said in a gentle voice, "You didn't mention to Ramsay that you were near the park around the time of the murder."

Posy shook her head. "I sure didn't. I like to think that it was because I was so shocked by what I'd seen that I didn't even remember to mention it. But maybe, somewhere deep in my subconscious, there was a little bit of self-protecting going on. And I wanted to cover for Cork, of course, and the fact that he'd gone out that night. I feel just awful about it. And now, if Meadow isn't mentioning the shovel to Ramsay, she's not being honest with her own husband."

"Did you happen to notice anything out of the ordinary while you were out? Anything that could help us find out who murdered Judith?"

Posy thought hard, then said, "I wish I could say that I did. About the only thing that I did that night that was useful at all was find Boris. I was on my way home from the wine shop and I saw Boris sitting by the side of the road. When I rolled down my window, he whimpered. It really wasn't like Boris at all—he was shaking and so sad-looking."

Posy continued. "I asked him what was wrong"—Beatrice tried to ignore this part—"and he looked at me like his heart was breaking. Of course, I thought it was because he was separated from his family. I opened up the car door and he jumped in, still talking to me about his problems with little whines. The poor thing erupted into wagging when he saw his mommy. He was wagging his whole body as soon as he caught sight of Meadow."

Great. So probably the only witness to the crime, besides the murderer, was Boris.

"Oh, and I saw Georgia out." Posy didn't look in the least concerned. "But she's always out at night. Like Judith used to be."

"I know that Judith needled everyone in earshot last night, Posy, but some of her barbs went over my head. I couldn't figure out exactly what she was trying to say. Can you remember anything Judith said specifically? I was trying to think of information that might help with the investigation."

Posy thought for a moment, then shook her head. "I'm afraid not, Beatrice, although you're good to try to help with the case. I think as soon as Judith mentioned closing the Patchwork Cottage, I just sort of tuned everything else out."

Posy reached out and softly stroked Noo-noo's head. "Noo-noo, I've got to head on home to Mr. Cork. Heaven knows what I'm making for supper tonight. Maybe we'll have breakfast for supper. That's always fun."

As Beatrice stood to walk her out, Posy gave her a quick hug. "Thanks again, Beatrice. I think you're going to be such a wonderful addition to Dappled Hills . . . and the guild, too. And if . . . if I can remember anything important about last night, I'll let you know."

The next morning, Beatrice peeped out her front door and was relieved not to see a glass bottle there. Of course, there was also the fact that there wasn't a real newspaper, either. The *Dappled Hills Dispatch* was just a slip of a paper, and she really didn't know any of the people *in* it. But still, she'd paid for a subscription.

She fixed a strong cup of coffee and sat in the backyard with Noo-noo, reading *Whispers of Summer* while she woke up. After a few minutes of reading, though, the silence was almost overpowering. Of course, she'd moved to the mountains to get a change of pace and some quiet. But this was *really* quiet. Sounds of traffic in Atlanta had provided a sort of white noise for Beatrice in the background. She'd gotten to the point where she didn't even notice it anymore. Maybe that's how the quiet of Dappled Hills would be, after a while.

Giving up on her book, Beatrice walked back inside her cottage. Maybe if she put up Posy's hummingbird feeder, she'd at least have the sounds of the little birds flying through. She held out the feeder directions to read the small print. Four parts water to one part sugar. Boiled to slow the growth of bacteria. Got it.

Soon the house smelled like cotton candy—not, actually, an unpleasant thing. The phone rang, and Beatrice was so deep in thought that the sudden noise made her drop the spoon she was using to mix the nectar.

"Mama?"

"Oh, hi, Piper." She reached down to the floor to pick up the sticky spoon, then grabbed a paper towel to clean up the spatter.

"Did I startle you? You sound a little breathless."

"I was in my own little world when you called. I'm making hummingbird nectar and I was thinking about a lot of different things."

"Hummingbird nectar? *You're* making it?"

Beatrice frowned. "I'm perfectly capable of making hummingbird nectar, Piper. Just because I haven't made it before doesn't mean I can't make it now."

"I'm thinking that Posy must have paid you a visit." Beatrice could hear the smile in Piper's voice. "She gave me a hummingbird feeder as a gift when I first moved to Dappled Hills, too. It's actually been a lot of fun to watch them. I set up the feeder outside my kitchen window and the birds fly right up to it. They fight like crazy over that feeder sometimes."

"That's what Posy was saying—that they're tiny but fierce." Posy was tiny herself. But Beatrice still had a hard time picturing her having anything to do with Judith's death, even with all she had to gain.

"I hate to ask," said Piper, "but if you're fitting making nectar so easily into your schedule, are you possibly a little bored?"

Beatrice repressed a sigh. Piper knew her well. Ordinarily she was juggling more than one thing at a time. Here in Dappled Hills, it was more like she was avoiding quilting, spending too much time thinking about a local murder and now making homemade bird food. It really didn't compare to setting up a traveling exhibit, giving a museum tour to a well-heeled patron and attending opening nights for new exhibits.

"What you need," said Piper thoughtfully, "is a jigsaw puzzle. That would keep you busy."

"I already *have* a jigsaw puzzle! This quilt block— I'm having a devil of a time trying to figure out how to put all the pieces together. No, it's really just frustrating me instead of keeping me entertained. I've decided that if I *do* end up working on it, I'm going to mess up a quilt of my own first before messing up a group quilt."

"Really? I'd have thought that you'd really take to quilting, considering your background."

"But I haven't taken to painting, Piper, and I know a lot about Southern painters. I haven't taken to folk art sculptures, and yet I dealt with a lot of sculptures."

"You really haven't given quilting much of a chance. You just bought your fabric and materials yesterday, so you couldn't have spent much time trying to quilt. You should work on a couple of different quilts and really get the hang of it before you judge it," said Piper.

Beatrice was opening her mouth to retort before she

stopped. "You're probably right, Piper. I always told you to hang with a hobby for a while before you made a decision about continuing with it. I'll keep plugging ahead." She looked morosely at the quilt block lying in a dejected pile across the room. If Piper was in a nagging mood, a change of subject was definitely in order.

"Is everything going okay with you?" Beatrice asked.

"Everything's fine, Mama. It's actually *more* than fine."

Ahh. Beatrice remembered now—Piper's date with Meadow's son, Ash. "Did y'all have a good time out on your date last night?"

Piper's smile came right through the phone line and warmed Beatrice's heart. "Mama, it was *more* than a good time. I felt as if I've known Ash my whole life. Have you ever felt really simpatico with someone, like you've got the same sense of humor, the same way of looking at the world?"

"I sure have, honey, but it's been a long time—since I met your daddy for the first time, probably."

Piper said, "You'll love him, Mama. Well, I know you met him, but you didn't get a chance to really talk to Ash at the quilting bee. He's got a great sense of humor and he's the perfect gentleman all the time."

"He sounds wonderful, honey. Are you planning on seeing him again today?"

"We're going out for a picnic lunch! That's why I wanted to go ahead and call you . . . I didn't want you to wonder where I was, since there's a murderer on the loose and everything. I'll have my cell phone, but I'll probably ignore it . . . unless you call. If you call me, I'll know it's something really important, since you'll know I'm on a date."

Beatrice felt happy and wistful at the same time. Yes, she'd felt like Piper before. But it'd been a long, long time.

As she hung up the phone, it immediately rang again. Thinking Piper had forgotten to tell her something, she picked right back up with a smile. But it was Savannah.

"Want to come along with Georgia and me to visit Felicity? Georgia called her earlier to give her the news about Judith, and she seemed really upset. We thought we'd pop by and make sure everything was all right. She had a rough time last night with Judith acting out, and then she seemed shaken up by the murder . . ." Savannah's voice trailed off.

And Beatrice knew things wouldn't get any better when Ramsay found out about the dispute over the antique quilt and wanted to talk to her about it. "Of course I'll come," said Beatrice.

"Would you mind picking us up?" asked Savannah in a brisk tone. "It's supposed to rain soon."

Savannah and Georgia lived in a small yellow, gable-front house that had a wraparound porch with two porch swings. Savannah sat in one of them, hands folded primly in her lap. When she saw Beatrice's car, she jumped up. "Georgia is running behind," she said with a *tsk*. "I do believe she lives in a different time zone from the rest of us. The sun is so bright out here. Want to come in for a minute while we wait?"

The inside of the little house was very tidy—almost to a fault, thought Beatrice. The wooden floors shone, and no dust dared settle on any surface in the house. Like Meadow's house, Savannah's and Georgia's walls and backs of chairs and sofas were covered with quilts. "These are mostly my quilts," said Savannah, noticing Beatrice's gaze. "Georgia keeps hers in her bedroom."

Beatrice could easily guess which of the quilts were Savannah's. She recognized the familiar patterns from the quilts she'd had at the folk-art museum: pinwheels, Dutchman's Puzzles, Windblown Squares, Pieced Stars, Flying Geese, Devil's Puzzles. The careful order of the patterns all must appeal to Savannah. Several quilts didn't seem to belong—they were covered with embellishments and boasted crystals and paillettes, beads and lace, buttons and ribbons. They were fanciful, dreamy, almost confectionary in nature. Clearly the daydreamy Georgia's quilts.

"Did you get started with your block for the group quilt that Meadow assigned at the guild meeting?" asked Beatrice. "My art background made me curious—I love the idea of putting symbols of things that are meaningful to different quilters on the blocks."

Savannah pressed her thin lips together tightly. "Not my favorite assignment of Meadow's. I usually favor very orderly, geometric patterns."

As if Beatrice didn't see that.

"But I'm giving it a go," said Savannah with a long-suffering sigh. "I couldn't sleep last night, so I got started with my block. Actually, I finished it." She walked over to a large notebook in a small bookcase. In it were three-holed plastic page protectors with finished squares in them. They seemed to be organized into sections with tabs. Beatrice blinked at the thought of the time involved.

Savannah carefully pulled out a block from one of the plastic pages and held it out for Beatrice to see.

There was a cat appliquéd on the block, although it looked like Savannah couldn't quite keep the geometric look out of her work—the cat's ears were Flying Geese.

"The little cat symbolizes Georgia, of course," said Savannah briskly. Beatrice must have been looking a little blank, because Savannah added with irritation, "Because of her little pet-clothing business. You know."

Beatrice said, "It must be nice for you to have your sister living here with you. I don't get to see my sister nearly often enough."

Savannah gave a vigorous nod. "Georgia needed a place to live after her divorce and this was the natural choice. It was hard at first because she and I have such different routines and habits. But it's worked out really well, and now I can't imagine her anywhere else."

It sounded like Savannah wasn't going to *allow* Georgia to go anywhere else. Maybe Georgia's marriage was the one instance where Savannah had let up on her iron control of Georgia and it had failed miserably. "Does Georgia's ex still live here in Dappled Hills? That must be awkward in such a small town."

Savannah put her hands on her narrow hips. "Well, it surely wasn't awkward for *Georgia*! That's what I kept telling her, anyway. I'd remind her that *she* wasn't the one who was cheating. *She* hadn't done anything to be ashamed of. He was the one who'd disgraced himself, after all. And, sure enough, he got so uncomfortable with everyone knowing what a cheating husband he'd been that he slunk out of town with his tail between his legs." Savannah looked quite ferociously pleased at the thought.

Georgia showed up breathlessly. "Sorry! Sorry! I'm all ready now." She opened a small closet near them and stuck her feet into some slip-on shoes. She turned around and saw Savannah holding a block. "Is that for the new quilt? You're so fast! How did you find the time to already finish the block?"

There was an indefinable edge to Savannah's voice. "A couple of nights ago. The night of the bee, actually. Sometimes when I'm worried and can't sleep, I quilt. And that was the least-peaceful quilting bee I've ever attended."

Judith's murder had clearly had an effect on Felicity. She wore none of the artfully applied makeup she'd had at the quilting bee and now she looked her age, which must be early seventies. Gone was the spunk and the strength. She wore a thick wool sweater and was covered up with a quilt, but was still giving little shivers as she clutched the covering around her, huddled on the sofa. Glancing around the room, Beatrice saw many other quilts that could be heaped on Felicity, if needed. The walls were covered with hanging quilts, and they were draped over sofas and chair backs, too. She hadn't been kidding when she'd said she had a huge collection of quilts.

Georgia was already clucking as soon as they walked in the door, her nurturing instincts in overdrive. "Let me make you some tea," she said, scurrying to the kitchen. "*Hot* tea, not iced."

There was some banging around in cabinets and then a crash as several things fell to the floor. "Sorry!" Georgia called out. Savannah muttered under her breath at her sister's clumsiness.

Beatrice said, "Felicity, is there anything we can do? Are you actually feeling ill, or are you upset about Judith . . . ?"

Beatrice trailed off as Felicity knit her brows at the mention of Judith. Georgia hurried in and pressed the cup of warm tea into Felicity's hands.

"Sorry," said Beatrice, feeling that she'd made things worse by bringing up the murder.

Felicity shook her head. "No, Beatrice, it's not your fault. This whole thing has put me in a state."

Georgia said sadly, "I think what's made me feel so terrible is how we left things with Judith. You'd like to think that your last words with a person before they die would be nice ones." Georgia's eyes grew misty and she rummaged in her pocketbook for a tissue.

"It's hardly our fault, Georgia. Judith is the one who riled everybody up! She made us all furious with her, then waltzed out the door and got herself murdered." Savannah sounded miffed at Judith's thoughtlessness.

"And no one was angrier with Judith than Amber," said Felicity quietly.

"You can't think that *Amber* would have anything to do with her murder!" Georgia's eyes were wide.

Felicity shrugged wordlessly, staring blankly across the room.

"Amber had absolutely *nothing* to do with it!" said Savannah, raising her penciled-in eyebrows to severe heights. "The very idea! Your daughter is no murderer, Felicity."

Felicity took a tiny sip of her tea and didn't answer.

"Why do you think," asked Beatrice quietly, "that Amber could be involved with Judith's death?"

Felicity looked down at the colorful quilt covering her, smoothing the fabric gently. "She was incredibly angry," she said. She raised her hand at Georgia, who was about to sputter something in Amber's defense. "No, you didn't hear all of it. She wasn't just upset at the quilting bee . . . She was absolutely furious while driving me home. She said hateful things about Judith . . . It wasn't like Amber at all," she said in a firm voice. "At least . . . it wasn't like Amber, the way she is *now.*"

Savannah clucked. "Don't bring up the past, Felicity. It doesn't have any bearing at all."

"But it *does*. The past *always* has a bearing on the present." Felicity sighed and looked directly at Beatrice. "Amber was a very difficult teenager. Her dad died in an accident when she was fifteen. It really seemed to change her. She started hanging out with the wrong kind of kids—not Dappled Hills kids. She was angry over everything. It was a very bad time."

"A bad time," reminded Savannah in a stern voice, "that happened long ago."

Felicity shook her head. "But Amber was so furious after the bee. It was just like when she was a teenager."

"We all have our triggers," Beatrice said.

"Well, this was clearly one of Amber's. She hated the idea that Judith tried to take advantage of me."

Savannah bristled with indignation. "As she should! It sounds like Judith planned to cheat you out of a good deal of money."

Beatrice said, "I have to agree with Savannah—any daughter would be upset about that, Felicity. It doesn't mean that Amber acted on her anger."

Felicity paused. "It's the second time that it's happened, though. Judith was right when she said that a swindler duped me with a pyramid scheme." There was a hard note in Felicity's voice now. "It's been five years now, but the whole episode still makes Amber livid. Plus, she was worried she was going to have to help me out financially, which is hard to do on a teacher's salary, especially when you're just starting out. I'd been supporting *Amber*, not the other way round. So I know that the thought of Judith cheating me out of money would be a trigger for Amber. I tried talking to Amber last night. I wanted to check back in with her because she was so upset. Terribly upset. And . . . she never picked up her phone." She rubbed the soft border of the quilt between her fingers as she spoke.

Georgia waved a hand in the air, indicating the nebulous nature of Amber's evening. "She could have been in the bathtub or something. Maybe she decided to go straight to bed and turned the ringer off the phone so she wouldn't be disturbed."

"Maybe." Felicity didn't look convinced. There were deep circles under her eyes. Beatrice quickly changed the subject, since Felicity didn't seem to have any other information to share. "Savannah was showing me her block for the new group quilt that Meadow is organizing."

"You did get a message from Meadow, didn't you?" Savannah cut in. "She was supposed to call everyone who wasn't at the guild meeting."

Felicity straightened in the chair a little. "Meadow did call me. I've got so much fabric already here at the house that I went ahead and got started. Quilting helps calm my nerves." She pointed to a basket across the room. Georgia gently picked up a block from the top of the pile in the basket, and oohed over it. "I love it!"

Georgia held it up for everyone to see. Felicity had used romantic pastels in her block and had started appliquéing delicate roses on the front. She had also cut fabric in the shape of what looked like a large house in the Tudor revival style. "That's Hampstead Columns," Felicity explained. She shrugged a thin shoulder. "Apparently, that retirement home is my new obsession."

"It makes for a beautiful block, though," said Beatrice. "If it's that pretty, I sure don't blame you for wanting to move there."

"It's a lovely place. It's not in Dappled Hills, but it's not a long drive, either. I've got the money for the current monthly rent there," said Felicity slowly. "But if any costs go up at all, I won't be able to afford it. And we know that costs always go up. So I really can't move there at this point, with no extra money to ensure against cost-of-living increases, because that would put Amber on the hook to help me out. I've got to get a cushion somehow."

This line of conversation also seemed to be a worrying one for the older woman. Since Felicity mentioned that quilting was calming for her, Beatrice switched over to some guild conversation. "By the way," she said, "Meadow has talked to me a little bit about taking the Village Quilters in a new direction—maybe accelerating the number of shows the group attends or focusing more on unique quilt designs. It would be really helpful if you could tell me about the kinds of things the Village Quilters have participated in in the past. Maybe that would give me some ideas about what direction to head in first."

This was an area that Felicity knew a lot about, since she'd been part of the guild for the past thirty years. As she happily prattled about charity events and bazaars and different regional venues, the stress seemed to fall away from her a little. Savannah would intersperse her monologue from time to time with small corrections or additions.

Finally, Felicity stifled a yawn and Beatrice said, "Why don't we let you get a little rest now? It looks like you didn't sleep well last night."

Felicity said drowsily, "Take some quilts with you as you go. Please. I really am trying to unload them, and I don't think I've got anything else valuable here. And if I do, I'm sure you'll let me know, Beatrice."

Beatrice said, "By the way, I jotted down some quilt collectors' names that I'm acquainted with from my work at the museum. Some of them might be interested in talking with you about your quilt, since you were thinking about selling it. Maybe Amber can help you get in touch with them." The older lady gave Beatrice a grateful smile.

Felicity wouldn't let her leave without a quilt in her hands—and she made Georgia and Savannah take one, too. Beatrice was able to assure her that they were *lovely* but not as valuable as the one she'd been planning to give Judith.

Beatrice had to admit that the new quilt looked beautiful on her bed. It inspired her to spend an hour struggling through some quilting herself. At first, the quilting was just as frustrating as usual . . . but then she discovered that she was actually improving. She wasn't *good*, but she was getting better. This gave her a sense of peace—which was quickly dispelled the next morning when she found another note on her front porch. *Don't be nosy*, it advised.

Chapter 4

Whether it was the mysterious bottle appearing on her porch again, the beautiful summer day, the reminder of life's sometimes untimely end that Judith's death prompted, or perhaps a small yearning to see the handsome minister again, Beatrice decided that church was in order.

She looked in her closet and wondered what to wear. She finally decided on a basic royal blue dress. Beatrice had an inkling that it might be the kind of church where the congregation still got dressed up on Sundays.

Beatrice spent a few minutes rummaging around in the remaining boxes for her Bible before giving up. They'd have them in the pews. She found her favorite straw purse with colorful raffia flowers splashed across it and headed out the door. The weather was fine for walking and she had on comfortable sandals, so she left the car in the driveway.

Will I ever get used to the stillness and quiet here? The silence was almost noisy. After a moment, though, she realized that there *were* sounds, just not the street sounds she'd gotten accustomed to in the city. One bird in particular was remarkable. It must have been a mockingbird, because the song jumped from one pattern to another. How many did the bird know? Beatrice started counting the unique songs.

Unfortunately, she became so engrossed with the mockingbird's song that she didn't notice the sound of a car engine behind her—until an old Lincoln came within about a foot of her and she scrambled off the sidewalk onto the grass.

She saw a fist waving on a skinny arm and muttered dark things under her breath. Miss Sissy was a public menace. How did she manage to keep a license? She must be paying Ramsay on the side.

Beatrice was relieved to finally make it safely to the church. Wyatt was at the huge wooden door, greeting worshippers as they came in. When she reached the door, Daisy was talking to Wyatt. She automatically put up a hand to smooth her hair and saw Daisy wink at her.

Daisy said, "So I designed that quilt to represent disappearing rural Americana. It's a wistful, poignant tribute. At least, that's what the judges said. Isn't that nice? Now it's going in a Southeastern juried competition among the best original designs in our region. I'm just pleased as punch—and feel so honored."

Wyatt was quick to compliment her on her accomplishment and wish her luck in the competition. He actually *seemed* interested in quilting when she was telling him about it. An amazing man, really.

Daisy started talking again, and Beatrice tried to shift her attention back. "I'm glad you're here, Beatrice, because I wanted to invite you to a dinner party I'm having tonight—in your honor."

"Oh . . . Daisy. That's really nice of you."

Daisy smiled at her. "It's just a small dinner with my friends, to welcome you to town and give you a chance to visit with some people I think you'll enjoy. I'd do something larger, but I think it would be inappropriate under the circumstances. Wyatt, I'd love for you to come, too. You always have such interesting stories about Dappled Hills."

"You've lived here a long time?" asked Beatrice with interest.

"All my life," Wyatt said. "Actually, I'm a third-generation minister for the Dappled Hills Presbyterian Church."

Beatrice was about to ask a little more about his family's history with the church when a shrill voice to the side of them said, "I'll come, too." When they all blinked at her in confusion, she added, "To the party. I'll come, too." Thankfully, Miss Sissy was on foot and so they weren't in any actual danger of being killed by her. Beatrice had to smile at Miss Sissy's announcement that she'd be at a party to which she hadn't been invited.

Daisy looked as if she had a sudden case of indigestion. There wasn't much she could say, though, not in front of the minister and Beatrice.

"I'd be *delighted* for you to come, Miss Sissy! But I'm

not sure you'd like my menu. Lots of exotic spices like cumin and saffron."

Beatrice wondered if *she* was going to like the menu.

Miss Sissy's lower lip stuck out and she looked even fiercer than usual.

Daisy gave a brave smile. "Of course you're invited, Miss Sissy. Six thirty tonight, y'all?"

Beatrice felt cheerier about going to a dinner party with Wyatt planning on going, too.

"Sorry, but it's time for me to go in for the service," said Wyatt in his gentle way. "Thanks so much for coming to worship with us today, Beatrice."

She could only beam in response.

Piper dropped in unexpectedly that evening as Beatrice was dressing for the party.

"You're not wearing *that*, are you?" Piper's face was scandalized.

Beatrice looked down at her black slacks and crisp white blouse. "What wrong with it?" she asked, fingering the strand of pearls she'd paired with her outfit. "And what are you doing here? I thought you were going out tonight."

"I was just checking on you before Ash and I went out. And, Mama, absolutely nothing is wrong with your outfit—if you're going to a nice lunch or a casual supper, or volunteering in the elementary school, or—"

"But this is supposed to be a last-minute, informal dinner party," said Beatrice with an exasperated sigh.

"Informal for *Daisy*, maybe. Trust me, you don't want to show up at her house unless you're in a dress. She's probably measuring the distance between place settings and putting out ten different forks and spoons."

"She takes it seriously, then." Beatrice frowned before hurrying to her pantry and peering in. "Somehow I didn't really get that impression from her. She said something about a small group of friends—something like that. All right, I guess I'll change." She looked absently into the pantry, forgetting what she was looking in there for.

She heard Piper saying behind her, "Now, you don't have any spectacular dresses hiding in *there*, do you?"

She finally remembered what she was looking for. "No, but I'm thinking I should take a bottle of wine, since she's such a stickler. Aha!" She turned around with a slightly dusty bottle of red wine.

Piper looked relieved. "Good idea. It's always nice to start off on the right foot, and Daisy is a great person to know—she's just a little particular. I'll dust off the wine bottle while you change."

"I'll put my black dress on," said Beatrice glumly.

"And the diamond pendant that Grandma used to wear!" called out Piper behind her.

Unlike the cute bungalows and charming mountain homes Beatrice had seen, Daisy and Harrison's house was an estate, a sprawling white mansion set in a tremendous, tree-filled yard with immaculate landscaping.

The inside seemed a testament to Harrison and Daisy's various successes: framed diplomas and awards for the doctor; blue ribbons for Daisy. Quilts were everywhere, but not in the haphazard way she'd seen at Meadow's. These were carefully arranged, with lighting to display them to best advantage. Daisy was definitely showcasing the quilts as works of art. Beatrice couldn't have done a better job herself at setting up the exhibit.

She was glad Piper had forced her into changing. Posy looked charming in a bright blue coat dress, and her husband, Cork, was wearing a suit (apparently under duress, since every so often he'd pull at the collar). Even former hippie Meadow had on a dress and a dab of makeup, and her long, gray braid was a little more orderly than usual. Miss Sissy looked rather witchy in a long black dress. Wyatt was in a suit (actually, he'd probably never changed from church), Harrison—Daisy's husband—wore a suit that perfectly complemented his silvery hair, and Ramsay had on his uniform (clearly, he was ready to jump out the door at a moment's notice). It seemed that Beatrice was the only one who hadn't gotten the memo that dress wasn't optional. Thank heavens for Piper.

The food was amazing and not, actually, spicy at all. Daisy must have been trying to keep Miss Sissy from crashing the party. The table was carefully set with old china and crystal and sterling silverware. A pretty centerpiece of what looked like flowers from Daisy's garden adorned the table. And it was all for her? Beatrice felt touched. And, perhaps, a little envious of Daisy.

Her home was perfectly decorated and immaculate. She had quite a flower garden, too. And—

"I wanted to point out that the vegetables we're serving tonight are all organically grown from our very own gardens here at Ambleside."

Oh. And an organic garden. Plus a named house. How manoresque.

Meadow was talking and laughing even louder than usual as her husband soberly drank ginger ale. "Are you on duty?" asked Beatrice.

Ramsay looked morose. "Possibly. If I get called. The North Carolina State Police are here, running the investigation. They'll call me if they need any assistance or want me to help question anyone."

Meadow patted her husband's hand. "It's been a rough time for Ramsay, y'all. He'd much rather be sitting around writing short stories than investigating a murder. Did you know he was a writer?" she asked Beatrice.

Beatrice shook her head. Meadow seemed oblivious to Ramsay's glower at the mention of his writing. How could he handle living with Meadow, who seemed to have no filter at all for what came out of her mouth? Beatrice shuddered at the thought.

Posy said in a small voice, "Such a horrible thing for this town. And for you, too, Ramsay. You're not any more used to dealing with murder than we are."

"Isn't that the truth?" Ramsay looked intently at his ginger ale, as if hoping to transform it into something a little stronger.

"Do you know more about what happened to Judith?" asked Daisy. "I heard that it looked like she'd been struck over the head by something."

Ramsay grunted. "It's sort of early to know much. But I guess there's no harm in saying that it does look like she was hit with some heavy object. The fatal blow was caused by a flat-surfaced object, nothing sharp. There are tons of things that fit that description. It could have been anything."

"Could you tell anything about the angle of the blow?" asked Beatrice. "Could you tell if her attacker was taller or shorter than Judith?"

Ramsay said, "We think it was someone about her size or slightly taller." There was a small murmur from Posy, and Ramsay smiled. "Yes, Posy, that takes you off the hook. Unless Judith was content to just stand there and wait to be murdered while you found a stepladder."

Posy beamed happily with relief.

"It was probably somebody mugging her," said Meadow with certainty. "Seeing a woman out by herself at night—they must have thought she was an easy mark. They just came up behind her and hit her over the head and took her money."

"Except," said Ramsay drily, "that her attacker was facing her. And there were no defensive wounds, so Judith wasn't expecting to be attacked. Both of these things indicate to me that she knew and trusted her murderer." Meadow sputtered an interruption, but Ramsay held up his hand to stop her. "Plus the fact that she had a fifty-dollar bill in her pocket that hadn't been taken from her. I don't see robbery as a motive."

"So the weapon wasn't found, then? And it could have been anything with a flat surface. Like a shovel?" asked Daisy. "Something like that?"

There was a gasp from someone at the table, but Beatrice didn't see who. "Most decidedly *not* a shovel!" said Meadow. "The very idea! How could someone go into a park late in the evening, carrying a shovel, and not look conspicuous? Maybe it was a fireplace poker or a baseball bat, or something like that."

Ramsay raised his eyebrows at his wife's fervency. "Or maybe it was a shovel. The killer might not have thought that anyone would be out to *see* him or her at that hour. Dappled Hills *seems* like a sleepy little town."

"But there sure isn't much sleeping going on," said Posy with a little sigh. "So many of my quilters say that they get most of their progress done on their quilts in the middle of the night. We all have trouble sleeping, I guess."

"I sleep like the dead," said Cork in a grouchy tone.

Daisy sat up a little straighter in her chair. "I know this isn't very pleasant dinner-party conversation, but it's probably inevitable that we'd want to talk about the biggest news story this town has ever seen. And I had a thought earlier today, Ramsay, which I wanted to tell you about."

Ramsay's face seemed to struggle to put a patient expression in place. He looked morosely again into his glass of ginger ale.

"I was thinking," said Daisy, tapping her French-manicured nails on the table, "that Judith and I had a lot in common."

"Oh, I don't think so," said Meadow, as if a question had been asked. "You were both into quilting, of course. Both fairly competitive." Meadow studied Daisy over the top of her red glasses. "You were both fond of heading up committees. You . . ."

"I meant," said Daisy firmly, "that Judith and I *looked* a good deal alike. Especially since Judith dyed her hair to match mine. And I *did* tell everyone that I planned on taking a walk after the bee. I frequently walk in the park at night."

Now that she mentioned it, she had said something after the bee about not wanting to run into Judith in the park while she was walking.

Harrison nodded sagely at his wife. "Exercise is good for you. For everyone. We're just now finding out how it helps with a variety of different processes, including mental sharpness and our general mood and well-being."

Daisy gave a fond laugh. "Always thinking of medicine, Harrison. Yes, it's good for us. But as I was saying, it would have been easy in the park to mistake Judith for me. Especially at night."

Ramsay said thoughtfully, "It's true that the park doesn't have much lighting."

Wyatt cleared his throat. "It was overcast, too. I remember thinking that it might rain that night. I put a couple of my houseplants outside in case it did."

"But it didn't rain," pointed out Ramsay, "or else all this late-night walking around wouldn't have taken place at all."

Daisy held out her hands. "You can see why I thought that perhaps someone mistook Judith for me. We were even wearing similar outfits that night." It almost seemed like she was *pleased* that she was important enough to murder. She was being a little silly about the similar-outfit thing, though—that was a bit of a stretch. They were both wearing the same *color*, maybe.

Wyatt said, "But why do you think someone would want to kill you, Daisy?"

Ramsay nodded. "If there's no motive, then there's no point in even considering mistaken identity as a possibility. Who would want to kill you?"

Daisy said, "I'm sure that plenty of quilters would, Ramsay. Jealousy is a very powerful motivator. I'm a top quilter—and that means others have to lose for me to win. Not only that, but I'm starting to do a lot of judging for juried competitions. Maybe one of our more ambitious quilters thought that with *me* out of the way, there'd be more opportunity for her to actually win a prize. Plus, I judge a lot of competitions myself. Someone could have thought I should have given her a higher standing. Maybe she thinks I have it in for her somehow."

"Daisy, I don't want you to go around thinking these kinds of things about yourself," scolded Meadow in between bites. "I've never heard a single quilter speak of you in a hateful way. I think we've all cheered on your success—both publicly and privately. We're *proud* of you because you're representing our guild well. Heck, you're representing our *community* well. This is all nonsense."

"Poppycock! It's poppycock," said Miss Sissy with sudden violence, waving a dinner roll to emphasize her point.

"Yes," said Daisy, with a concerned look in Miss Sissy's direction. "Well, I appreciate your saying so, Meadow, but I still think it's a definite possibility and I didn't want Ramsay to overlook it. I even got a threatening note the other day saying that I should be removed as a judge, that I should start rethinking the winners of these quilting competitions."

Daisy was getting anonymous letters, too? At least Beatrice wasn't the only one.

"Did you?" asked Ramsay with interest. "I'd like to have a look at it, then. Is it here at the house?"

"No. No, I burned it, Ramsay. At the time, I just thought someone was being hateful because they were jealous. Actually, I thought that Judith might be behind the note—that maybe she was trying to scare me. Anyway, my point is that maybe the murderer was really trying to eliminate *me*. I guess that note must not have been from Judith after all, if the murderer sent it."

Ramsay looked as if he was having a hard time following Daisy's logic. "At any rate, if you happen to get another note, do me a favor and don't burn it. There's a police department in Dappled Hills for a reason."

Daisy said, "I'll certainly let you know. And I'll be

watching my step, too, in case someone is determined not to make a mistake next time. You know, people were jealous of Judith, too, and she'd only won a fraction of the shows that I have. So they must *really* have been envious of me. This is what I think might have happened after the bee: Someone heard me say that I was going out for a walk, decided it was a good opportunity to take me out when I was by myself, saw Judith, took out a handy blunt object, and whacked her over the head. Maybe she left without even realizing her mistake—she could have just run off. But I really do feel that jealousy is at the bottom of it all. Thankfully, I decided not to take that walk after the bee."

"You're very fortunate," said Posy gently, "that you have the resources and time to be able to go to as many out-of-town shows as you do. Most quilters aren't able to pay for the entry fee or get a hotel room to attend the show."

"I'm blessed," said Daisy, bowing her head.

Ramsay said, "I'll keep your theory in mind, Daisy. And I'll pass it along to the state police as a motive, too."

"I just wanted to point out that there were more people with motives than poor Posy."

Posy looked miserably at her plate. Daisy leaned forward as if Cork were hard of hearing. "I was just saying that Posy had a strong motive for killing Judith. But there were other motives out there, too."

"Wickedness!" shrieked Miss Sissy. "Minister, rid this town of its evil!"

Wyatt didn't appear at all nonplussed at this. "I'll certainly do my best, Miss Sissy," he said in a soothing voice.

Ramsay said, "But as I was just saying, Daisy, Posy has been eliminated from the pool of suspects. She's too small to have struck the victim from the angle of the blow."

Beatrice said, "Posy, have you heard from Judith's daughter at all? I know all the quilters are hoping you'll be able to keep your shop open."

Posy's face brightened. "Yes, Meg called me early this afternoon. She said that for the foreseeable future she wanted to keep things exactly the way they are. She didn't want the trouble or worry of selling the property. So I'll just start sending the rent checks over to Meg. She was already here in town—she'd started driving to Dappled Hills as soon as she'd heard the news. She mentioned needing to go through Judith's things and settle her affairs."

"Posy, did Meg mention raising the rent?" asked Beatrice.

"Not at all. I guess her mother didn't talk to her about any of the plans for the building. I'm not sure how often they chatted with each other."

Daisy said, "Not often. Judith wasn't exactly the most nurturing mother in the world."

"I feel even worse that Judith's death solved my problem," Posy said sadly. "I feel simply awful about it. Now all that stress and worry has lifted and it's all because Judith is dead! I felt guilty just talking to Meg, and I haven't done anything!"

"Savannah and Georgia could say the same thing," said Daisy, buttering another roll. "Judith was baiting both of them at the bee. I think she knew something that they didn't want to have spread all over town. They're very private people, those two. And when you live in a small town like Dappled Hills, everybody knows your business or gets involved in your business. Don't you think so, Harrison?"

Harrison Butler said, "That's the truth. All people tend to do here is chatter about each other. You'd be amazed at the amount of gossip I hear by the end of the day. And if it's not gossip, it's people getting involved in other people's business."

"Don't these people think they're being helpful, though?" asked Wyatt with a smile.

"I'm sure they do. But they're meddling. I'm not even sure their motives are good."

"Sometimes meddling *can* be helpful, though," Daisy insisted. "I did some meddling of my own today for Felicity's daughter, Amber. She's talked about moving to a big city for ages, and I finally contacted my cousin in Atlanta—the one who works for the school district there. He said he'd be delighted to talk to her about teaching there."

Piper was going to hate to hear that Amber might be moving to Atlanta. And Beatrice couldn't help but think that Daisy wasn't just a Goodwill Ambassador for the town of Dappled Hills. What was Daisy Butler hiding? Savannah and Georgia hadn't been the only ones that Judith was picking on at the bee. She'd definitely alluded to something with Daisy, too.

Meadow was enthusiastically taking another helping of sautéed spinach, having already polished off her filet mignon au Bordelaise with shallots. "No one else is having seconds?" she asked in a huffy voice. She studied everyone's plate. "Y'all haven't even finished yet!" She knit her brows in consternation. "You know what's wrong with old people?" Everyone silently stared at Meadow, as if unwilling to concede that anyone in the room qualified as old. "They don't eat!"

Everyone took the cue and immediately continued eating again, except for Miss Sissy, who had completely cleaned her plate and sat there, cackling as if she'd just gotten confirmation that she wasn't old after all. Meadow continued plaintively. "Maybe it's all the talk about murder that's causing the loss of appetite. I don't like the fact that we're talking about our *friends* as if they were killers!"

"Although it sure sounds like everybody's been upset with everyone else lately," said Cork, yanking at his collar again. "Posy was telling me how upset Amber was about Judith trying to get a valuable quilt for free. Sounds like you saved the day, Beatrice. Felicity was lucky to be able to leave the bee with that quilt. Judith was a difficult woman to cross—I wouldn't have been surprised if she'd pulled that quilt out of Felicity's hands and run off with it. But, you know, Felicity has always wanted to have her own way. She's a very stubborn woman. That's how she did so well with those makeup sales—you couldn't get away from her!"

"I can see Judith ripping the quilt away from Felicity," muttered Meadow.

"Or she could have threatened to take Felicity to a small-claims court because she'd promised her the quilt and then didn't give it to her," said Posy.

"Possession is nine-tenths of the law, though," said Beatrice. "And Felicity had the quilt. Besides, she hadn't realized the value of the quilt when she'd promised it to Judith."

"That's what you and I say. But what would the *court* say? And Felicity would never have even made it to court. She wouldn't have wanted to pay for a lawyer. She'd just have been fuming at home," said Meadow.

Cork said thoughtfully, "Wasn't there some talk, a long while back, about Felicity's finances?"

Posy said, "Unfortunately, Felicity's never been really smart about money. Such a shame. She'd done so well for herself, too, selling makeup for years and getting that lavender Cadillac and all kinds of other bonuses. She was tough and strong—we all really looked up to her. She lost her husband in an accident; then Amber went a little wild, and she still ended up doing really well in a brand-new life in sales. But then it was gone all of a sudden—everything she'd worked so hard for."

"Didn't I hear somewhere that she trusted someone

who mismanaged her funds? Something like that?" asked Beatrice.

"Even worse than mismanagement," said Wyatt quietly. "She trusted the wrong person—someone who didn't have her best interests at heart and took advantage of her. The man she'd trusted with her money had all of her savings invested in a pyramid scheme. She lost everything. She wasn't the only one; a whole bunch of people lost their money. But she still remained remarkably upbeat and strong."

Posy sighed. "That's just Felicity. She's quite a lady."

Cork said, "Maybe Amber did it. Judith was trying to take advantage of her mom. You know what an angry teenager she always was. And she still gets all wound up over stuff even now. She was arguing with somebody in the shop one day over politics, and they hadn't even tried to be provocative. Judith might just have made her mad—that's all."

"I categorically reject that idea! Amber is my friend," said Meadow.

Miss Sissy gave another grating cackle. "None of you know what happened." She looked craftily around at the others gaping at her. "The police don't use their eyes or brains. But *I* do. And I know who did it. I might not have my teeth, but I *do* still have my eyes and ears and they still work fine. It's wickedness! And lies! And greed." She looked pointedly at Ramsay, and he shrugged.

Daisy rolled her eyes. "*Most* murders are committed over money, Miss Sissy. Everybody knows that."

Miss Sissy shook her head in impatience. "Greed!"

she repeated again sternly, wagging a bony finger at Daisy.

With that pronouncement, Miss Sissy seemed to consider herself done. She stood, drew herself up proudly to her full height of four feet, ten inches; gave everyone a malevolent look; and hobbled out of the door. A minute later, they heard a screeching sound as Miss Sissy pulled her Lincoln out of the driveway and, according to the sound effects they were hearing, through some of Daisy and Harrison's shrubbery.

"I don't know *how*," said Daisy in a tired voice, "you put up with that woman in your shop all day, Posy."

Posy sighed. "Some people have cats in their shops. I have Miss Sissy."

"She's completely mad," said Daisy.

The room was quiet for a moment. Meadow finally said, "Tell you what. Daisy, why don't you show Beatrice the block you're working on for the group quilt? You've probably already started on it, haven't you?"

"I've finished it."

"Of course you have," said Meadow. "Do you mind pulling it out? I know Beatrice is still trying to get the hang of quilting again."

"There's really no *again* to it," said Beatrice. "I've *never* quilted seriously. At least, not for many years." No one seemed to be listening to her, though.

Daisy quickly left the dining room and returned with a piece of fabric. "I'd be delighted to show it to you. Don't worry, Beatrice. We all had to learn sometime."

Daisy's block featured a bucolic scene that Beatrice guessed was Daisy's idealized view of country life. Did she fancy Harrison some sort of local squire? The block was amok with chickens, cows, ivy and skirted peasant women feeding sheep. There was also a medicine bag on the ground near a chicken that seemed startlingly out of place.

There was no doubt that Daisy had talent. Her stitching was immaculate and the block design was busy but riveting. "It symbolizes our life here in the country," said Daisy. "Very different from my life growing up in the cultural districts of Charleston, but still not without its pleasures." She patted Beatrice's arm. "We wouldn't expect you to be able to come up with a block like this, Beatrice. This is an example of advanced quilting. Maybe Meadow could help walk you through a block. I would, except I've got such a busy schedule the next few weeks with my different clubs."

Meadow bounced a little in her seat. "Isn't it exciting having someone new in the guild? And Beatrice has such an extensive background in folk art! I want the Village Quilters to really push themselves—we could have more fund-raisers to get the cash to enter more juried shows. We could then easily get more members. Maybe even quilters from other towns nearby would want to join our group. We could make more quilts for charities, too!"

The rest of the dinner party passed without drama, mostly featuring Meadow's grandiose ideas for the future of the Village Quilters, which seemed to include ruling the world. And she kept indicating that Beatrice was a critical part of the plan she was formulating.

An hour later, Beatrice was ready to turn in. Wyatt left the party then, too, saying he needed to get home and let his dog out. As they were walking to their cars, Wyatt gave Beatrice a sympathetic look. "You've got to think you've moved into the middle of a hornet's nest! I promise Dappled Hills is completely benign ninety-nine percent of the time."

"Honestly," said Beatrice, "I'm less concerned about my safety and more concerned about neighbors blaming neighbors for murder. You heard everyone tonight—considering the pros and cons of their friends and neighbors being involved. If this case isn't solved quickly, everybody in town is going to start being suspicious of everyone else. I'm going to do a little poking around."

Wyatt raised his eyebrows at her in surprise, making Beatrice laugh. "I've got my own selfish reasons for doing it. I'm retiring here, and Dappled Hills won't be nearly as much fun if all the neighbors are suspicious of each other. Besides, I've always had a knack for investigating."

Wyatt's eyebrows lifted even higher, disappearing into his hair. Beatrice said with a smile, "Well, I was investigating the background of some interesting art, but still. Poking around is poking around! I think I might be able to find something out."

Whenever she'd *thought* she'd gotten all the supplies she needed to make a simple quilt block, she kept realizing there was more still to get. Patchwork Cottage seemed to be becoming a fixture in her life. It made sense why all the quilters had been anxious that it might suddenly close.

As she walked up to the shop, Beatrice saw Amber coming out the door.

The murder investigation seemed to be getting to her. Amber had dark circles under her eyes and she hadn't dressed or done her makeup with her usual attention to detail.

Amber raised her eyebrows at Beatrice and said in a teasing voice, "So we haven't run you out of Dappled Hills yet, Mrs. Coleman? I'd have thought with all our murder and mayhem that you'd have run screaming back to Atlanta."

Beatrice said drily, "Right. Because Atlanta is completely crime free. Daisy mentioned that *you* might actually be moving to Atlanta. She's helping you find a teaching position there?"

Amber smiled, but it didn't quite make it up to her eyes. "She certainly is. Daisy is nothing if not efficient. I mentioned once or twice in passing that I'd love to check out the big-city scene, and next thing I know, she's networking with her contacts."

Amber almost seemed to be hiding something with her carefully blank face. Was there some reason why she *needed* to move from Dappled Hills? A reason other than wanting to meet new people and live in a larger city?

"And your mother? I suppose Felicity would stay here in the area," said Beatrice.

Amber rolled her eyes. "You couldn't budge Mother from North Carolina with a crowbar! She definitely wants to stay in the area, but she knows I'm sure not going to *meet* anybody around here. I haven't yet, and there aren't tons of single guys moving into town. Mother was forty when she had me, which was super late back then. Now I'm thirty-five and not even in a relationship. I'm sure she'd like a chance at having some grandchildren to spoil. If she's at a retirement home, then I won't be worried about her—I know they'll take good care of her." It all sounded pretty practiced. Maybe Amber was still trying to justify it to herself. Her actions *could* be considered a little selfish, although the desire to have a change of scenery and pace was completely understandable. Beatrice had done it herself.

"I'm sure they'll take care of her," Beatrice said. "And she'll be glad to know you're having fun in Atlanta. Mamas are always happy when their children are happy."

Now Amber's eyes seemed to really light up. "You know, I think Atlanta *will* make me happy. There's just so much I want to see and do—I want to eat great food and drink great wine and go to amazing parties and stay out all night and not have people wonder where I am. I just want to go out and *live*." The passionate nature that Beatrice had seen a glimpse of the night of the bee was really out in full force.

Beatrice said, "I'm surprised you've stayed in Dappled Hills all these years. Why haven't you left before now?"

Amber shrugged. "I grew up here. And when I got out of school, there was a teaching job just waiting for me. Then Mother ran into some financial trouble. I felt like I needed to stick around for a while to make sure she was going to be okay. But now the time has come to blow this joint."

As though misinterpreting Beatrice's thoughtful silence, Amber quickly added, "Of course, I wouldn't leave until all of this mess with the murder investigation is over. Especially with Mother being a suspect." She gave a short laugh.

Beatrice said, "I'm sure your mother isn't much of a suspect."

"I don't know about that. But I do know there are some people who make just as strong of a suspect as my mother." Beatrice raised her eyebrows questioningly at her, and Amber said in a quiet voice that Beatrice had to lean in to hear, "I've been really wrestling with telling Ramsay, but I guess I have to. I heard Savannah and Judith having a huge squabble a week before Judith was murdered." Amber looked down at the sidewalk. "And I love Savannah—I really do. I don't want to have to go tattling to Ramsay about this."

Somehow it was hard to picture the prim Savannah engaging in a shouting match. "Really? What were they arguing about?"

"It was probably a lot of built-up anger that finally set Savannah off. From what I hear, Judith has been picking on both Savannah and Georgia for ages. Then, about a week ago, I was sitting at one of the outdoor tables at the coffee shop, working on some lesson plans on my laptop, when I heard them arguing across the street. I don't think they even noticed I was listening, they were so wrapped up in their argument. Judith was talking in a really scornful voice about Savannah's quilts and blaming them for our losing a place in the last quilt show."

Beatrice said, "That sounds like exactly the kind of accusation that would be sure to get Savannah's goat. She seems to take a lot of pride in her quilting." She remembered Savannah's precise stitching and eye for detail.

"She takes her quilting *very* seriously. And, really, her work is *perfect*. There's not ever a stitch out of place."

"Why would Judith blame Savannah, then?"

"She said that Savannah's quilting was uninspired." Amber imitated Judith's harsh voice and condescending tone. "That maybe she was *technically* good, but to place in juried shows, you need to be *better* than good . . . You need to be creative."

"Is that true?"

"Well, it sure helps. Quilts are usually judged by category, and we'd like to have some quilts we can put in categories like Art-Pictorial or Art-Abstract. Creative composition can really help out. Yes, it's great that the piecing is accurate, but the theme and design is important, too. Of course, Meadow is always pushing us to do our best or try new things. Honestly, it's a little surprising that *Meadow* wasn't the one murdered," said Amber in a fond voice. "I can tell that Savannah has murder on the brain whenever Meadow forces her away from her geometric patterns."

"What did Savannah say back to Judith?" asked Beatrice

"She didn't just *say* it—she yelled it! With her hands on her skinny hips and her chin jutting out. She looked like she was about five years old . . . I thought she was going to stomp her foot next. Anyway, she said that Judith was jealous of her because she was a better quilter and Judith knew it. Then *Judith* became even more furious and told Savannah that Georgia was holding them back from winning competitions, too."

"That couldn't have made matters any better," said Beatrice.

"No. And the truth probably hurt, because even though Georgia is a much more creative quilter than Savannah will ever be, she gets sort of dreamy and forgetful sometimes and leaves things hanging that we have to fix later on a group quilt. And on her individual quilts, she'll make mistakes like not having enough space to let the judges' eyes rest, or needing more contrast, or not having consistent binding corners. Sometimes even her straight lines won't be all that straight." Amber shrugged. "Maybe Savannah recognized the truth in what Judith was saying, because suddenly she seemed really threatening. She told Judith to watch her back or she'd be sorry."

Beatrice said, "You'd probably better tell Ramsay about it, then, Amber. Especially since Savannah sounded like she was making a threat."

"At the time, it sounded sort of childish. I envisioned Savannah sabotaging one of Judith's patches . . . You know, something like that. Because, although she's very serious, Savannah is really pretty immature at heart," said Amber.

"But now you think maybe it wasn't an idle threat?" asked Beatrice.

"No. I think that maybe the final straw came on the night of the bee when Judith was taunting Savannah and Georgia. I think she snapped and ended up coming after Judith. After all, Judith announced to everybody in earshot that she was planning on taking a solitary stroll in the park to work off any frustration. Savannah could have biked home, stuck some sort of hammer or something in her bike basket, and biked over to the park to confront Judith. Georgia would never tell if she wasn't where she said she was. Instant alibi."

Beatrice said, "I know that Savannah is really protective of Georgia. Is Georgia the same way about Savannah?"

"Oh, absolutely!" It looked like Amber was going to say more about that, but then she pressed her lips shut as if to keep inside whatever gossip she'd been about to spill. "Absolutely," she repeated instead. Then she hurried on, "Although it's more obvious with Savannah and Georgia. Of course they're twins, but Savannah has always been the stronger of the two. The only time Savannah relinquished any of her control over Georgia, she ended up getting married to someone who cheated on her. After that, Savannah has been even more determined to keep an eye on her sister and make sure she stays out of trouble. That's why I'm saying that Savannah could have been involved in this crime. Judith might finally have pushed her too far."

"You said that other *people* were equally strong suspects. Is there someone else you have in mind?" asked Beatrice.

Amber shrugged. "It seems to me that the quilting bee was the final straw for Judith's killer. And Judith was really trash-talking. She said something about Daisy, too, didn't she?"

"She did," said Beatrice, nodding. "Judith made a comment about Daisy not being able to be a social climber anymore . . . something like that."

"I don't know about social climbing," Amber said, "but I know Daisy cares a lot about her quilting. That's how she spends most of her time, apart from all the clubs she belongs to. I've seen a lot of rivalry between those two. I'm not sure exactly what Judith was referring to at the bee, but it wouldn't shock me if old anger and jealousy made Daisy suddenly crack."

Quilting seemed like such a *tame* pastime at first. Beatrice was thinking this through when Amber took a look at her watch. "Sorry I kept you so long, Beatrice. I've got to get going."

The dried-out casserole was annoying on a couple of different levels, Beatrice decided. On one level was the time and money she'd spent at Bub's, getting ingredients for a dish she ultimately destroyed. On the other level was the regrettable fact that now she had nothing for supper . . . and the prospect of a lot more dried-out casseroles in her future until she got back into the cooking groove again.

She *thought* she'd chosen a foolproof recipe. She'd cooked it practically once a week at one point in her life. You'd think that making it would still be rote. But no—the pasta in the casserole was overcooked in some areas and crunchy at the top of the casserole where she'd forgotten to cover the dish. The chicken was rubbery and bland. The seasonings were all wrong. Beatrice made a face. She couldn't bring herself to choke it down. Not even with the promise of the peach-flavored ice cream she'd picked up as a treat from Bub's. Actually, she'd also gotten a basket of peaches there. Couldn't she cut some up over the peach-flavored ice cream and call that supper?

Her exploration of this philosophical question was interrupted by the doorbell and Noo-noo's eruption of barking. "Noo-noo!" she fussed at the ecstatically barking corgi. "Don't you think I can hear the doorbell?"

Beatrice peered out the peephole. It was Meadow, wearing a red caftan and a big smile. Beatrice wasn't feeling in a very Meadow-like mood. Could she hide? No, Meadow had probably heard her fussing at the dog. But what was that she was carrying—could it be food? It was a testament to Beatrice's hunger that she opened the door with such alacrity. Meadow was many odd and irritating things . . . but she was definitely a top-notch cook.

"Hello, neighbor!" said Meadow brightly. "I've brought you some goodies to enjoy. I know it couldn't be easy to move your household from one place to another. Do you mind breakfast for supper? It's one of Ramsay's and my most favorite things. I've got you a quiche Lorraine made with our free-range chicken eggs and some wonderful cured bacon that I pick up locally at the farmers' market. You'll love it! And I've got a chicken casserole that you can throw in the oven tomorrow for supper."

Meadow bustled in and found a spot for the casserole and quiche. "I think I'm going to have to regularly make some covered dishes for you. It was *too* fun skipping through the woods between our houses. I tell you, I felt exactly like Little Red Riding Hood in my red caftan. I shall have to buy myself a hooded sweatshirt!" She gave a booming laugh that reverberated through Beatrice's cottage like a skipping stone on a quiet lake. Her little house seemed so much smaller when Meadow was here.

Meadow sniffed the air. "But I didn't come in time! Have you been cooking? Did you make your own chicken recipe? Something smells absolutely delicious, Beatrice!"

"Does it?" Beatrice looked dubiously at the casserole. "Dinner didn't turn out quite like I'd planned. I guess it'll take a while to get back into the rhythm of cooking again."

"Could I have a bitty spoonful?"

"Be my guest." Beatrice handed Meadow a spoon.

Meadow took a healthy bite, then looked up at the ceiling in a considering manner as she tasted the food. "Beatrice, maybe you forgot salt and pepper. This might even be better over rice or over pasta al dente." She took another small bite off her spoon, then said thoughtfully, "You know who would love this casserole? Ramsay. He doesn't really care for spicy food. Gives him heartburn."

"And he likes crunchy noodles? And chewy chicken?"

"It won't bother him in the *least*. Ash might even fight him for it, because he's always scavenging for something to eat in the house. Mind if I take a plate home to him?"

"Meadow, please feel free to take the entire thing."

As Beatrice put some aluminum foil over the casserole and listened to Meadow prattling on with her usual exuberance, it occurred to Beatrice that her neighbor was being kind. Boris the dog would likely be the recipient of her casserole. But the small kindness warmed her heart toward her red-caftaned visitor.

"Have you started on your quilt block for our group quilt?" asked Meadow. "You've still got plenty of time if you haven't. But it's always good to go ahead and jump in and get started."

Beatrice turned to rinse out some of her dishes. "Well, no. No, I haven't gotten started with it."

Meadow had seen something on Beatrice's coffee table and had walked over to investigate. "What's this, then? Looks like the beginnings of a block."

"Oh, that? No, that's just practice. That's all."

Beatrice thought she saw a relieved expression pass across Meadow's face. "Practice is good, Beatrice! Keep practicing and you'll be an expert in no time. Actually, I guess you *are* a quilting expert, aren't you? Just not an expert in *making* them."

"Definitely not an expert in making them. Don't worry—that little scrap is simply for me to figure out my stitches and cutting. I decided I'd work a little on my own quilt first before I took a stab at a block for the group one."

"A whole *quilt*, Beatrice?" Meadow's heavy brows knit together. "Did you tell Posy that that's what you wanted to do? I'd have thought she'd have directed you to something smaller."

"I meant a *baby* quilt. No, I'm not starting out with a full-sized quilt. I *had* been going to do that, but Posy stopped me. She recommended a decorative hanging or a baby quilt for my first solo project."

Meadow nodded vigorously, making her red glasses slide down on her nose. "That makes a lot more sense. A *lot* more. You know, I still do a lot of experimenting myself. I've got plenty of abandoned quilts. Sometimes I'll decide to experiment with different prints and colors or add different embellishments, and then don't like what I end up with. Sometimes I'll even get excited about a new project, then lose interest in it. I've got lots of UFOs," said Meadow.

"I'll bet you do," said Beatrice softly.

"What? Oh, sorry. I mean unfinished objects. Quilts that I've started but never finished."

Meadow rambled on a little about quilting and the fleeting nature of inspiration as Beatrice loaded the few dishes into the dishwasher. She tuned back in to Meadow's monologue when she heard, "Ramsay is sure that Judith was murdered. I'm still not convinced, Beatrice. I keep telling him it's *got* to be a mugging gone wrong. I don't know why he's being so stubborn and won't acknowledge it as a possibility."

"I don't blame him, Meadow. After all, how many muggers do you know lurking in the bushes in Dappled Hills? I just don't see it. Now, if Judith had been some really *nice* person who never made folks mad, then maybe your theory would make sense. But she made too many people upset with her. Does Ramsay have any ideas about who might be behind it?"

"He doesn't suspect one particular person—or if he does, he's not telling me—but he's sure it's someone in the guild. Said the murder happened too soon after the bee for there not to be a connection. And he's heard me complain about Judith and how she upsets everybody in the guild. I know he and the state police are really focusing on the Village Quilters."

Beatrice nodded. "It does make sense, you have to admit."

"Does it? I think she could have upset a whole bunch of different people just being herself. I hope Ramsay will tread softly. I really don't want to lose any friends over this. I think he's so unhappy about having a major crime to investigate that he might take it out on the poor suspects! You know, he'd rather be writing his poetry. Or whatever he writes," she added, looking thoughtful.

"And you didn't see or hear anything that night?" asked Beatrice.

"Not a thing! Besides, we're not close enough to the park to witness anything, Beatrice. You know that."

"Well I *know*, but I was wondering if maybe you saw cars driving past or saw people out—besides Posy . . ."

"Now, how would I see people out when I was in?" Meadow was all puffed up now with indignation.

"Never mind," said Beatrice. She sighed, sensing her next question was just as pointless. "Did Ash mention seeing or hearing anything?"

"My poor boy turned in super early that night after I'd dragged him to the quilting bee. He was asleep in front of the TV when I got home from the bee, and I barely got him stumbling off in the direction of his room before he was snoring again. He'd had a big day rock climbing with that buddy from high school. And I think he was still a little jet-lagged."

"So you heard nothing and saw nothing," said Beatrice.

"Not a blessed thing!" said Meadow with an emphatic bob of her head that made her red glasses slip down her nose again and her long, gray braid swish.

But Beatrice wasn't so sure.

The next morning, Beatrice strolled out for the paper, and there was another Nehi bottle with a note on her front porch. *Stop asking questions*, it read.

Beatrice frowned and brought the note inside to look at it over a strong cup of coffee. She knew she *should* be really shaken up by these notes, but somehow she kept feeling that the thought behind them wasn't malicious. Maybe it's more of a friendly warning, she mulled. Or maybe an *un*friendly warning, but nothing that hinted of any danger.

Someone was definitely noticing her efforts to poke around in the case and dig up information. It sounded like maybe they thought she was onto something.

Could Miss Sissy be sending these notes? She thought of the little woman's gleeful face as she made her pronouncements on the case. It seemed like the kind of meddlesome thing she *could* do. Beatrice decided to pay a little social visit to Miss Sissy as soon as she finished her coffee.

There was a knock at the door, and Noo-noo started dutifully barking to show off her watchdog skills. But Beatrice knew that as soon as the door opened, Noo-noo would fling herself on her back for a tummy rub.

Piper was at her door. And—Beatrice put a hand up to her uncombed hair—Ash. "Mama, I thought I'd pop by and say hi before Ash and I go off hiking and picnicking for the day."

Beatrice smiled weakly but nurtured murderous thoughts toward her offspring. "Hi, Ash. You're hiking where . . . Grandfather Mountain?"

Piper nodded happily. "We're going to see the wildlife center and go on the swinging bridge, do some hiking and have a picnic." Her pixie face was lit up, and for a minute Beatrice could almost believe that she was six years old again.

Ash grinned at Beatrice. "Sorry we've dropped by so early. I know you're not set up for company at this hour of the morning. Piper saw you go back inside from getting the paper and she thought we should come by and say hi before we left."

Piper frowned at the bottle on the counter. "I didn't know you drank orange Nehis. Hmm. Start living in the same town as somebody and you find out all kinds of things. Unless . . . you didn't get another of those notes, did you?"

Beatrice shook her head and quickly changed the subject. She didn't want Piper to start worrying about her mother. "You're not making it back in time for the Village Quilters today?"

"No, I'm skipping it this time. Ash and I will still be gone this afternoon." Piper couldn't look less interested in quilting, which was a radical departure from a few days ago. Beatrice wondered where all this was going to lead. Meadow had said that Ash would be flying back to California at the end of the week.

"Have you even gotten started with your block for the group quilt?" asked Beatrice.

"I did, because I couldn't sleep the other night. But I'll admit I kind of cheated. I know Meadow likes us to put a lot of thought into our blocks and explore symbolism. I've been busy lately, though, so I used some appliqués that I'd cut out for earlier quilts that I hadn't finished."

"UFOs?" asked Beatrice archly.

Ash laughed and Piper blinked. "Wow, you're really getting into the quilting lingo, aren't you? Yes, I had some unfinished objects, so I repurposed them. One of them is a little ginger cat that looks a lot like my kitty." She suddenly blushed. "Of course, I'd have put you in there, Mama, if I'd actually been planning out the block instead of trying to cut corners."

Beatrice waved her hand dismissively. "No worries, Piper. I know you've got a lot of other things going on."

"Let me know," said Piper, "if you find out anything about Judith's murder when you're with the Village Quilters. It's a gossipy group, and somebody might know more than they even realize they do. The guilds and the Patchwork Cottage are the best places to learn what's going on in this town."

"I did learn some things yesterday," said Beatrice. "I went to Felicity's house and over to Posy's shop." She filled Piper and Ash in.

Piper whistled. "It sounds like you found out a lot of stuff. I had a feeling you might want to root around in this mystery a little. You never could resist a good puzzle. You're going to give Ash's dad a run for his money with the detective work."

"Sounds good to me. Maybe you can clear my mom as a suspect," said Ash.

"What?" asked Piper and Beatrice together.

"Why would Meadow be a suspect?" asked Beatrice.

Ash raised his eyebrows. "You mean word hasn't gotten around yet? Well, that's a miracle, considering it's Dappled Hills. Mother had an argument with Judith in the middle of the grocery store a week ago. Talk about your public places. Anyway, somebody at the store tipped off the police as soon as they heard Judith was dead. And then I understand that Mother let her have it again in front of a bunch of people at the quilting bee."

Beatrice thoughtfully took a sip of coffee. "No, she really didn't let her have it. Judith deserved more than she got, actually. Meadow was just trying to make sure that she kept order. She *is* the queen bee or beekeeper or whatever, after all. She saw an explosive situation and she defused it. That was my take on it, anyway." She looked questioningly at Piper, who nodded.

"Mine, too. Wow. I can't see Meadow clubbing somebody over the head, Ash. Besides, your dad isn't going to put her on the list of suspects."

"Are you kidding? Dad's fantasized for years about having Mom put away in the county jail!" Ash's eyes twinkled.

Beatrice returned his smile, but she couldn't help but wonder. *Somebody* had murdered Judith. And, judging from what she knew of Judith, it was likely someone Judith knew. Meadow, of course, hadn't been the only one to have an argument with Judith shortly before she was murdered. Had Amber ever told the police that she'd seen Savannah and Judith arguing?

Piper said, "I'm surprised that your mom let Judith get to her like that in the store. Actually, a lot of things have surprised me lately. I'm *really* surprised Felicity thinks that Amber had something to do with it."

Beatrice said, "Well, you have to look at it the way Felicity is. Amber had motive and opportunity, and anyone could have had the means. Obviously, Felicity is thinking about Amber's troubled past, too. Amber was awfully upset with Judith. I know it's hard to think about your friend having something to do with it. Think how hard it must be on Felicity. Felicity looked really awful when I visited her. Totally different than she had the night of the bee, when she was vivacious and strong. She was worried."

Piper shrugged her shoulders impatiently. "Yes, Amber *was* awfully upset with Judith. That doesn't mean that she was going to kill her, though. I don't care how many times she got suspended from school or how many inappropriate boyfriends she had when she was a teenager—that was fifteen years ago and she'd just lost her dad. Being mad at someone isn't the same as feeling homicidal. I've been just as angry, but the idea of murdering someone never crossed my mind."

Piper was silent for a few moments. "Amber has been really worried about her mom lately," she said finally, in a quiet voice. "The Wilsons were pretty important people in Dappled Hills when Felicity was a little girl. But her father made some bad investments . . . and her mom spent money like it was water. The family ended up with practically nothing. I think Amber is worried that the cycle is repeating itself."

"Didn't Felicity do all right selling makeup? I keep

hearing how she was this fantastic salesperson. I know she got a car, and they wouldn't hand those out if someone wasn't doing well."

Piper said, "I think she did do really well, yes, for a lot of years. She was the Eula May top seller for North Carolina and she has the lavender Cadillac to prove it. I think it was a source of pride for her that she was able to provide for Amber so well after her husband died. But in the past few years, she started making the same kinds of bad investments that Amber's father had all those years ago. That pyramid scheme, you know. That's another reason Amber is keeping an eye on her mom—she's worried about her making flaky financial decisions."

"Amber probably feels like Felicity is being cheated at every turn," said Beatrice thoughtfully.

Piper said, "Oh, I'm sure realizing that her mom was about to be taken advantage of again *did* make Amber mad. But she's not a killer. She's a teacher—and a quilter. Not exactly the kind of person who goes homicidal."

"I'm wondering who *is* the type of person who gets pushed over the edge and goes homicidal," said Beatrice. "Tell me a little more about Daisy. Judith was goading her at the bee, too."

"Daisy? She's great. She kind of swoops in and just tries to make people feel included in the town. Like the dinner party she had. She's a giver."

"Yes, I know. That was very sweet," said Beatrice, trying not to show her impatience. *Someone* at that bee killed Judith, but Piper seemed determined not to cast suspicion on any of the quilters. "But she also seems like she's very gung-ho about quilting."

"Everyone in the guild is," said Piper with a snort. "That's practically all they talk about."

"For Daisy, though, it seemed like it was more than just an interest," pressed Beatrice. "She put a lot of thought into the way she displayed her quilts at her home. Almost like I'd have done if I were setting up a show at the museum. That tells me she's pretty serious about it and maybe about winning prizes, too."

Piper shrugged. "I guess. She did seem sort of competitive with Judith. But Judith was always provoking people by bragging about her awards and quilts and stuff. It probably just got on Daisy's nerves."

"What I'm hoping," said Beatrice quietly, "is that whoever the killer is, she's satisfied with the outcome. If she's not—or if she still feels threatened in some way—then she might feel like she's got to kill again."

After Piper and Ash finished their coffee and left for their hike, Beatrice showered and dressed and decided to walk to Miss Sissy's house to see if she could find any evidence of crazed note writing or a pile of empty Nehi bottles. Noo-noo looked up at her hopefully. "No, Noo-noo. Usually I'd take you along, but I'm visiting Miss Sissy. I have a feeling she's not a dog person." Actually, Beatrice wondered if Miss Sissy was a person at all or just some cackling apparition.

A riot of thorny vines that blew menacingly about in the brisk breeze nearly obscured Miss Sissy's house.

The yard was choked by weeds, the trees were consumed by kudzu and the vines waved around Miss Sissy's door, threatening to wrap Beatrice up and hold her hostage. She looked for a doorbell, didn't see one, and rapped on the door. There was no answer.

She hit the door with even louder rapping, thinking that maybe the elderly lady was losing her hearing. But she remembered Miss Sissy's comment about her hearing being just fine. She could have been bragging, though, thought Beatrice uneasily as she rapped again. Miss Sissy's elderly Lincoln was parked right there in the weed-infested driveway, so she *should* have been at home.

Remembering how Miss Sissy had mentioned she knew who the killer was—in a roomful of suspects—made Beatrice leery. After giving another loud series of raps, she cautiously pushed the creaky, splintered wooden door open. "Miss Sissy?" she called. She had no desire for the old harpy to come running out at her, fists flying, berating her for trespassing. "It's Beatrice. I've come over for a visit." Still no response.

Now Beatrice felt a prickling of unease up her spine that had nothing to do with an angry Miss Sissy. She hesitated, then moved forward again, turning on overhead lights as she walked around the dark furniture crowding the small, dim house.

Finally she saw a small, huddled lump on the floor near the kitchen door. "Miss Sissy!" she cried out, hurrying across the room and hunching over the crumpled figure.

She was alive. Beatrice sighed with relief as she felt

a steady, thumping pulse in Miss Sissy's wrist. But she lay in a pool of blood and had a huge lump on her head. This was no natural fall. Beatrice was surprised to glimpse a cell phone on a nearby table, but instead pulled out her own with trembling fingers to dial 911.

Chapter 5

After the phone call, Beatrice hurried to find a clean cloth to hold to Miss Sissy's head until the ambulance came. Her attention was briefly diverted by a sheet of paper beside a thick Bible on a rickety wooden table. Miss Sissy's favorite pastime was apparently penning dire, cryptic proclamations. But the handwriting looked nothing like the careful penmanship and uniform lettering on the anonymous notes she'd received.

Miss Sissy had scrawled *The Wages of Sin are Death!* in large letters and put a few of her favorite of the Ten Commandments underneath. Beatrice had just read "Thou shalt not steal" and "Thou shalt not kill" and an out-of-place "The love of money is the root of all evil!" among other scribbles before the sound of sirens signaled the arrival of the ambulance. Beatrice gave up her futile search for clean linens—that weren't quilts or quilt fabrics, at any rate. There were many, many quilts in the house, and many seemed made of different fabrics. Beatrice was sure that Posy was kindly giving Miss Sissy extra scraps of fabric from the shop, gratis.

After the paramedics carefully lifted Miss Sissy's stretcher into the ambulance, one of the paramedics turned to Beatrice. "You're her friend? Are you riding with us to the hospital?"

"Yes, I'm coming along," said Beatrice, getting into the passenger's side of the ambulance. No one else was there, and she could at least offer the limited information that she had about Miss Sissy.

Fortunately, the regional emergency room had been able to take Miss Sissy fairly quickly. The ER doctor treated Miss Sissy's wound, then told her she'd need to stay for a few hours for observation before they'd release her.

After the staff had settled her in a small room, Miss Sissy had a brief interview with Ramsay, during which Beatrice was allowed to stay in the room. Unfortunately, the interview wasn't exactly illuminating, since Miss Sissy apparently remembered nothing about her attack. After Ramsay left, Miss Sissy surprised Beatrice with a wide, toothless grin. Beatrice leaned over and gently squeezed her hand.

"Feeling any better?" she asked softly.

Miss Sissy gave a small nod.

"Can I get you anything? I think Posy is throwing a couple of things in a bag for you. Probably a toothbrush and toothpaste and a change of clothes. And your Medicare card, I guess."

Miss Sissy gave another smile.

Beatrice hesitated. Ramsay hadn't gotten any information from her, but she wondered if it were possible that maybe the old lady knew more than she was letting on. Maybe she'd open up more to Beatrice. "Do you . . . do you have any idea who did this to you, Miss Sissy?"

Miss Sissy's face grew thunderous and she nodded slowly. "Barbaric!" she barked.

"Who? Who did this, Miss Sissy?"

"The Russians!" she hissed.

Clearly, Miss Sissy was shaken by her experience. And, a nurse later told Beatrice, sometimes people will have a little temporary amnesia after a traumatic event. In the case of someone Miss Sissy's age, the nurse said, it could take a while for her to recover. And she might *always* blame the Cold War Russians for her attack.

Beatrice had called Posy on the way to the hospital, knowing that of everyone she knew, she'd be the one who'd spent the most time with the old lady. Posy found someone to watch the shop for her, picked up some clothes for Miss Sissy to change into (since her own clothes had been covered in blood), and drove right to the hospital.

"I can't believe this happened!" said Posy, her gentle face creased with worry. "Do you think"—she looked over to make sure Miss Sissy was still asleep—"that someone meant to *murder* her?"

"Yes, I do. If they'd only wanted to scare her, they wouldn't have injured her so badly. No, I'm guessing the murderer believes she knows something and thought she was more fragile than she actually is. They left in a hurry, without waiting to see if she'd survived the blow. Remember how Miss Sissy was talking at Daisy's dinner party? I think it makes her feel important knowing something that no one else knows. She's probably been bragging about knowing information at other places, too."

"I'm really getting worried, Beatrice. I sure hope the police can figure out who's behind all of this," said Posy.

Beatrice nodded. "I've been poking around a little bit, too. I've never been able to resist puzzles, and this one threatens all of us—our safety and our friendships."

Beatrice saw Miss Sissy's dark eyes pop open and she motioned to Posy, who abruptly stopped talking.

"Hi, Miss Sissy!" said Posy, gently squeezing Miss Sissy's gnarled hand. "I'm so sorry this happened to you. Can I tell the nurses to get you something? Does your head hurt?"

Miss Sissy stayed very still, but moved her head slightly in what looked like a *no*. She opened her mouth and croaked, "It was the Russians!"

Posy looked at Beatrice worriedly. But Beatrice had noticed that Miss Sissy's gaze looked brighter and more focused than it had earlier. She couldn't help wondering if the old lady was trying to divert them. The canniness in her rheumy eyes made Beatrice think Miss Sissy knew more than she was letting on. Or maybe not. Maybe that bump on the head had made her even crazier than she'd been before.

There was a soft tap at the door and Wyatt Thompson poked his head around it. "Miss Sissy?"

The minister grinned when he saw Posy, and Beatrice felt a tingle when his grin widened at the sight of her. Then he strode over to Miss Sissy's side and pulled up a chair to sit next to her. He reached over and squeezed her hand, and Miss Sissy gave him a rather simpering smile and batted her lashes at him.

Posy and Beatrice left to let the minister visit Miss Sissy without an audience. They walked down the hall to get a soft drink from the visitors' lounge. Fifteen minutes later, Wyatt joined them.

"Miss Sissy was so appreciative of y'all being here." He turned his gaze on Beatrice and his eyes crinkled. "She said that you even rode in the ambulance with her, Beatrice."

Beatrice felt that tongue-tied sensation again and cursed herself for her clumsiness. "I did. I wasn't sure if she had any family anywhere close by. I didn't even realize she was really conscious during that ambulance ride."

Posy knit her brows. "I didn't think to ask if there was someone she wanted me to call. Since I'd never heard her mention any family, it didn't even occur to me."

Wyatt said, "Miss Sissy told me that she has a nephew who lives a couple of hours away—but she didn't want me to call him. I think she considers all of us her family."

Posy said sadly, "And she drives us batty most of the

time. But she can be really funny, too. She's definitely part of the Patchwork Cottage. A very *unique* part."

Beatrice cleared her throat and was relieved to find that she had some control of her tongue again. "I'm worried about her living by herself right now. She's already been attacked once. She'd been talking as if she knew something about Judith's murder." Wyatt frowned, and Beatrice added, "Remember at Daisy's dinner party? She was saying that she knew more than the police did."

Posy said, "She *could* have known something—and the murderer wanted to make sure she kept quiet. But now she's rambling on about the Russians."

"I don't know if she actually has any information about the murder at all," said Beatrice. "She reminds me of a child when she makes those statements—she *wants* to know something. Maybe it makes her feel a little superior to act like she knows something about the killer. But it's obvious that whether she knows anything or not, she convinced the murderer that she did."

Wyatt nodded. "The murderer must have decided to silence her for good. Luckily, he was unsuccessful. Miss Sissy certainly doesn't seem like she's a threat to anyone in her current condition. But, then, I guess if she *did* know something, then she's more likely to come right out and say it. There's no filter there at all now." He looked thoughtful. "She also seems very worried about her safety. Which is, of course, only natural. She acted a little skittish even with me, which I hated to see."

"I think Miss Sissy is clever enough to act crazy on

purpose. She might be rambling about the Russians as a way of protecting herself and making herself look like she's harmless. She could still know a lot more than she's letting on. We could"—and Beatrice couldn't believe that she was the one proposing this—"set her up on sort of a rotation for a couple of weeks. Just to keep an eye on her, you know. Each of her friends could host her for a few days and then she could go on to the next house."

Posy and Wyatt both beamed at her. "That's a wonderful idea," said Wyatt. "Miss Sissy is going to pop with pride that she gets to go on a two-week sleepover."

"I can make some phone calls," said Posy. "With a rotation, she won't be too much of a burden for one person. When she's released in a little while, she can go home with me. She knows me the best," she said, "and I can keep an eye on her in the daytime, too—she can come to work with me at the Patchwork Cottage like she usually does."

Beatrice grinned. "I'm sure Cork will really *love* that!" Then she took a deep breath. In for an inch; in for a mile. "Miss Sissy can stay with me for a few days, for sure." She only hoped she survived those days. . . .

When Wyatt left to go back to the church, Beatrice said to Posy, "He, uh, seems like a really nice man." Beatrice knew that at least Posy wouldn't be giving her any of the knowing looks she'd have gotten from someone like Piper or Meadow.

"He is. He's a really *good* man. We've been blessed to have him as our minister."

Beatrice hesitated. There really wasn't another way

to ask, so she said, "Does he have a big family? Is his wife very involved in the community?"

"Oh, he isn't married. He was—a long time ago. But after she passed away in a car accident, he never seemed interested in dating again." Beatrice was relieved that Posy sounded so matter-of-fact. If she'd asked *Meadow*, there would have been a whole game of Twenty Questions. And then the sly matchmaking. Beatrice shuddered.

Posy had piqued her interest in the minster even more. But she shook herself out of it. He's obviously still mourning his wife, Beatrice told herself sternly. She tried to ignore the wave of warmth that she felt at the thought of him.

It was evening before Beatrice got back home. The hospital had quickly decided to release Miss Sissy, but the discharge process had taken longer than Posy and Beatrice had expected, as they wanted to give instructions on how to care for her wound. Finally, Posy left with both Miss Sissy and Beatrice, since Beatrice had arrived at the hospital by ambulance.

When Beatrice arrived home, she was completely exhausted. She tramped straight to her bedroom, put up her feet, and fell fast asleep without even changing into her pj's or climbing under the sheets.

When her cell phone rang, she wasn't sure at first where she even was. Then she scrambled for the phone, which she'd set down by her back door when she'd first walked in.

It was Piper. "Mama? Were you asleep already? It's only eight o'clock!"

Beatrice filled her in on the events of the day, finishing with, "So I'm going to end up with Miss Sissy as my houseguest at some point soon. After Posy isn't able to manage her anymore, I guess."

"Boy, when you move to a new town, you start off with a bang, don't you? Poor Miss Sissy! I'm glad that y'all are going to keep an eye on her until the police catch whoever is behind all this. It sure sounds like somebody thinks she knows something about Judith's murder."

Although Piper sounded concerned about Miss Sissy, there was still a lilt to her voice, as if she might break out in a smile at any moment. Finally Piper said, "Mama, is it okay if I come by for a few minutes to talk?"

Beatrice had a feeling she knew who the subject of this conversation was going to be. "Sure, sweetie. Come on over." She got up and moved into the kitchen for a glass of water and to try to wake up a little.

Piper came in bubbling with excitement but also looking a little apprehensive. "I don't know where to even start!" she said.

Beatrice smiled at her, but inside her heart was sinking a little. "Why not tell me how your hiking trip and picnic lunch went today?"

"Fantastic! We had the best time, Mama . . . We laughed over the littlest things, and the view from the top of the mountain was beautiful. And romantic. Our

picnic was at a lookout point with an amazing vista—
and he'd packed shrimp for an appetizer and this wonderful artichoke salad that had prosciutto in it that was
the best thing I'd ever put in my mouth! There was Brie
and fruit and this delicious chocolate cake. And wine."

"So it's fair to say you had a reasonably good time,"
Beatrice said drily.

"Oh, Mama." Piper's eyes shone, and Beatrice felt a
little moisture welling up in hers. This alarmed Piper.
"You're upset! I knew I should have brought Ash over
to visit with you tonight."

"No, honey, I'm not upset at all."

"I've been so wrapped up with Ash that I feel like I
haven't even spent any time with you at all." There was
a guilty flush on Piper's pixieish face. "I'd planned that
when you moved in, we were going to go hiking and I
was going to introduce you to different people and get
you involved in clubs and groups. I haven't done any
of those things. I haven't even offered to help you out
with your quilting block or given you any pointers."

The idea of having even *more* activity made Beatrice's head swim. "Are you kidding? I've been crazily
busy since I moved to Dappled Hills. I surely couldn't
handle more things to do. The quilt block has been a
disaster, though. I'm not cut out for quilting." Piper
started to jump in and Beatrice held up her hand. "I can
still *participate* in the Village Quilters, which is a great
group. Meadow has mentioned a couple of times that
they'd need some direction regarding design and planning for shows, and I'm happy to help with that. But I

won't be the one who contributes horrible quilt blocks to an otherwise beautiful work of art."

Beatrice continued. "I never knew how completely inadequate I could feel. There are folks here in Dappled Hills who grow their own food, whip up minor gourmet masterpieces, and make fabulous art in their spare time. It's pretty stressful."

"That's because you're taking it all too seriously," said Piper coolly. "You don't have to be a blue-ribbon quilter, and you don't need to know how to keep a garden alive and you don't need to be able to cook gourmet cuisine."

"So why do I feel that I *do* need to?"

"Because you like to do a good job. When you were working at the museum, you wanted to be the best curator you could be. That was the best-run museum in the Southeast. And now that you're retired and living in the country, you think you've got to be the best retired mountain resident you can be."

"All I know," said Beatrice, patting her book sadly, "is that I want some time to read *Whispers of Summer*."

"Dappled Hills is the complete opposite of Atlanta, Mama. You're the one who's putting all the pressure on yourself. You need to learn how to relax. You know what's really helped me to de-stress? It's meditation."

Beatrice indulged in an eye roll.

"Now, don't look at me like that, Mama. Meditation is a great way to loosen up. I like to use mantras."

Beatrice's head started to hurt.

"My favorite one is 'Peace, calm, kindness.' You

should try it sometime. It's very basic and calming. I was using it today because thinking about the murder was making me tense. I felt my tension melt away the more I said it."

Beatrice managed a smile. "Thanks for sharing it with me, Piper. It's nice of you to be worried about me."

"I want you to *try* it. Promise me that you'll give it a try the next time you think you're not measuring up or when you're stressed out."

"I *promise*." Beatrice was ready to move on to another subject. "But enough about me. I'd rather talk about you and how happy you are with Ash. He sounds like a really special man."

A shadow passed over Piper's face. "I *am* happy, Mama. But there is one thing that's been on my mind. The night Judith was killed, I had a really hard time sleeping. So I decided to peek out the door and see if I saw any of your lights on. I thought I'd pop by for a quick visit if they were. Maybe share a glass of milk with you."

Piper's visits did seem to happen at some unusual times.

"Anyway, I opened the door and stepped outside, and there was Meadow. She didn't see me because my porch was in the shadows. But she was acting sneaky." Piper looked miserable.

"Sneaky?"

"She was peering out toward the street. Then she went inside real quick, then hurried back outside and rushed off down the street at a pretty fast clip. Later on, I was still awake and heard her car driving off. I can recognize that Jeep's engine every time." Piper shrugged. "She might have had trouble sleeping, too, I guess."

It sure didn't sound likely, though.

Chapter 6

Did she feel a certain satisfaction or trepidation about Piper's revelation about Meadow? She *had* longed a little for the excitement of Atlanta in comparison to Dappled Hills. Everyone seemed so *nice* in Dappled Hills. It was all almost too pat—the quilting, the cheerful residents, the daily life centered around the church's activities, the gardening.

In some ways, it was a relief to find that the little town was every bit as quirky and exciting as the big city had been.

In other ways, though, Beatrice couldn't help but worry. Piper was getting emotionally close to Meadow's son. Ash seemed like a nice man and Ramsay was the chief of police, so Ash was probably raised right. But what about Meadow? Was she as open and honest as she seemed? Or was it all a sham to cover up a quick temper . . . and murder? It was very deflating to think that her usual strong instinct for first impressions might have gone so wrong.

Daisy was someone else who was hard to figure out. Judith herself had said that Daisy wasn't everything she seemed to be. She seemed generous with her time and eager to make Beatrice feel at home and settle into the little town. But Beatrice couldn't help but feel like she was hiding something. Judith's taunts the night of the bee had really seemed to affect Daisy. Daisy seemed to put a lot of stock into her quilting and winning quilt shows. What if she wanted to be the best quilter from Dappled Hills? Getting rid of Judith would have been a great way to accomplish that. Or did Judith have some damaging gossip about Daisy? She'd said something about Daisy being dethroned and ending her days of social climbing.

Beatrice hadn't moved far from her front door since Piper had left, which was why she could hear the rustling sound from the bushes near her porch. She froze. Even if Piper were coming back inside to tell her something, she wouldn't be coming back by way of the bushes. Beatrice reached over and turned off the front porch lights and decided to wait. She'd had enough anonymous notes to last a lifetime. She stood to the side of her window and found that she could see at an angle across the porch. Her line of sight included the area right in front of her door, which was where the other notes had been. Noo-noo sat next to Beatrice, head cocked to the side and looking puzzled.

After about ten minutes, Beatrice's waiting was rewarded when she heard a squeaking floorboard and some quiet footsteps on the front porch. Noo-noo gave a low growl, which Beatrice quelled with a warning look at the corgi. Beatrice crept closer to the window and peered slowly around the curtains . . . and saw Georgia gently setting down a glass Nehi bottle with a note sticking out of the top.

As Georgia quickly slipped away, Beatrice released the pent-up breath that she hadn't realized she'd been holding. Georgia? Why was Georgia behind these notes? Beatrice had thought that they were becoming friends. But, really, how well did she know Georgia? She'd apparently had a very rough divorce after she'd found out her husband had been cheating on her. Her life hadn't been very stable, and she was still obviously adjusting to rooming with her sister and doing things Savannah's way—and Savannah seemed very bossy about having things done *her* way.

Satisfied that Georgia had left, Beatrice opened the front door and brought in the bottle. *Stay out of it!* said the note. Stay out of what? Investigating Judith's murder? Why would Georgia care about Beatrice looking into the truth . . . unless maybe Georgia was the one who murdered Judith? Or she was worried that Savannah had. Or *knew* that she had.

Beatrice's sleep that night was spotted with nightmares of a menacing Meadow lurking in her azalea bushes while Georgia peered around the corner of her house, holding a bag of glass bottles containing pithy warnings written in blood.

Beatrice nearly jumped out of her skin when she

woke up to scratching at her front door and an odd, moaning cry. Noo-noo barked a sharp warning in the living room.

Trembling, Beatrice clutched her nightgown together at the neck and hurried to the door, her blood pounding in her ears. When she peered anxiously out the side window, she didn't see anyone; then she jerked back when the scratching started again with increased desperation and vigor. This time she could tell the moaning was coming from a dog. Noo-noo looked at her with worry in her brown eyes.

Beatrice unlocked the bolt and opened the door, and in bounded Meadow's huge beast, Boris. The Great Dane/Newfoundland/corgi mix whined like a baby and looked at her pitifully, as if to say, "I shouldn't be here. Can you take me home?"

Beatrice sank onto her sofa in relief that there hadn't been some crazed killer scratching at her door. Noo-noo took one look at the size of the dog and scampered off to hide under Beatrice's bed. Beatrice glared resentfully at Boris and he wagged his tail sympathetically, agreeing that his predawn visit was a little over the top.

"What I don't understand," said Beatrice with her hands on her hips, "is what you're doing here at all! You couldn't possibly be lost—your house . . . barn . . . whatever . . . is in plain sight. Why aren't you scratching on your own door?"

Boris looked innocently at her, then loped into Beatrice's tiny kitchen and proceeded to poke around.

"Now, where," said Beatrice under her breath, "did

I put Meadow's phone number?" Did Meadow write it down on the Village Quilters' info she'd handed to her? And how was it possible that she'd *just* moved into this cottage and she already was losing things?

It was while she rummaged through her bedside-table drawers that she first heard the unusual noise. Beatrice frowned. What was that? It sounded like . . . chewing.

She hurried back into the kitchen and was greeted by the sight of Boris finishing off a loaf of bread he'd snagged from the counter. As she watched in horror, he reached out a huge paw and batted the sugar canister off the counter . . . and quickly gobbled up the contents.

"Bad Boris! No!" Beatrice put her arms around Boris's neck and pulled him back away from the sugar. Noo-noo peered around the door, watching the proceedings with interest. It must have been the corgi blood Meadow claimed Boris had that was making him scavenge like this. Corgis were tummies with feet. Noo-noo was probably calculating her risk factor for dodging the huge dog and digging her snout into the pile of sugar on the floor.

For all she knew, sugar was poisonous for dogs . . . At the very least, it would certainly lead to diabetes and dental problems. She pulled hard at Boris, who was stubbornly determined to dive into that pile of sugar and broken ceramic. Finally, he gave up and stopped lunging for it. Beatrice, panting from her struggle with the huge animal, backed onto a kitchen stool to catch her breath.

"We'll forget the phone call and just walk there," said Beatrice grimly, pushing a strand of hair from her eyes. She gripped Boris by his collar and yanked him into her bedroom so she could quickly change clothes. Then she took Noo-noo's leash off the nail by the door while the corgi watched her dejectedly. She could tell that *she* wasn't the one who was going on a walk.

Boris joyfully pulled Beatrice behind him as he galloped to the barn, which was visible through the foggy mist of the dawn. She finally resigned herself to a brisk jog behind the dog, and they made quick time.

Ramsay was climbing into his police car when he stopped short at the sight of Boris bounding toward him. Beatrice gave up trying to hold the leash and the dog leaped up, putting his arms around Ramsay's neck and leaning his massive chest against the policeman's.

"Off! Boris, off!" And Beatrice watched in amazement as the dog obediently dropped down and sat on its haunches, grinning at his master.

Ramsay said, "Early-morning visitor, Beatrice? I'm sorry. I didn't even know he'd gotten out. That dog is too smart for his own good."

Beatrice was feeling a wee bit sour. Ramsay was a nice enough man and definitely a more stable neighbor than his flighty wife (although he did live in a barn, apparently without protest), but still. Dealing with other people's gigantic beasts before breakfast—or even coffee—was above and beyond the call of duty. "I'm not sure he's so smart, Ramsay. I believe he's done something that might make him feel sick later on today. I was trying to find y'all's phone number, and before I knew it, he'd scarfed down a loaf of bread and half the contents of my sugar canister." She crossed her arms over her chest.

Boris blinked at her as if butter wouldn't melt in his mouth.

"That rascal. My profuse apologies, Beatrice"—she noticed he didn't *give* them, though—"but I've got to get in to the station. Let me holler at Meadow and she'll pick up on the apologizing for me. Ash is still sound asleep, of course." He opened the door to the barn and bellowed, "Meadow! It's Boris and Beatrice." Apparently thinking that was explanation enough (and not at all worried about waking up the allegedly sleeping Ash), he pulled the door shut, gave Beatrice a kind but distracted smile and hurried off to his police cruiser.

Beatrice's eyes widened as Meadow approached. She had on a pair of navy blue pajamas with large, neon peace symbols covering the fabric. Her eyes danced behind her red pair of glasses. "Boris!" she cried delightedly, and the dog jumped up and licked her face ecstatically, knocking the glasses askew.

Meadow beamed at Beatrice, apparently not noticing the sour look on Beatrice's face. Meadow pushed her glasses back into place and said, "Aren't you smart! Finding Boris when we didn't even know he was out loose!"

"Really, it was a matter of Boris finding me. And, Meadow, I was thinking maybe we should call the vet.

Or maybe even Poison Control—they'd be able to tell us if large quantities of sugar are dangerous for dogs. He consumed most of my sugar canister. And a loaf of bread on top of that." And she'd been planning to have that new jar of blackberry jam on toast this morning. Darn it. Another trip to Bub's.

Meadow wandered to the kitchen, looking either absentminded or sleepy—Beatrice couldn't decide which. "So he's hungry? Let's see. Maybe I should put some peanut butter in his kibbles. Peanut butter always sticks to my ribs—that would probably fill him up."

"For heaven's sake, Meadow! The dog ate several cups of sugar! Don't you think we should find out if that's a problem?"

Meadow narrowed her eyes. "Was it *sugar* or was it artificial sweetener?"

"Sugar."

"Well, that's all right, then. I mean, I wouldn't want to feed a dog sugar on a *daily* basis, since it'll be a problem for them just like it's a problem for us . . . cavities and obesity and all. But I don't blame you, Beatrice, for giving him a treat. That was nice of you, even if it wasn't the best *choice* of treat available."

Beatrice ground her teeth.

Meadow, happily unaware of the consternation she was causing, cheerfully mixed up some peanut butter in Boris's dog food for his unnecessary second breakfast, then beamed as the dog devoured his breakfast in a matter of three or four gulps. She then put a tremendous mug of coffee in front of Beatrice and pushed a large sugar bowl down the counter to her.

"I'm reading a book about choices," said Meadow. "I started reading it last night, and at two o'clock I was shocked at the time and had to turn off my light. It's really good, Beatrice. I'll lend it to you when I'm through with it. It talks about *everything* being a choice . . . that really, we make hundreds of choices in a day. Hundreds! I used to think that a choice was something like, *Where do I go for vacation this year?* But no—we make deliberate choices every day when we decide what we're having for breakfast or whether we have that second cup of coffee before or after we read our paper. We need to *realize* we're making choices and live more *deliberately* . . ."

Beatrice tuned out at this point as Meadow continued her earnest rambles. Actually, mused Beatrice, this seems like an excellent opportunity to bring up Meadow's choice to act odd on the night of Judith's murder. "I wanted to ask you about something," she interjected into Meadow's increasingly beatnik-leaning monologue.

"Hmm?" Meadow picked up the milk carton and poured at least half a cup into Beatrice's coffee mug. Really! Had she already forgotten Beatrice was drinking coffee?

"About the night that Judith was murdered. I remembered your saying that you were inside the whole night. And you've already said that you didn't see or hear anything except when Posy dropped off Boris, and that Ash was sound asleep. But when I was talking to Piper, she mentioned that she'd seen you outside. She thought that you looked . . . well, a little odd."

Piper, of course, had said that Meadow looked suspicious, not odd. Meadow, thought Beatrice as she looked at the other woman's pj's, was *always* odd.

Meadow's round face grew pink. "Why ever would Piper say something like that? She must have gotten her nights confused. I was in the bed that night. Reading!" She spun around, bending to pick up Boris's water bowl and refill it.

"Reading about choices?"

"Yes! I was totally absorbed," said Meadow in a blustering voice.

"But you said that you'd started reading your book on choices *last* night." Beatrice tried not to be smug about the fact that she'd actually listened to some of Meadow's blathering. "Besides, Piper seemed certain that it was the night of Judith's murder that she saw you."

"Oh. That's right. It was my other book."

"Which book was it? I could use another book right now." Especially since *Whispers of Summer* didn't seem to be holding her interest.

Meadow spilled some of Boris's water on the floor and cursed at it. "Well, the book is— Well, what do you know? I can't remember the title."

"Or the author?"

"I *never* remember the author, Beatrice. My memory isn't that great." Meadow sounded dignified about her shortcoming.

"I'm sure I can figure out what the book is," said Beatrice. "Just tell me what it's about. Maybe then the title will come to you."

A flash of irritation crossed Meadow's broad face. She tilted the bowl too much and the water was once again spilling out onto the floor. "It's a story about a woman. She's trying to . . . you know . . . discover herself. She's middle-aged and her marriage broke up and she discovers God and her artistic talents. And food." Meadow stopped and looked hopefully through her lashes at Beatrice.

Clever. That was the plot for at least a dozen different books. But then the water bowl, Meadow's own personal lie detector, slipped completely out of her hands and fell with a metal clanging onto the wooden floor. Meadow reached over and pulled handfuls of paper towels off the holder as the unconcerned Boris lapped the water right off the floor.

Meadow sighed. "It's no use. I never could fib, even to save my own soul. You might as well have a seat. I haven't even offered you any coffee! Where are my manners?" Beatrice opened her mouth to remind her that she'd already had a huge mug, but then realized resistance was probably futile. More coffee? Beatrice not only envisioned herself in the restroom very soon, but she also had visions of hot coffee in Meadow's shaky hands, splashing all over her, and Meadow quickly added, "Without spilling it, I promise. I'm putting my sins behind me!"

A few minutes later, Beatrice perched on Meadow's

sofa, drinking some very black coffee. Meadow looked sheepish. "You won't say anything, Beatrice, will you? Because I don't want to get anyone into trouble."

"But, Meadow, what about Ramsay? Have you told *him* what you were doing that night?"

"It's just that Amber came by that night. After the quilting bee. She was riled up and wanted to fuss about Judith. She felt like Judith was robbing Felicity of money she could have made from the quilt. Felicity hasn't had a whole lot of extra cash on hand lately, so she's reached the point in her life where she wants to make things *simple*. But *simple* can still be *expensive*. She needed that money, and Amber took Judith's trick personally."

"Well, the money from that quilt wouldn't be enough to be able to put Felicity in a top-notch retirement home. It wasn't *that* valuable."

Meadow hesitated, drinking some of her coffee, then made a face. "Too strong. Would you rather have some iced tea?" Beatrice shook her head and waited. Meadow sighed. "It wasn't just that the money from the quilt would help with expenses. That was merely the final straw. A developer approached Felicity and Judith about their properties. He wanted to buy both their lots for an office building. But he needed *both* of them to agree to sell the property to make it worth anything. He couldn't do anything with just one of the properties; the space would be too small."

"Judith wasn't interested?" asked Beatrice.

"She wouldn't *budge*. Wouldn't even *talk* to the developer about it. If Felicity had gotten that money, then she'd have been able to move into any retirement community that she chose."

This put things in a more serious light. So Amber had several grievances against Judith. No wonder she'd been furious about Judith's attempt to swindle her mother.

"Amber wanted to talk. That's *all*," said Meadow. She lifted her cup to sip her coffee and spilled some on her lap. She looked sadly at the telltale spill. "Okay. Well, maybe she was interested in drinking a bottle of my Chardonnay, too. But that was only to take the edge off."

"*Did* it take the edge off?"

Meadow shook her head. "It sure didn't. Nothing I said seemed to help, actually. Amber left just as upset as she was when she came. Maybe even more upset."

"I know you've mentioned that Amber used to be a real hothead. But she doesn't seem that way anymore."

"She's usually not. But she's really protective of Felicity."

Beatrice asked, "How did you and Amber end up being such great friends?"

"I'm her confidant and mentor. We've been friends since she was a teenager." Meadow looked pleased with herself.

The idea of Meadow being anyone's mentor made Beatrice smile. "So, you decided to cover up the fact that she'd been over to visit you."

"Well, not originally. But after I found out about the murder, I decided not to say anything about it. After all, it's not like Amber could *murder* anyone." Meadow gave a halfhearted laugh. "I'd practically be derailing Ramsay's investigation if I mentioned Amber's visit. It'd take him off on the wrong tangent. Better to have him investigating true leads and finding out who the real killer is."

"But you were out in your yard later? That's when Piper said that she saw you looking or acting odd," said Beatrice.

Meadow looked guilty, but then looked away. "I was out looking for Boris. He'd gotten out at some point and I couldn't find him. Before Posy returned him I walked a little ways down the street; then I came back in. But then you'd understand that, since you've just brought him back to me." She bent over and covered the Great Dane with kisses. He grinned with delight, his tongue hanging out of his mouth.

Meadow set her mug down on the coffee table with great determination and focus. There was now no indicator for her truthfulness, but Beatrice still couldn't believe what Meadow was saying. "Who do you think would want to murder Judith, then, if not Amber?"

Meadow raised her eyebrows. "Everybody in this town, girlfriend. Nobody liked her. She was a major busybody, which doesn't win friends or influence people when you live in a small town. Plus the fact, of course, that she blackmailed people."

"*Blackmailed* people? I thought Judith had plenty of money. She owned her own shop, and it seems like she'd sell her property to the developer if she needed money."

"She had plenty of money. She just enjoyed being mean," said Meadow. "I had an old high school friend here for a visit a few months ago. We were having a good time reminiscing over a bottle of wine. Judith came by out of the blue." Meadow looked irritated. "She was always really nosy."

Coming from Meadow, that was really saying something.

Meadow said, "She was probably out driving around, looking for trouble, and spotted my friend's car in the driveway. She popped by for a visit and to see who was with me."

Beatrice asked, "Did she even give a reason for being there?"

"She said she'd dropped by to pay me back for some fabric I picked up at Posy's for everyone in the guild. But she didn't have to pay me back that *minute*. The guild was meeting in a couple of days, anyway. Judith was being nosy. Like I said."

"So your friend was sloshed and started spilling secrets?" asked Beatrice.

"She was laughing and cutting up and blabbing all our youthful indiscretions to Judith. Judith, of all people! Telling her that she and I had smoked pot in college." Meadow rolled her eyes. "I tried to cut her off, but she was bound and determined to tell some funny story about something silly we'd done."

"And I bet," said Beatrice drily, "that Judith was a really attentive audience for your friend."

"I'm sure Sally must have been flattered to bits having Judith hanging on her every word like that. Of course, she didn't know Judith was going to try blackmailing me over it."

"What did Judith do?"

"She was so smug," said Meadow, making a face. "She automatically assumed that I'd be happy to pay her to keep her from telling all of Dappled Hills that the town police chief's wife used to smoke pot."

"How much money did she want?"

"Believe it or not, considering how greedy she is, she didn't actually want any money. No, Miss Judith wanted to be president of the Village Quilters."

"What?" Beatrice frowned. "Was the presidency something you could arrange for her?"

"Not really. It would be bending the rules. The guild votes on the president. Judith wanted me to step down with some kind of excuse about being busy and appoint her as president in my place. I kind of doubted that the others were going to go for it, though. They'd have thought I'd flipped my wig."

Beatrice tapped her finger against her coffee cup. "Why on earth would Judith care so much about being president of the Village Quilters?"

"Judith wanted the position because she knew she'd never get it through our guild elections. And she took it very personally whenever someone else was voted as president. Nobody liked her, and that was reflected every year at elections. If she'd ended up as the guild president, she could have really rubbed it in everyone's faces."

Beatrice sighed. "None of it makes sense to me. I can understand somebody trying to get rid of Judith, especially if she was trying to blackmail them or reveal a secret they had. But who on earth would try to kill Miss Sissy? She seems harmless enough. Well, not exactly *harmless*, and she's clearly crazy as a coot, but . . ."

"What?"

Beatrice blinked. "Oh, for heaven's sake. I completely forgot to mention what happened yesterday in all the bother with Boris and thinking about Judith's murder. Besides, I'm surprised Ramsay didn't tell you. Miss Sissy was attacked in her home yesterday and left for dead. She was unconscious when I discovered her yesterday morning."

Beatrice had the distinct pleasure of seeing Meadow struck speechless for the first time since she'd met her.

Beatrice continued. "It must be the same person responsible for killing Judith. I find it hard to believe such a tiny town would have *two* murderers running around in it. But what could her attacker have been trying to accomplish?"

Meadow found her tongue finally. "Could she have known something or seen something? Miss Sissy honestly doesn't even seem like she knows what's going on half the time."

But Beatrice wondered. She sometimes glimpsed a cunning look in Miss Sissy's eyes that made her think that the old woman knew more than she let on. "A couple of days ago, I was at the Patchwork Cottage while Miss Sissy was there. She was rambling about greed and acting smug."

Meadow snorted. "Miss Sissy's pet peeve is greed. She's totally obsessed with it. She's even called *me* greedy before, and I live in a barn and am married to a cop. It's her personal mania. But who knows? Maybe she did know something. Good luck getting anything out of her that makes sense, though. Honestly, I'm going to kill that Ramsay for not telling me about this yesterday." Meadow reached down and absently rubbed Boris's head. Boris half closed his eyes, and Beatrice wondered for a moment if the Great Dane was going to start purring.

"You know what you could do?" said Meadow. "You could take Miss Sissy her favorite treat. I think food is definitely the way to her heart. She'll probably spill whatever's on her mind right away."

"What's her favorite treat?" asked Beatrice.

"Peanut brittle. The homemade kind."

"Peanut brittle? Miss Sissy doesn't have any teeth!"

"She certainly does! Maybe they're not over at Posy's, though. No, I'm sure Posy would have packed them. And Miss Sissy would definitely pop them in if she had peanut brittle handed to her." Meadow snapped her fingers. "And I just thought of something. This attack on Miss Sissy should prove that Amber had nothing to do with Judith's murder. Can you picture Amber hitting Miss Sissy over the head?"

Beatrice couldn't. But, then, she couldn't actually picture *anyone* doing it. She did wonder, though, how Meadow knew Miss Sissy had been hit over the head during the attack. Was it just because that was how Judith had been killed? Or did Meadow know more than she was letting on?

Chapter 7

Peanut brittle, thought Beatrice. She was still trying to find her way around her tiny kitchen and remember where the plates and cups were. And her recipe box. She was pretty sure that her mother's peanut brittle recipe was in her battered recipe box somewhere.

Beatrice finally found the box tucked in the same cupboard as her pots and pans. Really, she had to wonder sometimes where her brain was. She'd been a curator at an art museum, for heaven's sake. She was great at arranging things so they made perfect sense. Ordinarily.

There was a knock at the door, so Beatrice scrambled off the floor where she'd perched in front of the pots and pans. She peered out to see Daisy there, holding a tremendous planter with a collection of different flowers and green plants in it. "A welcome-to–Dappled Hills gift," she said with a smile as she walked through Beatrice's tiny living room and put the planter by the backdoor.

Beatrice wished she had thought to put on something nicer that morning. Here she was in a disreputable pair of old jeans and a T-shirt that never made it out of the house (for good reason). Daisy was wearing a pair of dark slacks and a crisp, lilac-colored blouse . . . with too many buttons unbuttoned. Daisy came back into the living room and seemed to be waiting for something. Beatrice quickly said, "Oh, Daisy. Please . . . have a seat."

Daisy sat down on Beatrice's gingham sofa, and Beatrice said, "Can I get you a coffee or a snack or anything?"

"I'm fine, Beatrice, but thanks."

"Well, thanks so much for the plants. They're lovely, and, really, you've done enough, anyway—the dinner party was such a treat." How long was she going to be able to keep those poor plants alive? She hadn't been blessed with any gardening genes.

"It's my pleasure, Beatrice! It's such a pity we had this terrible tragedy right after you moved to town. And to think that we've got some sort of deranged killer in our midst! It hardly seems safe to go outside right now."

It was actually hard to picture a more benign place than Dappled Hills. For the town residents, though, it must seem a lot more alarming to have a murder in such a pastoral place. Beatrice said, "I'm sure Ramsay will figure out who did it; then everything will return to normal. I'm curious to see what normal is like here, since I haven't really experienced it yet."

Daisy gave a small shrug. "It's usually a little slow. I try to liven things up by having different parties. And I travel around a lot with the quilting."

"Oh, right—your quilting competitions."

"They're really like juried shows," said Daisy mildly. "My family is from Charleston, South Carolina, and I try to make it down there fairly often, too. The entire family are patrons, so we'll visit museums and galleries when I'm there. It's very refreshing."

There wasn't art in Dappled Hills? "There are galleries here, too, aren't there? I'm sure I saw them downtown."

"There are . . . Well, there *is*. There's one gallery. I'd like to see a lot more, of course, but I don't know if this area can support more than one." She glanced around thoughtfully at Beatrice's bare walls. "Funny, because somehow I thought with your background as a curator, you'd have more artwork on your walls."

Beatrice felt an annoying flush crawl up her neck. "I do, actually, have a nice collection of Southern folk art. I haven't unpacked everything, though. I did downsize a lot when I came here, realizing that I was moving into a smaller place. Which is funny—I was only in a condo in Atlanta, but this cottage is still smaller." She hated feeling defensive.

"Soon you'll have your own art up on the walls." Beatrice blinked at her, and she continued. "Your quilts, of course!"

"Oh. Of course. Quilts everywhere."

"Did you start on your group block for Meadow?"

"No. No, I decided to start out with a quilt of my own first. That way I could practice and make mistakes and not mess up a group quilt for my first project."

Daisy pursed her lips thoughtfully. "I suppose that's one way of doing it. Although I'm sure you wouldn't mess anything up, Beatrice." She peered innocently at the shelf under the coffee table. "What's this?"

"It's my practice quilt," said Beatrice. Her voice sounded stiff to her ears.

"It's really lovely, Beatrice. It really, really is." The number of *really*s seemed to increase with the level of insincerity in Daisy's voice. Beatrice hadn't realized the quilt was *that* bad.

"Were you . . . well, were you just being ingenious here?" Daisy pointed a red-lacquered nail at one block.

"Ingenious?"

"Where you put the patch on upside down. Sometimes there are quilters who sort of *wink* with their patches. An inside joke between them and their audience."

"Oh. No, that would be a plain old error. I didn't plan any winks in the quilt." Darn it. And *audience*? As if quilting was in the entertainment realm?

"We all do things like that, Beatrice. It's easily fixed." Daisy's voice seemed to indicate that she was perhaps telling a little white lie to make Beatrice feel better.

After seeing Daisy off a few minutes later, Beatrice sat back down on the gingham sofa and looked grimly at both the potted plants and her quilting mistake.

There was nothing like a setback, especially when you thought you might be getting the hang of something.

Daisy's visit had knocked her completely off course. She finally remembered that she'd been planning on making Miss Sissy some peanut brittle. Noo-noo watched with great interest as she pulled out the recipe box to find the recipe. The box was more packed than she'd remembered. There were scraps of yellowed newspaper peeping out, ancient index cards with smudges on them, and pages ripped from old magazines.

Finally she found her mother's peanut brittle recipe. The card was so old that it looked like it had been written on parchment paper. She popped the card in her pocketbook and looked out the window. It looked nice enough to walk to Bub's, and the recipe didn't call for many ingredients. Noo-noo looked hopefully at Beatrice. "Not this time, Noo-noo. You wouldn't be able to go inside the store. But I'll bring you back some treats."

Beatrice was halfway to the store when she saw a tremendous old-model Lincoln shuddering down the road toward her. She quickly hopped out of the way. Miss Sissy, behind the wheel already? Hearing a cheerful toot-toot of the horn, she noticed the car was actually within the parameters of the road and that Posy was behind the wheel with a bandaged Miss Sissy sitting ferociously beside her in the passenger's seat. As the car passed, Miss Sissy brandished a cane at her through the back window. Since Beatrice was such a road hog, walking in the grass.

Beatrice set a meandering pace, taking in the sights of the little town along the way. It was really almost *too* picturesque. But it was all completely genuine, she knew—there were no tourists here until the fall leaves changed. There was the old-timey grocery store with three old men in rocking chairs cutting up in front. There was a *full-service* gasoline station with another coterie of old boys (this time in gas-station uniform). The little art gallery, bookstores, and toy stores dotted the main road. And then there was the Patchwork Cottage . . . very cottagey indeed with gingham curtains hanging in the window. Nothing at all like Atlanta. Beatrice felt a little stirring of sadness for the big city she'd left as she looked at the bucolic scene ahead of her. There had been real excitement in the city. Then Beatrice frowned and squinted a little bit. Off on the side road there. It was Amber, sitting in her car with the engine off. She acted like she was waiting for something. Or someone. Maybe it was the fact that Felicity had mentioned Amber's rebellious past, but Beatrice couldn't help but get the feeling that Amber looked furtive. Could it be that some of her past behavior was resurfacing?

Beatrice saw Amber suddenly lift a phone to her ear as if she'd gotten a call. She started the motor and drove away. What was Amber up to? Just looking for some excitement in the small town? Or was there something more troubling going on?

Suddenly the little town of Dappled Hills didn't seem quite so sleepy.

After the peanut brittle had cooled and Beatrice had put it in a container, she called Posy's house. It was past five, so surely Posy and Miss Sissy were back at the house by now. Sure enough, Posy's cheerful voice answered the phone and she urged her to come on by. "Miss Sissy will be so thrilled!" said Posy. "And it's so thoughtful of you to do something nice for her."

It made Beatrice feel a little bit guilty about her motives. But, after all, it *was* important to solve this case. It wasn't healthy for such a small community to be looking over their shoulders for very long . . . wondering which neighbor was a killer.

Miss Sissy *was* thrilled by the peanut brittle, actually. She crowed loudly and clapped her withered hands as soon as she saw the treat. The next thing Beatrice knew, she'd snatched the container out of her hands and disappeared into the back of the house, presumably to reunite with her teeth.

Posy's husband, Cork, shook his head as he watched the cronelike figure scamper away. "When did you say that it was your turn to host Miss Sissy, Beatrice?"

"Now, Cork! It's our pleasure to have Miss Sissy here with us. You know she gives back a lot . . . in her own way."

Cork put the heels of his hands over his eyes and pushed as if to relieve the pressure there. Beatrice said,

"Well, whenever you do need a break from Miss Sissy's giving, give me a call."

Cork growled, "I'm still not convinced that there's some murderer after her, anyway. Maybe it was a burglary gone wrong. Somebody could have broken into Miss Sissy's house looking for money, she surprised them, and they conked her on the head. Could've been as simple as that."

Beatrice sighed. "Ordinarily I'd agree with you, Cork. But, really. If you were a burglar, would you pick *Miss Sissy's* house to break into? The place is in shambles. You can barely even *get* to the front door with all the vines and thorns surrounding the house. It's the last place I'd choose if I were looking for money."

Cork waved his hand irritably. "Looking for prescription drugs, then. She's an old woman. Probably got tons of prescription drugs in there. You know what drug users are like these days. All trying to get ahold of those prescription drugs." He pushed his chair back abruptly. "Got a great red wine today from the store . . . It's been decanting. Want a glass, Beatrice? I sure as heck need one."

"I'd love one. Thanks."

Cork disappeared into the kitchen, and Posy sighed. "Cork sometimes isn't quite as patient with Miss Sissy as I'd like."

Cork was apparently still within earshot, because he stuck his head back through the doorway. He had a couple of empty wineglasses in his hands. "Miss Sissy isn't patient with *me*, Posy. She hisses at me."

"Only when you're not friendly, Cork!"

Grumbling, Cork disappeared again.

"Don't let Miss Sissy come between you," Beatrice said quickly. "If her visit becomes too much of a strain, just let me know and she can stay with me for a while. I do think it's important to keep an eye on her, though. There's no way anyone would have imagined that she had designer prescription drugs in her house. I'm sure she was targeted because she knew something. How is Miss Sissy doing, by the way?"

"You know, Beatrice, she's not really doing so well. That's why it was especially nice of you to bring over a special treat for her. *Physically* she's doing all right, but *mentally* it's another story. It's really so sad—she jumps at the slightest little thing. That feistiness isn't there. I actually called Wyatt to see if he had any suggestions. She seems to respond so well to him. It was all a really traumatic experience for her."

"Well, if anyone has a solution to Miss Sissy's fears, it would be the minister. He does have a very calming influence on her," said Beatrice. "Most of the rest of us seem guilty of riling her up."

The kitchen door opened again, and Cork arrived with a tray bearing the wine decanter and three glasses of wine. Unfortunately for Cork, Miss Sissy reappeared simultaneously. She had some very obvious peanut brittle crumbs on her mouth and dress. And, apparently, she'd overheard some of the conversation. Or, maybe, just the word *guilty*. "Posy isn't guilty," she bellowed, shooting Beatrice a vicious look. "But the guilty know their transgressions. *Wickedness*."

Cork gave a long-suffering sigh, put the tray firmly down on the coffee table and took a glass and the rest of the decanter with him as he disappeared into the back of the house.

Posy said, "Now, Miss Sissy, you're getting yourself all excited again! You know the doctor said that wasn't good for your blood pressure. What are you talking about—wickedness?"

"It was wickedness that killed Judith," spat Miss Sissy.

Beatrice resisted the urge to roll her eyes. Miss Sissy wasn't exactly trotting out a new idea, after all. She didn't want to lose the footing she'd gained with her, though. "Do you know something about the killer, Miss Sissy? Did you see or hear something?"

She looked at Beatrice balefully with bloodshot eyes. "I saw them kissing."

"Saw *who* kissing?" asked Beatrice.

But Miss Sissy wasn't ready to spill what, if anything, she knew. She gave Beatrice a cunning look. "Their evildoing will bring contagion! Contagion on Dappled Hills!"

Miss Sissy looked on the verge of foaming at the mouth, and Beatrice had to give Posy points for her enormous patience as she gently squeezed Miss Sissy's crippled hand. "It's all right, dear. Don't worry about it now. Would you like a glass of milk to go with your peanut brittle?"

Surely someone with the patience of a saint couldn't have acted out of spontaneous anger against Judith.

There was a gentle knock at the front door, and Miss Sissy went pale. "Bolt the door!" she said, scampering into the kitchen and peering around the door into the living room. As Posy trotted to the door, Miss Sissy hissed, "Don't open it!"

Posy carefully pulled the curtain over the door aside and looked through. "Miss Sissy, it's just Wyatt. Is it okay if I open the door and let him in?"

Miss Sissy nodded reluctantly, but did come out of the kitchen, smoothing her dress a little.

Wyatt was dressed casually in a golf shirt and jeans. He gave Beatrice and Posy a wink when he saw them, but focused his attention mainly on Miss Sissy. "Miss Sissy, I'm glad to see you up and around again."

She preened.

"I wanted to bring something by for you. I can only imagine how scary life might seem to you now after being attacked. I'm sure it's one of those things that can make you jump at shadows or unexpected noises."

Miss Sissy nodded and looked curiously at the paper bag he held.

"So I went by the hardware store, and they had this great selection of whistles in their camping section." He reached into the paper bag and pulled out a shiny whistle on a bright red cord.

Miss Sissy's eyes brightened and she reached out a gnarled hand, snatching the whistle away as quickly as she had the peanut brittle.

"So now you don't have to worry," he explained in a rush, apparently realizing that she could disappear at any moment. "Whenever you're out and you don't feel safe, you blow that whistle. Blow it as loud as you can and help will come running. That's the nice thing about Dappled Hills, right? Help is never very far away."

Miss Sissy glowed with appreciation. She put the red cord around her neck, stuck the whistle in her mouth . . . and blew as hard as she could.

Beatrice felt her heart leap into her mouth at the piercing blast, and saw that Posy and Wyatt looked equally shaken. Duchess, Posy's beagle, barked frantically. Beatrice could only imagine how the noise must have hurt the dog's ears.

Miss Sissy looked pleased at the noise she'd produced. Cork appeared in the kitchen door, his expression thunderous. He stared at the whistle, as if unwilling to believe his eyes. Miss Sissy bounded to the back of the house, cackling. Cork looked at Wyatt with narrowed eyes.

"Cork, Wyatt gave Miss Sissy a whistle so she wouldn't feel so scared anymore. Isn't that helpful?" Posy explained.

Wyatt smiled weakly at Cork.

"I suppose so," drawled Cork. "Wouldn't want Miss Sissy to feel scared, I guess. So long as she's not blowing that whistle all the time—" The last bit was cut short by the shrill blast of the whistle and the beagle's frantic barking in response.

Cork reached into a drawer, pulled out an iPod and earbuds, plugged his ears and disappeared.

Wyatt cleared his throat. "Well, I'm sure that as Miss

Sissy gets used to the whistle, the novelty will wear off and she'll feel more secure."

He looked sheepishly at Posy and Beatrice, and Posy hurried to say, "I think it's such a thoughtful thing to have done, Wyatt. She really has been in a state, and that whistle is the perfect way of handling it."

As another piercing shrill of the whistle penetrated the house, Wyatt winced. "I hope so, Posy. At least we know she won't be attacked. No one would be able to get within a couple of yards of her if she's blowing that whistle."

Chapter 8

The sun shone cheerfully on Beatrice's backyard as she and Noo-noo enjoyed a late-morning brunch. Noo-noo nibbled her kibble and looked hopefully at the fluffy, buttered biscuits Beatrice was having with her coffee. Beatrice dearly loved homemade biscuits. But why worry with baking your own when the refrigerated ones were practically as good?

It had been hard to wake up this morning. The soft quilt that Felicity had given her had formed a comfy cocoon, Noo-noo had snored gently next to the bed and the morning light bathed the room with a gentle glow.

There was something to be said for a morning ritual . . . and Beatrice loved the beginnings of her outdoor-breakfast ritual. She brought out a carafe of coffee, a china cup, sugar, cream, spoons and napkins on a tray with the biscuits, and set them out on the little wrought-iron table. Relaxation had definitely felt strange at first—she was so used to the fast pace of her life and job in Atlanta. But as she tilted her face up to feel the warmth of the sun and relaxed in the yard with the scent of magnolias filling the air . . . it all conspired to convert her to a simpler way of life.

With a happy sigh, Beatrice added an extra scoop of sugar to her coffee. Noo-noo gave up on the biscuits and rolled onto her back for a little nap. Beatrice took in a deep, cleansing breath, held it, breathed out, took a sip of her coffee . . . then froze as she heard a tremendous crashing through her bushes by an unseen intruder. Noo-noo rolled over, jumped up, and started furiously barking in the direction of the noise. Beatrice, thinking of uncaught murderers, snatched up the carafe of coffee, ready to fling the hot liquid at whatever perpetrator charged into the yard.

Then she saw Boris's goofy grin and relaxed, even as Noo-noo got tenser. The huge dog bounded into the yard with delight, blue leash trailing along behind him. A moment later, there was more rustling in the bushes and Meadow appeared, leaves snagged in her braid and a beaming smile on her rosy face. "Boris!" she panted. "Bad boy! Shouldn't run off." Thoroughly winded, Meadow plopped down into the other lawn chair and seemed oblivious to Beatrice's less-than-welcoming look.

Beatrice knew from past experience with people who trespassed on her time that you can only have your time abused if you *allow* it to be abused. Meadow, she reminded herself, was a likable person. But boundaries had to be set. Visits before breakfast just couldn't become routine. For heaven's sake, Beatrice was only now starting to get the hang of relaxing and enjoying her solitude!

"Meadow"—she used a firm but kind voice—"I would love to invite you to have coffee with me, but . . ."

Meadow, leaning over and fumbling for Boris's leash, looked up at Beatrice with such tremendous gratitude on her face that it stopped Beatrice's little speech more effectively than anything else could have done.

"Oh, Beatrice, *thank* you. I'll take you up on your offer of coffee. Crazy morning. I swear, some days I can't seem to do anything right. I couldn't even hold on to Boris's leash this morning! And I'm worried sick about the murder and the attack on Miss Sissy. I mean, *really*? Who attacks a helpless old lady like Miss *Sissy*? I was up half the night worrying over it all. And wondering who was behind it." Meadow blinked at the tray. "Were you having a tea party, just you and Noonoo? I'll run in for another cup if you hold Boris."

Somehow, Beatrice found herself clutching the huge beast's leash and looking into his grinning face. Noonoo stared reproachfully at her. She'd have to mend some bridges with her later today. And Meadow was clearly delusional. Miss Sissy, a helpless old lady? In what alternate universe? Miss Sissy was only slightly less alarming to Beatrice than the murderer. Boris drooled delightedly at the sight of Beatrice's last remaining biscuit, and before she could anticipate his next move, he'd reached his massive head over and gobbled it up.

Beatrice gritted her teeth. "Peace, calm, kindness," she grated out, using Piper's mantra. Boris burped.

Meadow ambled up, humming off tune, with a china cup in her hand. She poured herself a generous cup of coffee from the carafe, put several teaspoons of sugar in her cup, and set it on the table before taking the leash from Beatrice. Winding it around her chair leg, she gave a deep chuckle at the fluffy biscuit crumb on Boris's face. "Had some more breakfast, big boy? I was wondering where that other biscuit had gotten to. You should thank Beatrice for spoiling you with goodies. This is the second time she's done it! Beatrice, it's official—Boris is your number one fan. He runs over here every chance he gets. You can tell he loves you."

Meadow took a gulp from her coffee with enough of a slurp to set Beatrice's teeth on edge. Boris continued grinning at her lovingly. "Now, *this* is good coffee! You'll have to give Ramsay some coffee-making lessons. He was up before I was this morning, and the coffee was absolutely ghastly. I think it was his revenge for my forgetting to tape *Wheel* again."

Peace, calm, kindness. She was feeling a little prissy sitting so straight in her wrought-iron chair, scowling at the sprawling, slouching Meadow. Before she could try to move past her reserve, Meadow said in a quiet voice, "You have a gorgeous backyard, Beatrice. The magnolias, the azalea bushes, the Knock Out rosebushes. What a peaceful oasis."

Beatrice hurried to speak before Meadow started spouting some mantras herself (and Beatrice had a feeling that Meadow's might take a while). "It certainly is—I'm very lucky. You seem . . . stressed-out, Meadow. Is it Judith's murder or Miss Sissy? Or something else?"

"It's everything. I'm completely shocked about Judith and Miss Sissy. You'd think I'd be immune to trouble, being married to the police chief. But all Ramsay usually has to deal with in Dappled Hills is barking-dog complaints or bringing old Mrs. Towne her prescription, since she's shut-in. And he has to help put up the Christmas lights downtown and take them down again. It's not as if I've gotten hardened to some dark criminal underbelly of Dappled Hills. It doesn't exist!" Meadow moved restlessly in her chair, and Boris laid his head on her leg with concern.

"I don't *like* wondering which of my friends or neighbors might be some crazed killer, either. A murderer! In the Village Quilters!" Meadow shook her head.

Meadow gave a small sniff, and Beatrice realized with horror that she was on the verge of bursting into tears. "It might not be someone in the guild," said Beatrice quickly. "Who knows? It could be anyone. No one liked the woman."

Meadow's lip quivered. "No, it's someone in the Village Quilters. It has to be, Beatrice. I started out so angry with Ramsay for suspecting my friends in the guild. It makes me so sad to think of it. It's taken all the fun out of the group for me. I'm not even looking forward to our meeting today."

That was right—there was a guild meeting today.

"You know, Meadow, since I'm sort of an outsider, maybe I can look at the situation with a better perspective and a little distance. Maybe I can help to solve the case."

Beatrice blinked in surprise when Meadow leaped up, nearly upsetting the table in the process, and hugged her. "Would you? I was thinking that as guild president, maybe I had a responsibility to get to the bottom of it. Not that I don't have faith in Ramsay and the state police, but I *know* these women. I should be able to pinpoint who might be capable of murder. But the fact that I *do* know them has put blinders on me. I *love* these ladies, even the ones who sometimes get on my last nerve. I simply can't picture anyone as a killer or someone who'd beat up old ladies."

"I'll be at the guild meeting today," said Beatrice. "I'm hoping that as I spend more time with the quilters, something might jump out at me that doesn't seem right."

Meadow smiled. "Will you be quilting at the meeting?"

"Well, I'm not so sure about that. You know, I tried to do a small quilt, just to practice, but Daisy saw it and was pretty appalled. I might decide not to give you a block for the group quilt. I think I need some more practice first."

"Your quilt will probably end up a lot better than you think," said Meadow. "I bet you'll be an ace quilter in no time!"

Beatrice had her doubts, though. Her experience

with quilts was of looking at them as works of art . . . and she knew that her quilting couldn't measure up. It was frustrating.

"By the way," said Meadow with a sappy grin. "Ash has loved spending time with Piper. They really seemed to hit it off! Wouldn't it be fantastic if we weren't simply neighbors and in the same quilting guild . . . but if we were family, too?" Boris grinned at her, as if agreeing with Meadow.

Peace, calm, kindness.

"If y'all don't mind," said Amber in a hushed voice, "could you keep the conversation off the murder? Mother hasn't really been feeling well today, and I'm hoping she can relax this afternoon."

It was Felicity's turn to host the guild, and she'd insisted on going through with the hosting. Felicity and Meadow were in the kitchen, putting together a tray with snacks and drinks.

Daisy's face puckered with concern. "Is your mama doing all right, Amber? It seems like Judith's death has really shaken her up."

Amber's expression darkened and she shrugged.

"I'm sure she'll be fine," said Daisy kindly. "My husband always talks about how many of his patients' problems are really just a side effect of stress. Maybe it's the stress of the murder that's taking a while for her to get over."

Beatrice made a mental note to avoid being Harrison Butler's patient at all costs. It would be highly annoying to go in for gout and be told her problems were all due to stress.

Amber pressed her lips closer together, apparently to keep any ill-advised words from popping out.

Minutes later, they were all sitting together in Felicity's living room, pulling out their blocks and needles for hand piecing. And so far, Felicity seemed relaxed.

Daisy said, "Y'all, I'm going to make a pledge to you right here and now. I will never do yard work again. Ever! You've got my word on it." She pulled up her sleeve a bit and there was a nasty rash on her arm. "Poison ivy. Right there in my yard! That's the thanks I get for gardening."

Meadow made a face and seemed to scoot away from Daisy on the sofa. "That's a nasty rash, Daisy. Has it been bothering you?"

"It's been giving me absolute fits!"

Posy's face crinkled with concern. "Have you tried oatmeal on it for the itch? Poison ivy is so miserable!"

"I've been plenty uncomfortable, but Harrison has been such a doll. He's fussed over me like a mother and promised that he'd get me a yard service starting immediately to take care of the yard. No more weeding or hedge trimming for me."

Amber appeared deeply engrossed in her appliqué. Her block for the group quilt was a luscious square with sumptuous colors. It featured a sun with curled scarlet, amber, and crimson rays licking out from the curlicue base. She told Beatrice it symbolized the sun and vacation, but Beatrice wondered if it was more of a symbol of Amber's passionate nature.

Meadow, who seemed grossed out by Daisy's poison ivy, said, "Posy, give us all an update on Miss Sissy. Is she doing any better?"

Felicity frowned with concern, and Amber rolled her eyes. Beatrice guessed, though, that Amber was probably used to Meadow's sticking her foot in it. Meadow had been in the kitchen with Felicity and hadn't heard Amber ask them not to mention the murder.

Posy said, "She's doing pretty well, I think. She's still got a huge knot on her head, but other than that, she seems like she's back to her old self again."

Beatrice thought of the malevolent, elfish face and shuddered.

"So she's walking around, quilting and doing all her usual activities?" asked Georgia with interest.

"She sure is. Except . . . well, she acts a little crazy." Posy shrugged a thin shoulder. "She seems to think she's back in the 1930s. Cork told her *Little Orphan Annie* had gone off the air and she tossed the radio in the trash can. Poor thing."

Beatrice winced. "And you didn't call me to say that Miss Sissy needed another place to stay? I'd have thought that would have been one of the final straws for Cork."

"Oh no. Besides, that radio hasn't worked for at least ten years. We use our iPods. Poor Miss Sissy just turned that dial and turned it . . ." Posy shook her head sadly as she made an expert stitch in her block. "She even called my cordless phone an instrument of the devil."

Savannah said, "If she's convinced she's still living in the twentieth century, her house must be like a museum. I've never been in there. Does she even *have* a television? She probably has one of those rotary phones, too, right? Not that I have a cell phone myself, but it seems like everyone else does."

"Actually," said Beatrice slowly, "she did have a cell phone."

"A cell phone?" everyone chimed in.

Beatrice paused with her stitching before she ended up missing even more stitches than usual in her distraction. "She did. She had a cell phone. I saw it sitting on the table but used my own phone to call for an ambulance."

Posy knit her brows. "That's so odd. She hasn't asked me to fetch it for her. And, really, who on earth would she call?"

"Maybe," said Georgia slowly, "it's one of those things that someone told her she should have . . . in case of emergency. In case she's driving around and that old Lincoln of hers breaks down and she needs to call for help."

Beatrice rolled her eyes. "From what I've seen of Miss Sissy's driving, the only person likely to need to call for help is any pedestrian who gets in her way."

The others laughed, except for Posy, who still frowned. "In all the rush and worry for Miss Sissy, I don't think I've done a good job looking after her house. When you called me on the way to the hospital, Beatrice, I put together a small bag of her things and hurried back out again. She seemed happy with the things I brought over and she hasn't asked to go by her house and pick up anything else." Posy blushed. "You know, Beatrice, I don't think I even locked the door. I guess I figured I'd be going back over there again to get more things. But that hasn't happened." Her small face looked miserable.

"It's all right," said Beatrice briskly. "You're doing enough just handling Miss Sissy's *Little Orphan Annie* fixation. I've got a couple of errands to run after I leave here, anyway—I'll pop by Miss Sissy's on the way home. I'll grab the phone, in case she wants it, and lock the door behind me."

Posy smiled in relief and started hand-piecing again.

The *Sleeping Beauty*–like aspect of Miss Sissy's yard had gotten decidedly worse. Maybe Daisy could send her new yard man over to give Miss Sissy's house a haircut. Because that's what the house looked like it had: hair. There were vines all over the roof and descending along the brick sides—thorny vines, flowering vines, vines of every description. Beatrice carefully edged her way through the unlocked door and into the dimness of the house.

Although the day was a hot one and Miss Sissy's house had no outward signs of having an air-conditioning unit, it was surprisingly cool inside. Must be because no daylight could penetrate through the windows with all those vines covering the glass.

There was the spot where Miss Sissy had lain on the floor. There was that massive old table where the phone had been . . . Beatrice blinked. The phone was no longer there. But it *had* been there—Beatrice hadn't dreamed it. Had someone come in and stolen it? Surely, though, a burglar would have taken other things? Not that the other things were modern, valuable . . . or even clean. The heavy layer of dust in the house played havoc with Beatrice's allergies and her eyes watered.

Remembering back to that day, though, it wasn't only the cell phone that was on the table—there had been a stack of papers there, too. In fact, it had been amazing that she'd even seen the phone with all the papers surrounding it. All fire-and-brimstone ramblings about the wages of sin or some such. Beatrice edged closer to the table. The papers were missing, too. Now she really was starting to feel like she was losing it. She'd *seen* the phone and the papers. Could the police have taken them? No, probably not. She had the feeling that Ramsay was determined to treat Miss Sissy's assault as a break-in gone wrong. He certainly didn't want a murder attempt on *his* watch. He wouldn't have thought twice about seeing a cell phone there.

As she was standing, looking down with irritation at the spot where the papers and cell phone *should* have been, the hairs on the back of her neck rose and an ominous feeling grabbed hold of her. She twisted to look around behind her, but only got the sensation of some presence there before she felt a terrific blow to the back of her head and slumped to the floor.

Chapter 9

As Beatrice lay on the floor, she felt a thin grasp on consciousness. She was aware enough to realize, though, that she needed to look as dead as possible. Her attacker leaned in close to her; she could hear the panting breath. Beatrice lay perfectly still. There was a strong, strange odor in the air. She couldn't place it, but it smelled familiar. As the panting presence leaned in closer, Beatrice held her breath to seem as convincingly dead as she could. Apparently convinced, her attacker hurried out the door, and Beatrice closed her eyes . . . just for a minute. And completely blacked out.

Beatrice wasn't sure how much time had passed when she groggily came to again. It could only have been minutes, she thought blearily. Or it could have been hours. When the house was as dark as Miss Sissy's always was, who knew?

She shifted on the hard floor to reach a hand into the

pocket of her slacks for her cell phone. It looked like about half an hour had passed. She clicked on her contacts list and poised her thumb over Piper's name, then paused. No, she'd call Ramsay first. Especially since he'd not connected Miss Sissy's attack with Judith's murder.

Beatrice gingerly sat up, holding the cell phone to her head, and dialed Ramsay and Meadow. Meadow picked up, sounding cheery. Typical, thought Beatrice, closing her eyes briefly. "Meadow?" she said. "Is Ramsay there? There's a problem . . ."

Minutes later, Meadow and Ramsay arrived. Meadow bustled around, arms flapping like an angry mother bird, burbling in concern while Ramsay surveyed the scene with a sour look on his face.

Beatrice said calmly, "Ramsay, I was attacked by Judith's killer. There's no other explanation. And I think it was probably by someone I know, too. I mentioned at the guild meeting this afternoon that I was going to run by Miss Sissy's to get her cell phone and lock her door. I don't think that cell phone I saw was Miss Sissy's; I think it must have been the murderer's. Whoever the murderer was didn't want me to have that phone as evidence."

Ramsay shook his head in an automatic no. "Beatrice, I hear what you're saying. But it really doesn't make any sense. If the murderer was in your quilt guild and knew you were going straight over to Miss Sissy's, then why risk being seen? And how did she manage to get here first and swipe the phone?"

"Because I said that I was coming here after I ran some errands. Which I did."

Ramsay said in a gruff voice, "I'm just not buying it, Beatrice." Beatrice started a hot retort, and Ramsay blurted, "I'm not saying you weren't attacked. But I don't believe for a second that it was some crazed killer. I think it must have been this same burglar, coming back for more stuff."

Beatrice's head throbbed and she said more crossly than she would have liked, "For heaven's sake, Ramsay! *What* stuff? More mildewed wooden chairs that need to be caned? A wobbly table? Whatever decomposing food is going rancid in the ancient fridge? This isn't stuff that's going to tempt even the most desperate thief. She was here to cover up her attack on Miss Sissy. And she attacked *Miss Sissy* because she thought Miss Sissy knew something about her involvement in Judith's murder." Just because Ramsay didn't want crime to happen didn't mean that it wouldn't.

Ramsay rubbed his face tiredly. "It just doesn't seem like something that could happen in Dappled Hills," he said. "It's so much more likely that we've got an unpremeditated murder because Judith drove someone to it. And then Miss Sissy's attack was probably a burglar who came back for more stuff and was surprised by your being here. I can't see Dappled Hills being the home of some homicidal maniac."

Meadow clucked. "Let's get out of here, y'all. It's getting spookier in here by the minute, and Beatrice probably needs to run by the doctor's."

Beatrice shook her head, then winced at the sharp pain that resulted. "Oh no. Not me. I'm not heading out to visit the good doctor tonight." The thought of spending time with Daisy's pompous Harrison wasn't making her headache any better.

Ramsay gently pushed her hair aside to look at the lump. "I don't know who did this to you, Beatrice, but you're a very lucky lady. If that blow had happened just a fraction of an inch to one side, we really *might* have been investigating another murder. And I do think you should have that lump looked at."

Beatrice really just wanted to crawl under the covers and go to bed. "I know it's not bedtime, but I'm exhausted," she said. "The last thing I want to do is to drive out of town and go to an urgent-care unit and wait for hours to be seen." She lifted her hand as they opened their mouths to protest. "And y'all know that's what would happen. Dappled Hills doesn't have an urgent care, does it?"

Meadow shook her head sadly.

"One thing I will insist on, then," said Ramsay sternly, "is that we keep an eye on you for the rest of the night. In case you change your mind about that doctor. And because you've just been attacked, no matter the reason."

"I could go to Piper's house . . ." But then Beatrice stopped with a shrug. She'd moved to Dappled Hills to keep an eye on *Piper*, not the other way around. She was enjoying the mothering role too much to have the roles switched around. Besides, Piper lived in a one-bedroom duplex. It wasn't the kind of togetherness that she liked.

Meadow clapped her hands. "A houseguest! Perfect! Boris will be so pleased," said Meadow with a wink at Beatrice. "We'll run by and pick up Noo-noo on the way so we can have a little sleepover soiree."

Ramsay looked at Beatrice apologetically.

"What about Ash, though?" asked Beatrice, feeling as though she had lost control of the situation. "Isn't he in the guest room?"

"We've got a three-bedroom barn, Beatrice! Plenty of room for all." Meadow looked pleased with herself.

"I know one thing," growled Ramsay. "We're locking Miss Sissy's blasted door this time."

Beatrice was sure that sleeping the night in an unfamiliar place (and a barn, at that) would mean a restless night or a few disoriented awakenings. She was amazed when she woke slowly to the sound of birds chirping at the Downeys' feeder and soft sunlight coming through the sheer curtains in the guest room.

Meadow was up and enthusiastically humming an off-key version of a *South Pacific* song. Her pajamas were as bright and mismatched as usual, and she was busily cooking enough breakfast to feed at least a dozen houseguests.

The eggs, bacon, grits, sausage and biscuits lured Beatrice into the kitchen, and her stomach growled to remind her that she hadn't remembered to eat supper before she'd stumbled, exhausted, into the Downeys' guest bed.

Meadow stopped humming as she spotted Beatrice. "There you are!" she exclaimed, pressing a mug of steaming coffee into her hands. "Here, have a seat." Meadow shoved a cushioned kitchen chair her way and peered anxiously at Beatrice's head. "How are you feeling? I very quietly tiptoed into your room a couple of times last night to make sure you were all right, and you seemed to be sleeping like a baby. And Noo-noo was, too, right at the foot of your bed. Guarding you well, the little furry angel."

Actually, thought Beatrice, I'm feeling surprisingly good. Except for this unexpected vengefulness that's welling up in me, that is. What *had* been an intellectual exercise for her was transforming into something very different. Yes, she was feeling a bit like Zorro this morning . . . She frowned at her flight of fancy.

"The throbbing has stopped," said Beatrice. "Now my head is sensitive to the touch . . . so I'm keeping my hands off it."

Meadow nodded, seeming to be only half listening. "Mmm. When will people learn," she wondered aloud, "that violence is never the answer? Never! They should give peace a chance."

Beatrice, fearing that Meadow might start rambling out some 1960s-inspired peace manifesto (or start singing some folk songs), quickly interjected, "Breakfast smells wonderful, Meadow. You've really outdone yourself!"

Meadow beamed and scooped heaping helpings of everything onto a large plate with an aggressive rose pattern on it. "If you have a full breakfast, then your day goes smoother. It does. Did you eat breakfast yesterday? Maybe you wouldn't have even ended up getting attacked if you had, you know? Maybe you'd have had the ability to outrun or outthink your attacker." Meadow mulled this over, absently stirring the eggs. Beatrice bit her tongue to keep from defending the biscuits she'd had for breakfast yesterday. Before Boris got to them. It wasn't worth arguing with Meadow.

Ramsay trod heavily in on the old, creaking hardwood floor and looked around him, bleary-eyed. He looks to have a much worse headache than I do, Beatrice thought. Probably because the realization is sinking in that he really does have a dangerous person on the loose.

Meadow handed Ramsay a plate that was loaded down with eggs, sausage, grits and biscuits, and Ramsay shook his head. "Coffee?" he asked gruffly. "I only want some black coffee this morning."

This was apparently unacceptable to Meadow. "Now, Ramsay, breakfast is the most important meal of the day! You need to gird yourself for a day of mental and physical exertion!" Ramsay was already at the coffeemaker, pouring a generous amount of coffee into a travel mug.

"Not this morning, Meadow. Not hungry." As he headed to the back of the house to get ready for work, he had a clucking Meadow following behind him, still carrying the plate of food and insisting that she would foist it on him.

Beatrice jumped at pressure against her leg and looked down to see that Boris had placed his massive head on her lap and was looking into her eyes with a love-struck expression that Beatrice was fairly certain had to do with the slice of bacon on her plate.

Meadow trotted back into the kitchen, a look of satisfaction on her face. "There. Now we're all going to have fuel to take on our day! Beatrice, I'm going to go out and weed the garden before the sun gets too hot. Take as long as you want over breakfast and eat as much as you'd like—there's plenty of food on the stove, and Ash won't eat but a little." She picked up a children's sand bucket with a spade and gardening gloves in it and hurried out the back door of the barn, humming a song from the musical again.

Beatrice gently moved her leg from under Boris's head and took a deep breath of relaxation. It was quite peaceful in the barn without Meadow's lively presence. Sunlight shone through the skylights and illuminated the cheerful colors of the assorted quilts below. The food *was* very good. Beatrice had always thought that there were only really a few ways to *make* breakfast, but somehow Meadow's meal was delicious. Maybe there was cream cheese in the scrambled eggs?

As peaceful as the room currently was, Beatrice was restless to get back to her cottage and figure out what was at the bottom of these Dappled Hills attacks. What had yesterday evening been about? Had her attacker intended to kill her? Had she been at the point of discovering the murderer there in the room with her? Or was the attack simply intended as a warning, like Georgia's notes in the soda bottles?

Could *Georgia* be behind something like that? She was such a gentle person that it seemed hard to imagine. But if she felt as if she were protecting Savannah, she might think she had no other choice. And she *was* behind the warning notes, after all. Beatrice frowned. She couldn't picture it. But what if Savannah had attacked her? What if *Georgia* was behind Judith's murder and Savannah was desperately trying to keep anyone from nosing around enough to find out? Beatrice could picture Georgia murdering Judith in the heat of the moment (it was difficult, but she could see it), but she sure couldn't imagine Georgia sneaking up behind her in Miss Sissy's house.

The ringing of the doorbell made Beatrice lay down her fork. Wasn't it sort of early for a visit from someone? She felt an unfamiliar apprehension before brusquely dismissing the nervousness. Ash was somewhere in the house, after all, and surely would wake up if she started screaming. The chief of police was mere yards away, getting ready for work. Not to mention a tremendous beast who seemed to be deeply in love with her, as well as her own Noo-noo, who was at her heels at all times now. She should be safe to answer the doorbell.

When she peeked out the heavy wooden door and saw Georgia standing there, holding a plastic bag with quilting materials sticking out the top, Beatrice wavered for only a moment before unlocking the door.

Georgia blinked in surprise and then looked around her, as if making sure she hadn't arrived at the wrong house. "Beatrice! I wasn't expecting to see you here," she said. "You must be an early bird like me. I knew Meadow and Ramsay would be up, so I thought I'd run by the quilting blocks for the new group quilt."

"Why don't you come on in for a few minutes, Georgia? If you have time, of course. Meadow is weeding out back, and Ramsay is getting ready for work. But Meadow cooked me breakfast and seemed to be under the mistaken impression that I am a three-hundred-pound body builder. There's no way I can eat even a fraction of the food, and I know she'll fuss."

Georgia allowed herself to be led over to the kitchen table. Beatrice pulled out another of the rose plates and heaped it with food. "I'm sure you are surprised to see me here," said Beatrice. "Especially considering I'm in my pajamas."

Georgia nodded solemnly as Beatrice put the plate down in front of her. "I was sort of wondering about that. Although," she said hurriedly, "it's nice to be comfortable, isn't it? That's the first thing I do in the evenings is to get my pj's on and my fuzzy slippers."

"To tell you the truth," said Beatrice, watching Georgia carefully for her reaction, "I was here all night. The Downeys thought it was a good idea for me to stay over because I was attacked yesterday when I went back to Miss Sissy's house."

The color drained from Georgia's face. "No! Oh no!"

"I'm afraid so. You might remember that I told everyone at the guild meeting yesterday afternoon that I was planning on running by Miss Sissy's house after I finished my errands. There was a cell phone at Miss Sissy's house that we thought belonged to her, and I was going to get it and lock the door. But when I got there, the cell phone was gone—and someone hit me on the back of the head and knocked me out before I could do more looking around."

"No!" said Georgia again, in her broken-record fashion. She paused. "You're all right?"

"Well, I *could* be better. But at least I'm not dead." Beatrice sniffed.

Georgia stared down at her eggs. Beatrice scooted her chair a little closer to Georgia's, looked up to make sure Ramsay wasn't about to come out from the back of the house and said softly, "Georgia, you look like you have a lot on your mind. Wouldn't you like to tell someone what's worrying you?" She hesitated, then continued. "I know you're the one who's been leaving notes on my porch at night."

Georgia's round eyes opened wide; then she raised her hands in front of her face to cover them. Beatrice said gently, "Why don't you tell me what's been going on? I know you couldn't have had anything to do with Judith's death. And I don't think you could have attacked Miss Sissy or me, either."

Georgia lowered her hands, and Beatrice saw her eyes were full of tears. "Beatrice, I've been so worried."

"About Savannah?"

Georgia nodded. "She's always been a little . . . well, different. But I didn't really understand *how* different she was until recently. She was *so* angry with Judith. When we went home that night, she was fussing the whole way. I couldn't hear all that she was saying, but she was *not* happy. She went straight into her room, and I figured she was worn-out with being upset and went right to bed. She says that she was quilting like crazy because she was anxious and worried after the bee. But what if she *wasn't* quilting? What if she went out and murdered Judith?" Georgia paused, swallowing hard. "It's all that's been on my mind."

"Do you have any reason to think she might have gone out? Because that quilt looked pretty complete to me. When else would she have squeezed in that much work on it?"

"When I came back that night—" Georgia hesitated. "You know why I was out?"

Beatrice nodded. "You mean when you came back after leaving a note on my porch."

Georgia turned a splotchy red. "Yes. Yes, I left you a note. Well, when I came back, Savannah's bedroom door was open. I called for her, but she didn't answer."

"You weren't worried enough to go looking for her?" asked Beatrice.

"Not really. I figured she was in the bathroom or something like that. That maybe she just couldn't hear me. Besides, I was so exhausted by that time that all I wanted to do was to lie down and sleep. Lately, though, I've been wondering where she *was*."

"But she might just have been sound asleep in her room, right? Or brushing her teeth in the bathroom. It might have been something very innocent," said Beatrice. Georgia looked so concerned that it was impossible to keep from comforting her. Georgia slowly nodded.

"About the notes. You were worried I was being too nosy, weren't you?" asked Beatrice.

Now Georgia looked a little wary. "That's true, Beatrice. But I never would have attacked you in order to stop you. Yes, I left the notes for you. I was trying to distract you," said Georgia, looking down again. "Folks who've been in town for a while just overlook things. Maybe they don't even see what's happening in front of them. But someone new to town, they might be more curious. You seemed to be very interested in the investigation and were asking a lot of questions." She looked up at Beatrice, then glanced down again.

"I got my first note the night of the bee—*before* Judith's murder was discovered. What did I do to make you leave me a note?"

Georgia didn't meet Beatrice's eyes. "You were making Judith all riled up, Beatrice. You pointed out that she was trying to cheat Felicity. Then once Judith got mad, she started saying all this awful stuff . . . about Savannah, too. I wanted to make sure you weren't going to keep being an instigator."

"What is it about your sister that you're trying to

hide, Georgia?" asked Beatrice. "I know that Judith was hinting at something at the quilting bee about Savannah."

Georgia gave a deep sigh. "My sister has . . . a problem. It's not *always* a problem," said Georgia in a hurry. "But when she gets really stressed-out or deals with changes . . . she borrows things."

"Borrows things?"

Georgia said with a studied carelessness, "You know. She goes into a shop and might come out with something. Something small," she added quickly. "Something that . . . she didn't pay for."

Beatrice's eyes widened.

"It's not as bad as it sounds," said Georgia insistently. "I know all the shopkeepers and we have a special Savannah account with them. Most of the time when she's taking things, it's just a small thing that's hardly worth a dollar. They know to keep an eye on her when they see her come in the shop, and they put the item's cost on our tab. If I find the merchandise at home, then I'll return it and get a refund. Otherwise, they just send me a bill for the outstanding tab once every couple of weeks." She shrugged, but Beatrice could see the strain on her face. She didn't feel that casual about it.

"Has Savannah always been a . . . Well, has she always borrowed things?" asked Beatrice.

Georgia said, "Oh no. At least, not as far as I'm aware. I'd have been more on top of things if I'd thought she was doing it. No, I think this is something that's just come up in the past five or six years. At least, that's what the shopkeepers were telling me. It's not like she was doing this when she was a teenager or anything. I talked to Dr. Butler about it and he said it's a manifestation of stress."

Beatrice had a difficult time picturing Dappled Hills as stressful. Unless trying to avoid getting murdered qualified. "What kind of stress does Savannah have?"

"The doctor said it isn't that she has a very *stress-ful* life, just that she doesn't know how to *handle* the stress she comes across. She finds interacting with people stressful, for instance. But she loves quilting, so she's spending time with other people who enjoy it. Maybe she doesn't handle personal relationships very well. Plus, well, it seemed to start when I got married and moved away. She and I had always been very close up to that point. We're twins, after all."

"But she bicycles everywhere. How would she *physically* be able to leave with these things she's . . . borrowed."

"It's always small things," said Georgia in a hurry. "And, well, she does have her backpack with her on her bike. You know."

"Was Savannah's borrowing," said Beatrice slowly, "something that Judith found out about?"

"She did," said Georgia in a hard voice. "But I guess it was inevitable, since she owned the building where some of the shops were located. Posy wouldn't have said anything to Judith, but some of her other tenants would have. She held it over me. I don't think Savannah even realizes that she's *doing* the borrowing. Maybe on some level she does; she was upset at the bee. But, really, Judith was picking at Savannah to get at *me*. She knew exactly how to get under my skin."

Beatrice said gently, "You've had a rough time, haven't you? Your divorce must have really unsettled you—for good reason. So you moved in with your sister, thinking finally you've got a little stability in your life . . ."

"Exactly!"

"And you find out that your sister isn't quite as stable as you thought."

Georgia shook her head. "No, she *is* stable. She's fine. And we've been happy and *will* be happy, as long as everything stays the same. But what if Judith had decided to tell Ramsay about Savannah?"

Beatrice remembered Ramsay's stress when faced with a tough problem. "You know," she said, "I'm not sure Ramsay would have done anything about it."

"He would have if Judith had been making a big stink about it. If she said she didn't like having someone stealing on a regular basis from her tenants. Think about it—he really wouldn't have had a choice if she'd lodged a complaint." Georgia stared blankly out the barn window, completely oblivious to the sight of Meadow vigorously weeding the garden and singing to herself.

"Well, but he wouldn't have arrested her. Not for something like that."

Georgia turned her head and her tired eyes looked

directly in Beatrice's. "No. But he would have had to take her for a mental-health evaluation. And what if it was determined that she needed to go to some kind of hospital or a group home or something?"

That seemed really unlikely. Savannah certainly hadn't become any kind of public menace—unless she *had* murdered Judith. She decided not to pooh-pooh this idea, though, since Georgia was clearly worried about it.

"You don't think that Savannah had anything to do with Judith's death, do you?" she asked quietly instead.

Georgia looked down at the wooden floor. "I don't know. I don't think so. But Savannah was so upset— she seemed to know exactly what Judith was hinting at, so I guess maybe she *does* somehow realize what she's doing. But I know she just can't help herself—she feels driven to doing it. I could tell how upset she was when we went back home. She didn't even answer me when I was talking to her."

"Do you see your sister attacking Miss Sissy?" asked Beatrice. "Or me?"

Now Georgia looked a little more confident. "No. No, I really don't. Unless." Georgia stopped talking and chewed her bottom lip for a second. "Unless she was doing it to protect *me*. If she thought I'd killed Judith to keep her from telling Savannah's secret."

Georgia looked a little sick at the thought. But it seemed like a distinct possibility to Beatrice. After all, Georgia was trying to protect Savannah, and Judith had made what amounted to a threat. She could picture Georgia moving to eliminate a threat and protect the status quo. And she could certainly see Savannah returning the favor by trying to scare off or eliminate Miss Sissy and herself.

"So these notes you've been leaving, they're just your way of trying to protect Savannah. You were trying to warn me off so that I wouldn't find out about Savannah's problem and you'd be able to keep things as they are."

Georgia gave a vigorous nod and said eagerly, "Yes, that's exactly it. *That's* my way of warning someone off . . . not by hitting them over the head. You just seemed to be goading Judith, and she got in more and more of a foul, retaliating mood. I just hoped that you'd stop poking around." Then she spread out her hands. "But lately, I realized that you weren't goading Judith that night . . . you were being kind. And I think you're investigating because you're being kind and trying to spare us all from suspecting each other. I've just been worried about what you might find out. And now I guess you'll have to go to Ramsay and tell him what you know." She looked anxiously at Beatrice.

Beatrice blew out a sigh. Kind? She thought of herself as a bit cranky, a little impatient. Eager to keep to herself and stay out of others' business. Was she really this person . . . someone who investigated things? Who was . . . kind?

"I wouldn't dream of saying anything about it," said Beatrice finally. Georgia's face relaxed.

Beatrice now realized that Boris's loving display was motivated not by the bacon but by his desire to get closer to the plate of biscuits. Beatrice scowled as he grabbed one with his teeth and scampered off with it to the other side of the room.

"Have you always done this kind of thing, Georgia? Left anonymous notes?" asked Beatrice.

Georgia shifted uncomfortably and had a forkful of scrambled eggs before answering. "I've never been one who liked confrontation. To me it was a good way to get my message across without having to come right out and discuss it with someone. But I haven't sent one for at least a year before I started sending yours."

"I noticed at the bee that you were playing a peace-making role when Judith started acting out."

Georgia said, "I do try to smooth things over when I can. I could tell that Judith was getting really fired up about Felicity's quilt—and when Judith got angry, then she'd always start throwing out accusations. Like that hint she made about Savannah." Georgia flushed, then asked quietly, "Are we still friends, Beatrice? I'm sorry that I scared you."

"Of course we are," said Beatrice.

"Thanks," said Georgia, smiling. "Actually, I have something for your little furry friend here. I carry everything around in my backpack . . ." She rummaged through the bag, finally pulling out a little bandanna with a whimsical corgi patch stitched to the back. "Hope you like it," she said shyly.

Beatrice stooped and tied the bandanna around

Noo-noo's neck as the corgi grinned at her. "I love it!" she said truthfully. "And I think Noo-noo does, too."

Ramsay trod heavily into the room, putting on a watch. He looked a little bemused by Georgia's presence there. "So you've got some quilting blocks for Meadow?"

"She's going to hand them out at the next guild meeting. It's for the new group project. I guess you'll be getting a block, too, Beatrice?"

Ramsay looked at Beatrice with interest. "Somehow I don't see you as a quilter, Beatrice."

For some reason, this made Beatrice feel defensive. "Why not?"

"I don't know exactly. Maybe the fact that you don't seem very patient. I know *I* couldn't quilt," he said. "I'd never be able to get past threading the needle."

How could Ramsay possibly handle living with Meadow if he was such an impatient person? Maybe all his patience went toward not killing Meadow.

Remembering the way that each quilter's different blocks gave her little insights into their characters, Beatrice said, "Georgia, did you bring your block with you? I know y'all seem to go everywhere with them. I'm still trying to get some ideas for mine."

Georgia pulled out a frothy-looking block embellished with lace and shimmering crystals around a very distinctive face. "It's Mama," she said, choking a little as Beatrice looked a little desperately for a tissue, and Ramsay looked longingly at the door. "It's a photo transfer that I did for the block."

"Is that hard to do?"

"Not a bit. You can scan old pictures like this one and then print it right onto treated fabric with an inkjet printer. I don't like colored pictures as much, but you can put any picture in grayscale and make it look like a classic picture." Georgia seemed to recover a little from her sentimental journey as she talked about the technique.

"I'll say hi to Meadow out back and walk around the house to the driveway before I go," said Georgia, standing. "Thanks for the breakfast, Beatrice. Hope you're feeling better soon."

Ramsay picked up his car keys, his reading glasses and a notebook, then noticed Boris licking his lips. "Oh, and Beatrice? Boris isn't allowed to eat table scraps. You probably give them to Noo-noo and didn't know better. Just an FYI. I know you thought you were being nice," he said quickly, raising his hand as Beatrice started sputtering a protest, "but those are the house rules."

Ramsay and Georgia left, Ramsay in his cruiser and Georgia on her bike. Boris grinned toothily at Beatrice from across the room. Instead of her mantra, Beatrice indulged in a little profanity instead.

Chapter 10

Meadow came back into the kitchen, her plaid apron full of tomatoes. "Can you believe it? What a haul!" she crowed. "And I only went outside to weed, not to pick. We'll have tomato sandwiches for lunch. And *maybe* even tomato sandwiches for supper, too! Heck, we could have tomatoes in our eggs for breakfast tomorrow!"

Time to set some boundaries. "Meadow, I really appreciate you and Ramsay letting me stay here last night. And for the big breakfast . . ." Beatrice waved a hand at the huge amount of food still on the counter. "But . . ."

"Did you enjoy it?" asked Meadow eagerly. "Weren't those grits lip-smacking good? There's a booth at the farmer's market where I buy stone-ground grits, and they're *so* scrumptious. I even stirred in some cream cheese. And a little cream, too."

Beatrice was going to have to get out of there just from a weight standpoint. She might be lanky now, but after a few all-dairy Meadow Downey meals, she'd have a lot more meat on her bones. "It was wonderful. Really, really good, Meadow. But now it's time for Noo-noo and me to go back home. I feel fine—I really do," she said quickly as Meadow opened her mouth to interrupt. "I had a touch of a headache, but that's pretty good, considering how much worse everything could be. So I'll go home and touch base with Piper."

Meadow's face fell comically. "Oh, that's a shame. I was hoping we could have a nice lunch together. Well, I'll send you home with the tomatoes—that'll work. Did Georgia have some breakfast, then?" She looked at the plate, which still had a bit left. "It looks like she barely had anything at all! I tell you, I worry about those girls. All that biking and not much eating."

They were hardly girls. But Meadow was an Earth Mother, so maybe she mothered everyone.

"I suppose Ramsay didn't end up eating his breakfast?" asked Meadow with a long-suffering sigh, looking at the full plate Ramsay had laid back down in the kitchen. "I've about given up on him. You'd think that if he were faced with a delicious breakfast year after year, he'd have given in by now. Instead it's black coffee every day. He'll end up with an ulcer—that's what I tell him." She sorrowfully started scraping pots into the garbage while Boris drooled nearby.

"Did you and Georgia have a nice conversation? What did you two find to talk about?" asked Meadow, valiantly moving on from her despair over Ramsay's eating habits.

"Oh . . . you know," said Beatrice. "This and that." Did Meadow know anything about Savannah's klepto-mania? Beatrice felt like she'd been given information in confidence and didn't want to reveal too much. After some hesitation, she said, "It seems to me that Georgia worries a lot over her sister. I thought at first that Sa-vannah was the one taking care of Georgia, but it seems more like it's the other way around."

Meadow turned around from her pot scrubbing, and Beatrice smiled at the sight of her red-framed glasses fogged up from the hot-water steam. "Yes, Beatrice! You've got it. That's exactly what their relationship is like. Savannah seemed like the one who had her act together and took in poor Georgia with the failed mar-riage. Instead, though, Georgia is the one who has to keep her eye on her sister. And she worries like the dickens over her."

Beatrice said casually, "Why do you think she's so worried?"

"Oh," said Meadow in just as casual of a voice, "be-cause Savannah steals things. Not big things, and she doesn't really mean to. But she does—believe me. I've lived in Dappled Hills for a million years and I know almost everything there is to know about it."

Beatrice blinked at this offhand revelation. "Do you think Judith knew about Savannah, too?"

"Well, now, no one would have told *her* about poor Savannah. Not like I just told *you*. And that's because Judith was nasty. But I think she somehow must have found out—maybe she was in one of the shops in her building one day, meeting with a tenant, and *saw* Savannah nab something. I could tell at the quilting bee that she was making these veiled hints about her." Meadow's voice rose in indignation.

"Do you think Judith was blackmailing Georgia or Savannah, the way she tried to blackmail you?" asked Beatrice. "After all, she had to know that Georgia would do anything to cover up for Savannah. And Savannah might want to do some covering up, too."

"I'd be shocked if the harridan hadn't tried it. Nasty thing." Meadow looked as if she'd tasted something sour. "Savannah and Georgia didn't even have two pennies to rub together, either. They depend on the little income they get from Georgia's dog and cat boutique and Savannah's part-time accounting. If Savannah had lost her job because of Judith spreading rumors, it would have had a real impact on their standard of living. Georgia doesn't make enough money to keep a parakeet alive."

It sounded like there were lots of reasons for Savannah and Georgia to want to get rid of Judith. A financial motive was another one to add to the list. Georgia was also worried about being left on her own or having Savannah taken away from her for some kind of treatment. And Georgia had clearly been desperate enough to write warning notes to try to scare Beatrice off from discovering the truth. Or. . . what if Georgia had killed Judith for all those reasons and *Savannah* had been the one to attack Miss Sissy and her? While Beatrice couldn't picture the gentle Georgia hitting old ladies

over the head, she sure wouldn't put it past the calculating, enigmatic Savannah.

"I'm a little surprised to hear you talk so vehemently
about Judith," said Beatrice. "I thought you'd gotten
along fairly well."

Meadow raised her eyebrows in surprise, and Beatrice said, "Someone was telling me that you'd even
given Judith some friendly advice about dyeing her
hair—that she should become a redhead."

"Certainly not! I avoided conversation with Judith
as much as humanly possible. I certainly wouldn't
have been giving her advice on her hairstyles."
Meadow put the last pan on the drying board and
wiped her damp hands dry with the dish towel. "I'm
furious with her for stirring all this up. For throwing
suspicion on *my friends*!"

"Meadow, Judith didn't *plan* on being murdered,"
said Beatrice.

"Well, she certainly *should* have! Blackmailing people and cheating people out of their money and being
nasty about rent! She *should* have!"

After returning home, Beatrice realized she was a lot
more tired than she'd thought. She spent the rest of the
day with her feet up. The next morning, Beatrice realized with annoyance that she felt jumpy inside her
home. It didn't help that the cottage was at least fifty
years old and had its little idiosyncrasies. The house
groaned and shifted from time to time like an old lady
with aching feet. Beatrice had barely even noticed the

settling sounds before, but now every time the cottage made noises, her heart pounded harder in her chest.

Beatrice puttered around. Ordinarily she wasn't much of a putterer, but in her present shape, she was moving slower than usual. She put the few dishes from the day before away, tidied up inside, and settled down into her cushy sofa. She took her reading glasses out of their case, put them on, and picked up *Whispers of Summer.* She'd have a nice little read with her feet up before she did anything else. Reading had always been a relaxing activity.

But *Whispers of Summer* had reached a bit of a boring part. There was some big flashback with one of the characters and a whole lot of description about a beach house. Beatrice sighed and put the book down. She used to have a longer attention span than this. Now it seemed like all she could do was think about this murder. And wonder if she might be the next victim.

Annoyed, she collected her pocketbook and keys. She'd go to the Patchwork Cottage for a while. There were some books and magazines that might be helpful if she was going to try to guide the guild into new directions for juried shows. Besides, Posy was going to put out some new jelly rolls. Maybe she could take a fresh stab at that quilt she was trying to practice with.

Beatrice was out in the driveway, fiddling with the key to lock up the cottage, when the sound of a curt voice behind her made shriek. Turning, she saw Savannah, the high collar of her dress up around her neck in self-defense. "Beatrice!" she scolded. "What on earth were you thinking, screaming like that? You took ten years off my life."

Beatrice took a deep breath. "You have to put your sudden appearance in context, Savannah. You see, I was attacked the day before yesterday in much the same way Miss Sissy was, but with less serious results. So people creeping up behind me when I'm not aware of it is probably not the best approach."

Savannah looked piqued instead of scandalized. "Yes, yes," she said briskly. "I know all about that. Georgia told me about it when she got back home from Meadow's house yesterday. I don't know what you think you're doing, getting attacked like this. You must have done something to provoke it all."

Beatrice's mouth opened and closed, but nothing came out.

"But enough of that. We all make mistakes," said Savannah, ignoring the spluttering sounds Beatrice was starting to make. "And the best thing to do is learn from them and move on. I've brought you some salve," she said with a stiff bob of her head as she dug a small container out of her backpack. "Made from healing herbs that I grew in our garden. You'll want to put it on twice a day. It will," she said fiercely, "work wonders."

At least the salve appeared completely homemade. Otherwise, she might be worried that it was some of Savannah's booty from downtown Dappled Hills.

"Thank you, Savannah," said Beatrice. Savannah was definitely not a very affectionate person—the gift was probably the closest thing to a hug that Savannah would give. "I did have a question for you," she said quickly as Savannah moved to get on her bike. "I was talking to someone the other day and heard that you and Judith had been having an argument not long before her death."

Savannah pressed her thin lips together and nodded. "Is that someone saying I killed Judith?"

"I think we're all racking our brains to figure out the case—that's all. And gathering any information that might help solve it."

"Well, Judith and I did have an argument. She's always gotten under my skin, and that particular day she was doing an even better job at it than usual. Criticizing my quilting and saying I was the reason that the Village Quilters weren't winning at shows!" Savannah's tone was affronted.

Beatrice said soothingly, "I've seen your work and it always looks perfect to me. Your appliqué stitches are small and even; your edges are crisp. Your work is beautiful."

Savannah seemed only slightly mollified. "Apparently, Judith thought that people like you—artsy people—wanted to see more art quilts."

"Quilts that almost look like canvases with paintings on them?" said Beatrice. "I've come across them before, yes. But surely that would be only one category of quilt at a show. There would also be many others— traditional quilts, whole cloth, pictorial—"

"Sometimes that's true," Savannah cut in. "Sometimes it's not. Some shows have really basic categories like small, medium, large, and miniature. So in those kinds of quilt shows, all the quilts would be lumped in with all the others in terms of size. Those art quilts might stand out in a group." She looked up at Beatrice uncertainly.

Could it be possible that this supremely confident quilter was having a little self-doubt?

"But I heard you were very upset with Judith for being so critical."

"Maybe," said Savannah grimly, "that's because I thought there might be some truth to it. But I've been making my traditional quilts with their geometric patterns for years. I'm not really the most creative person in town . . . I'm just a precise stitcher. Besides, she was complaining about Georgia's quilting, too, which was most irritating."

Beatrice was trying to think what to say to that when Savannah continued. "None of this matters, anyway. I didn't kill Judith. I didn't kill Judith because she insulted my quilt making. I didn't kill Judith because she taunted and bullied Georgia and me. I didn't do it. Besides, I wasn't the only quilter that Judith butted heads with. She and Daisy never saw eye to eye on the guild's direction. And they were always jealous of each other and bragged about which one had won more awards."

Savannah put her backpack back on and climbed onto her bicycle, giving Beatrice a nod and saying, "Hope the salve helps," before pedaling busily off. Perched on her bicycle, sitting stiffly in the seat, she bore an eerie resemblance to Miss Gulch, who turned into the witch in *The Wizard of Oz* film. Beatrice wondered how on earth that long dress didn't get caught up in the various bike parts.

Peace, calm, kindness.

Chapter 11

At the Patchwork Cottage, Meadow sat on one of Posy's overstuffed floral sofas, thumbing through a book of blocks and putting sticky notes where her favorites were. Posy had brought doughnuts into the shop. The jelly-filled kind were Beatrice's favorite. The doughnuts made for a nice late-morning snack. "Beatrice! How are you doing now? No headaches? Pains? Wrenching anxiety, perhaps?"

Beatrice ground her teeth a bit and shook her head.

Posy walked around the counter to give Beatrice a big hug. "Meadow was telling me about your ordeal! I'm so, so sorry you had such a scare. I declare, I don't know what is happening to Dappled Hills. It's an absolutely delightful town. It really is."

"Posy, I don't think I've seen your block for the group quilt yet. Have you started it?"

Posy smiled. "Oh, I've actually finished it. Thanks for the reminder. I can give it to Meadow, since she's here. I've got so many hours here at the shop, you know. Most of the time it's busy . . . except when it's not. That's when I'm glad I've got such a time-consuming hobby."

Posy's block was stunning. It featured a vibrantly colored, bright-eyed male hummingbird taking a drink from a delicate flower. In the background was a cheerfully painted birdfeeder on a post. "It's beautiful," said Beatrice in a sincere voice.

"Well, honey, I own a quilt shop! So I have gobs of time to practice and think about design and fabrics, you know. I'm here staring at them all day! But thanks so much—I'm glad you like it. You know that gardening and bird watching are just about as important to me as quilting is."

The shop bell rang, and Meadow said in a clearly audible voice she apparently thought of as a whisper, "For heaven's sake! It's Felicity. And doesn't she look like something the cat dragged in?"

She did. In fact, she looked nearly as bad as she had the day Beatrice, Savannah and Georgia had visited her right after Judith's death. Her makeup was completely AWOL—surprising, since she'd once sold cosmetics. And had she slept in those clothes? It certainly looked like it.

"Y'all, distract me," said Felicity in a faint rendition of her usually commanding voice. "Being home alone is just making me worry about everything. I had to get out."

Posy scurried over to Felicity. "Here, honey. Why don't you have a seat over here? And I've got the comfiest quilt for cuddling up in—it makes me feel better whenever I touch it. It's a baby quilt, which is why it's so soft and sweet . . ." Posy went on prattling and covered the shivering Felicity with a beautiful baby quilt scattered with whimsical storks and dimpled babies.

"Whatever is the matter, Felicity?" breathed Meadow, her large face crinkling in worry. "Has something awful happened? It's not Amber, is it? She's my protégée, you know."

Felicity looked at Meadow with sad eyes before breaking down in tears. Posy enveloped her in a hug and rocked her back and forth, cooing something comforting. Beatrice, not able to think of anything else that might help, hurried to find a Coca-Cola, and Meadow, seemingly unconcerned about anything but her protégée, continued urgently asking questions about Amber's well-being.

Finally, Felicity seemed cried out enough to talk for a while. "Meadow, no, Amber's fine. At least physically she's fine. I guess. But, y'all, she killed Judith."

"What!" A collective exclamation came from the women.

"That's right. She killed Judith in cold blood. You just don't know how furious she was the night of the bee. It was like all the anger against Judith that had been bottled up was coming out in this awful tirade. She was livid that Judith had tried to cheat me out of a fair price for the quilt. And she was devastated that Judith has been blocking the way for a real estate developer to buy both our properties and develop them. It's the money—she knows I don't have much, and it'll make a huge difference whether I get to move to Hampstead Columns or not. And I've had my heart set on Hampstead Columns for ages. But I can't move there unless I have enough extra money, in case the rent there goes up. Selling my property and getting some money from that quilt would really help a lot. And she knows I'm stubborn—I don't want to give up on moving there."

Meadow said in a huffy voice, "Well, we've known this all along, Felicity. Yes, Amber had a motive. So did a lot of other people. Judith wasn't exactly on the Dappled Hills' Most Popular People list."

Felicity sat stiffly with her hands folded in her lap. "I *called* Amber that night—and, yes, I know she was with you for a little while, Meadow," she added quickly as Meadow's mouth popped open. "But I also *drove* over to see Amber. I was that worried about her because I had never seen her that upset. And her car wasn't there. It *wasn't there.*"

Posy and Beatrice shared a look. Maybe that's where Felicity was going when Posy saw her drive by the night of Judith's murder.

Meadow blustered, "That doesn't mean a thing, Felicity! Why, Amber could have been . . . well, she could have been going to the drugstore. Or she could have suddenly wanted to have a burger or something." But Meadow looked worried now, too.

"Amber *could* have been doing something completely innocent. But you're doubtful too, Meadow. Aren't you? You remember how she was in her teens and early twenties. She still has that really willful streak—it hasn't gone anywhere," said Felicity. "She got suspended from school a few times, started hanging out with the wrong friends, wrong men. It was a disaster. She just made all the wrong choices."

"There was a reason for her behavior, though. When her dad died, she was just a little lost. That's all behind her now. I just don't see Amber driving to the park and murdering Judith," said Meadow in a strident tone.

To be completely honest, Amber did sound like the perfect candidate to have killed Judith. She was furious with the woman and *did* have a financial motive: with Judith out of the way, the path would have been cleared to sell her mother's land. Not only would Felicity go to the retirement home she'd dreamed of, but there would likely even be a little left over to help Amber out, too. Or maybe Amber had thought that Daisy was Judith? After all, Daisy had mentioned at the bee that she also planned on walking in the park. Amber might have been riled up enough by the whole Judith episode that she took it out on Daisy, who would have looked quite a bit like Judith in the dark. Felicity looked very much in danger of crying again, and now it appeared that Meadow was going to start howling alongside her. Beatrice said briskly, "I know a good way to get to the bottom of this, ladies. We'll call Amber. Here we all are accusing her of something horrible, and she doesn't have the chance to defend herself."

She pulled out her cell phone, and Felicity gave her Amber's number. Beatrice dialed it, and Felicity's pocketbook started ringing. "What a coincidence!" said Felicity. "Maybe that's Amber calling me now." She pulled out her phone and her brow wrinkled. "No, it's *you*, Beatrice! Your name is coming up on my phone." Then she put a hand to her forehead. "Oh, for heaven's sake. Of *course* your name is coming up. I misplaced my phone, and when I mentioned it to Amber, she insisted on giving me hers. Said it wasn't safe to have me tottering around everywhere with no way to call for help in an emergency."

Meadow said, "What a thoughtful daughter you have."

"She is. She's very thoughtful and she's been good to take care of me. She couldn't have had anything to do with this, could she?" Felicity's blue eyes pleaded with Meadow.

"Absolutely *not*," said Meadow.

As Posy and Meadow hurried to reassure Felicity, the door to the shop flew open, the bell jangling loudly. Miss Sissy stopped her loud snoring, waking with a start and blowing her whistle as hard as she could. They all put their hands over their ears and rolled their eyes at each other. Dogs barked in the distance.

Piper rushed through the door, wearing a mixture of concern and exasperation on her face.

"Mother!" she said, forgoing her usual, fond *mama*, "I just heard about your attack from *Ash*! You didn't call me? Why didn't you call me?" Her voice throbbed with outrage.

Beatrice swallowed. "I did call you yesterday when

I got home, but you were out and I didn't want to leave a message about something like that. Piper, there was nothing you could do. I knew you were probably out with Ash, and I was *fine*. I stayed with Meadow and Ramsay as a precaution—that's all. There was absolutely no reason to spoil your day."

"You didn't think I'd want to know something like that?" scolded Piper.

Felicity frowned. "What's all this? Has something else happened?"

Beatrice said in a rush, "It's nothing. I was messing around in Miss Sissy's house before locking the door and surprised a burglar or something. She struck me over the head with something hard. But I'm *fine*, as I was just telling Piper. The swelling is down, and Savannah gave me some kind of herbal salve to help with the cut that she claims works miracles."

"You could have stayed over at my house that night, Mama," said Piper, still sounding upset. "I could have kept an eye on you, too."

"Piper, no offense, but your duplex is the size of a Cracker Jack box."

"I could have stayed with *you*, then!"

"And I would have messed up your whole evening. Believe me, sweetie, I would call you if I needed you for anything. I love having you so close. Everything worked out fine. Noo-noo even enjoyed her sleepover at Boris's house."

"Surely Amber wouldn't have beat up on *Beatrice*," said Felicity, almost to herself.

"Wickedness! Pure evil!" Miss Sissy wagged her finger inexplicably toward the ceiling.

Beatrice realized suddenly that she felt very tired again. And she really had some reading to do at home. And perhaps a short nap to take.

The nap apparently took longer than Beatrice had originally intended. The sun was starting to dip down in the sky when there was a hesitant knock on the front door, jolting Beatrice from her sleep. Heart pounding, she looked apprehensively at the door as Noo-noo barked a warning. Silly. Attackers don't come knocking. She peered out the curtain and saw a hesitant Posy and a ferocious Miss Sissy. She fumbled with the bolts and opened the door.

Miss Sissy had an old-fashioned, scruffy suitcase that closed with a plastic snap. There were several garments peeking out from different spots of the suitcase. She hoisted up the bag, heaved it inside, and deposited it in Beatrice's little den.

Posy seemed reluctant to speak in front of the old lady. "I'm sorry, Beatrice. I hope you weren't still taking your nap. Miss Sissy, why don't you . . .?" Miss Sissy never waited for the rest of the sentence, instead marching directly out to the backyard, climbing nimbly into Beatrice's hammock and promptly falling asleep. Noo-noo inexplicably had followed her and stretched out on the grass beside the hammock for his own nap.

"Beatrice, I am so sorry!" said Posy with wide eyes. "Cork thought . . . well, he thought that it might be a good opportunity for Miss Sissy to make a new friend. And she does seem really fascinated by you, Beatrice," Posy ended weakly.

It was that darned whistle. She couldn't really blame Cork, though—all the wine in his wine shop wasn't enough to make that shrill whistle go away.

"*Does* she like me? The only thing I've heard her say to me is 'road hog.'" With friends like those . . .

"I think so. It's enough, you know. She really *doesn't* like Cork, and it's made his life with her very difficult." They both looked out the back window in time to see a wary squirrel creep up to Beatrice's backyard feeder. As it slunk by the corgi, he woke up with a yelp. Miss Sissy jumped in the hammock, reaching for the whistle and blowing it emphatically. Noo-noo barked louder, and the rest of the dogs in the town appeared to join in as Miss Sissy swung her head from side to side, peering suspiciously at the bushes.

"You're welcome to drop her by the Patchwork Cottage as soon as we open," said Posy in a hurry. "She mostly naps there all day in the chair, you know. Then you'll just have to pick her up at closing time. She's actually a wonderful cook—if you butter her up a little, she'll cook these fantastic meals."

Stiff upper lip, Beatrice reminded herself. This would be a good opportunity to practice Piper's mantra. Peace, calm, kindness.

Daytime wasn't the problem. It was definitely evening that presented more of a challenge. All the buttering up in the world hadn't budged Miss Sissy toward the kitchen or persuaded her to cook. Grumbling under her breath, Beatrice had decided to make them omelets. She still had some of the tomatoes and eggs that Meadow had brought her, a couple of green onions, and that lovely bacon from Bub's. Unfortunately, the pan had apparently gotten too hot and she'd forgotten to spray it before she put the eggs in. The underside of the omelet scorched.

Maybe Miss Sissy isn't very picky, mused Beatrice. She took some extra bits of the tomato and bacon filling and scooped it on the top, covering up some of the scorch marks. Miss Sissy crossed her arms as Beatrice set the plate in front of her. "Isn't edible!"

"Maybe not, but it's supper," said Beatrice, feeling cross. Beggars couldn't be choosers.

Miss Sissy clicked her tongue at her, finally motivated to cook. Beatrice had to admit that she'd never eaten a fluffier omelet. "How did you get the eggs so fluffy?" she grudgingly asked.

"You have to whip air into the eggs with a whisk." She ate a healthy amount. No old-lady appetite for her.

Posy hadn't seen fit to fill Beatrice in on the fact that Miss Sissy prowled the house at night. Beatrice lay in bed and sighed as she heard the old woman moving around the kitchen, fixing herself something to drink, then turning the television to a very high volume and cackling loudly at whatever she was watching. Beatrice pulled her pillow over her head and dozed for a little while.

She woke up again about an hour later and knew she wouldn't be able to roll over and fall back asleep again. She pulled on her navy blue robe, cinching the belt tightly around her waist. Girding my loins, she thought with a sigh. Time to face the indomitable Miss Sissy, which was never a pleasant concept, and even less so at three o'clock in the morning.

There was no sound from the television now. She guessed Miss Sissy had tired of the racket, although not of the images—there was still some sort of B movie playing with what appeared to be a lot of sweaty, shirtless men with machine guns looking grim and overacting. Beatrice noticed with irritation that Miss Sissy was bent over the collection of squares that Beatrice was working on. She wore a puzzled expression as she lovingly ran her hands over the blocks. Hearing a creaking floorboard, she jumped and popped the whistle in her mouth, but stopped when she saw Beatrice there.

"Your blocks are a mess," she said with a shrug.

"Yes," said Beatrice. "They are."

"The colors, though. The colors and the *ideas* are very good. Nice texture. Interesting detail. Well balanced." Miss Sissy nearly sounded sane when she talked about quilting.

"Too bad they won't work in a quilt." Beatrice sighed. It was frustrating not being able to bring an idea to fruition.

"These are for the *group* quilt? For the Village Quilters?" Miss Sissy frowned ferociously.

Beatrice waved her hand impatiently. "No. Just for

practice. I was going to make my own quilt and screw it all up to death before messing up someone else's quilt."

"You have a template?"

"I drew a template." Beatrice gestured to the stiff paper on her coffee table.

"Not enough seam allowances," said Miss Sissy in a gruff voice, studying the paper.

"It figures."

"Show me," said Miss Sissy, making a wild gesture toward Beatrice's fat quarters and notions.

"Show you?"

"How you cut things. How you piece them. What you're doing. Show me."

So Beatrice did. And with lots of clicking of her tongue and big sighs, Miss Sissy showed *her*. Showed her where to put pressure on the ruler so that she could cut her fabric in a straight line. How to measure a true quarter-inch seam. She showed her how to hand-piece, her old hands expertly guiding Beatrice's.

Beatrice had chosen something cheerful and comforting for her first quilt . . . something that, if it were good enough, could find a home in her cozy living room. Posy assured her that the snowball quilt pattern would be easy for a beginner, although it hadn't been until Miss Sissy jumped in. Beatrice had loved buying the different fabrics, though. She had lavender and navy florals, cherry colors with a lush green, periwinkle with a soft lime. Shopping had been the best part of all . . . until now.

Feeling excited, Beatrice asked more questions. Miss Sissy, eyes glowing, gave her tips on putting a quilt top together.

Not feeling in the least tired now, Beatrice picked up her blocks again with new enthusiasm. "So now we've got all the pieces for the block cut out. So if I put them like *this* . . ." And the next thing she knew, three hours had gone by. What was more, she felt revitalized instead of weary.

Chapter 12

The next day, Beatrice was on a full-fledged quilting marathon. Miss Sissy had shown a surprising degree of patience as a teacher. And quite a bit of skill—her block for the group quilt featured appliqués of several miniature quilts, showing their importance in her life.

Beatrice reached a turning point when she decided to let go of her perfectionism. She was used to appraising quilts and studying them as folk art; she shouldn't expect to create art herself when she really should just be in the beginning phase of learning how to work with different fabrics and patterns. As she gave herself permission to fail, she found that her creativity reached its peak. Even Miss Sissy decided to stay with her the next day—watching her with sharp eyes and jumping in impatiently from time to time to show her where she was going off course. When Posy called to tell her she'd bring her to the Patchwork Cottage, Miss Sissy turned her down flat.

In fact, it was one of the nicest days Beatrice had had

since moving to Dappled Hills. Miss Sissy took regular naps, and Beatrice even managed to fit in one (although she'd been trying to read *Whispers of Summer* again. She was finding a connection between her reading time and naptimes now).

The day passed in a very lazy way with a quiet companionship between the women. Miss Sissy helped her make supper, which was fine with Beatrice. Learning one thing at a time worked for her.

The next morning, Beatrice was reading the Dappled Hills wispy weekly paper when the doorbell rang. Noo-noo barked with alarm at the sudden sound. "It's all right, Noo-noo," said Beatrice, reaching down to pat the dog as she walked to the door.

She looked out and saw Daisy. Drat! The plants that Daisy had given her were flamboyantly perishing in her living room, a sunbeam illuminating the planter like a spotlight. Beatrice bolted across the room, flung a bag of batting over the pot, and hurried back to the door. She opened it, smiling as she brushed some Noo-noo fur off her pants and tried to catch her breath.

Miss Sissy, whose middle-of-the-night rambling had spurred her decision to go back to bed instead of going with Posy to the quilt shop, peered from the door of the spare bedroom, glowering at Daisy as she sailed into the living room. "Russians!" she spat.

Great. It looked like it was going to be one of Miss Sissy's demented days.

Daisy seemed to be completely ignoring Miss Sissy's

hissing. Beatrice felt a grudging admiration. Anyone who could blithely block out the old lady's mutterings and Noo-noo's continuing barking deserved kudos for composure.

"After the guild meeting, I was tied up with the Women's Auxiliary. Then yesterday I was bouncing from one meeting to another and didn't hear anything about your accident until late last night, when it was too late to call. Harrison had heard about it." She pursed her lips tightly together in disapproval, either at the failure of the Dappled Hills gossip network or at the attack. Then she said, "I'm completely shocked. Absolutely appalled."

It sounded like Daisy was out of pocket during the time she was attacked. At least, she was insinuating that she was. "I guess you heard, then, that it *wasn't* an accident." Daisy looked a little uncomfortable, as if the thought of an attack was of the utmost vulgarity.

"Maybe it was a warning?"

"Deceiver!" Miss Sissy injected inexplicably. Daisy rolled her eyes.

"I suppose it could have been a warning," said Beatrice. "Or it could have been that whomever I surprised in Miss Sissy's house was trying to leave without being detected and knocked me unconscious to make her escape."

Daisy looked even more uncomfortable at the *her*. "Why on earth would someone be in there in the first place?"

Beatrice grimaced. "Well, I rather stupidly mentioned at the guild meeting that I'd seen a cell phone in Miss Sissy's house. And Posy confirmed that we had forgotten to lock up the house. I suppose that whoever left the cell phone at Miss Sissy's house was her attacker and she went back to remove the evidence."

"I'm glad you're all right," said Daisy with a warm smile. "That's the important thing."

Beatrice said, "Actually, I think the important thing is to stop the person who is responsible for Judith's murder and the attacks on Miss Sissy and me. I've been trying to help the police get to the bottom of it all."

"You're working with the *police*?" It sounded as if Beatrice's invitation to join Daisy's various clubs might be rescinded.

"Not working *with* them. And they're completely unaware that I'm trying to figure it out. But I am. It's too important not to."

Daisy said in a musing voice, "Hmm. You might be right. You're probably aware that people are saying that it's an odd coincidence that all this violence seemed to start as soon as you came to town. I'm sure you'll be glad when the case is solved."

Beatrice felt cold. "People are blaming *me*? Why? They couldn't think that I had anything to do with it! I didn't even know Judith!"

"Villainy!" offered Miss Sissy.

"Oh, you know how these provincial people in villages can be—very tight with each other. And maybe a little superstitious." Daisy was carefully avoiding looking at Miss Sissy.

Beatrice put her hands on her hips. "Well, no one has mentioned anything to me about it. And the idea that someone would think I'm the kind of person who would move into a community and randomly start killing and attacking people is absurd. For heaven's sake, I was attacked, too!"

"Of course it is! I'm simply letting you know what you're up against, Beatrice—that's all," said Daisy in a soothing tone.

Beatrice was about to expand on the absurdity of it all when Daisy smoothly changed the subject. "Anyway, Beatrice, now that you've had some time to settle in to Dappled Hills a little bit," said Daisy, "I thought I'd check in with you."

Had she gotten settled in? "Check in about what?"

"Just to see how your quilting for the group quilt is coming along and if you needed any help. I thought you might want to visit a few of the groups I'm part of, too. You must have been much busier and active in Atlanta than here . . . I didn't want you to get bored with our little town."

Apparently, Beatrice's previous indiscretion of investigating a murder mystery had been forgiven if Daisy was bringing clubs back up again. "What kinds of groups are you part of?" asked Beatrice.

"Friends of the Library, the Dappled Hills Women's Auxiliary, Dappled Hills Garden Club, the historical society . . ."

"Have mercy," muttered Beatrice

". . . and, of course, I'm a member at the DAR—the

Daughters of the American Revolution, you know—but you're on your own if you want to attend meetings there. In the interest of time, I'm a sustaining member there instead of an active one."

For some reason, the talk of clubs seemed to rile up Miss Sissy even more. "Russians!" she bellowed again, and Noo-noo, who had finally quieted, started barking again in earnest.

Daisy finally acknowledged Miss Sissy's presence with a cold stare. "Anyway," she said, "if you're interested at all, I wanted to extend a personal invitation to you to visit one or more of these organizations with me. We're always looking for new members and help with our fund-raisers and community efforts. Since Harrison is a community leader, I feel it's really my duty to champion the rights of the less fortunate where I can."

This all sounded about as much fun as quilting.

"Speaking of fund-raising and community efforts," said Daisy quickly, "I really did want to check with you on your progress for Meadow's group quilt."

Beatrice felt a rising panic. She hadn't even decided on a theme for her block yet. "We've only just gotten the assignment, Daisy!"

"I know, but Meadow called me this morning and said that we needed to speed up production on it. Apparently, she's heard of a group-quilt show that's going to be in Asheville and she'd really like us to have an entry in it. So we're to finish up our blocks and then assemble the quilt. That was one of the reasons why I dropped by."

Daisy *sounded* like she was only trying to be helpful, but it sure seemed like she was looking for another opportunity to snicker at Beatrice's quilting. She watched in dismay as Daisy strode over to the Patchwork Cottage shopping bag containing the batting, bent down, picked up the bag and uncovered the crippled plants. Daisy stared down at her housewarming gift in horror. "The poor things!" she said.

Beatrice cleared her suddenly dry throat. "You know, Daisy, somehow I never really got the hang of gardening. In fact, I probably need the name of the yard guy that Harrison set you up with. I really did love your housewarming gift. So thoughtful. Sadly, though, it was doomed as soon as it was brought in this house. Its days were numbered."

Daisy pursed her lips. "So where is your block?"

This ignited Miss Sissy. "None of your business!" she bellowed. Noo-noo growled softly.

"The group block *is* part of my business, Miss Sissy! We're planning on auctioning that quilt off. Which means we need to ensure quality control." Daisy's glance darted around the room, looking for any evidence of quilting. "Besides, Beatrice might need my *help*, since she's new to quilting."

Miss Sissy rose to her full height of under five feet. "*I'm* helping her," she said with dignity. "That's all the help she needs."

Daisy's face acknowledged the truth in that statement and she picked up her car keys from the table where she'd laid them. "As long as you're getting some help," she grumbled. "Beatrice, I'll see you soon." Without so much as another glance at Miss Sissy, she was gone.

By evening, the steady rain that had started in the afternoon had turned into a downpour, which always served to make Beatrice feel sleepy. Around ten o'clock, she was about to call it a day when the doorbell rang. She hurried to the door, wondering who would be coming by at such an hour. Miss Sissy grabbed a brass candlestick and stealthily crept to the side of the door, holding it aloft. Beatrice peered out the side window and saw Meadow standing there. Of course. It would have to be Meadow. Beatrice unlocked the door quickly and opened it.

"Hello there!" said Meadow. Beatrice blinked at Meadow's somber expression—and the brightness of Meadow's yellow rain slicker that covered her from head to toe

"We're going to find Amber," she said in the way of someone outlining a mission.

Meadow had brought her van and Beatrice hurried out to it, rain pelting her as she ran. Miss Sissy demurred, looking out at the cold rain. Felicity was waiting in the front seat. "What's happened?" asked Beatrice with gasping breaths. "Has Amber disappeared?"

Felicity turned to look miserably at her. "I think so. I think she's on the lam."

Meadow made a tut-tutting noise. "She certainly isn't. She's *not* on the lam."

"Why," asked Beatrice, feeling the need to ask the reasonable question, "isn't *Ramsay* investigating this? Wouldn't it make more sense to use a police officer and his resources?"

"I don't want the police involved until I understand what's going on!" Felicity said in a loud voice. "All I know is that I haven't been able to reach Amber all day and haven't seen her at all. I tried to call her at home a little while ago and she didn't answer. So I called Piper on her cell phone to see if maybe Amber was out with her. But she wasn't; Piper was at supper with Ash." There was a faint accusatory note there.

Meadow said good-naturedly, "Well, of course Ash and Piper are out to supper. He's leaving for California tomorrow morning, early. Besides, *you* have Amber's cell phone, remember? So no wonder you haven't heard from her today."

"She should certainly be home by nine thirty at night, though. Where else would she be?" Felicity's voice rose shrilly in agitation.

"I guess we should just drive around for a bit?" asked Beatrice.

Meadow cleared her throat and said slowly, "I'm wondering if maybe we shouldn't try over near the Butlers' house."

Felicity frowned with confusion. Meadow added slowly, "I'm pretty sure tonight is Daisy's bridge night. I was just thinking . . ." She stopped with an embarrassed shrug as the car sped over to Daisy's house.

Sure enough, they saw Amber's small car driving in

their direction. Meadow flashed the van's lights several times, and Amber pulled over to the curb, parked, then ran over to the van and jumped into the back.

"What is it? Did something happen to Mother?" She pushed a blond strand of hair from her eyes as she saw Felicity there. "Mother? What's going on?"

Worry made Felicity furious, and she roared at Amber, "I should ask you the same thing! I didn't see or hear from you all day. Then I tried to call you at home a few minutes ago and you weren't home to answer. Now I've pulled my friends out of their beds on a night no animal would want to be out in, and we see you leaving Daisy's house. Why don't *you* tell *me* what's going on?"

Amber looked alarmed. Beatrice said quickly, "Amber, I think there's more to it than the fact that your mother was concerned about your safety. She's been worried sick that you murdered Judith. Your mother saw your car missing that night, and she knows how upset you were at the bee the night Judith was murdered. She's been thinking the worst."

Amber gave a huge sigh. "Mama, it's nothing. I *was* gone that night. But it's not what you're thinking. I wasn't outside in the park, murdering Judith. I haven't wanted to tell you because I know you wouldn't approve." She hesitated, then continued. "I've been seeing Dr. Butler. Meadow, I know you've got to be disappointed in me, too. That's what's been happening and that's why I've been acting sneaky. He called me after the bee and said that Daisy had gone out, and I went over for a little while. That's it."

Amber hugged her sobbing mother, then the inconsolable Meadow, who'd apparently found the scene very touching. "It's a good thing," said Amber, "that I don't get this upset about not being able to reach *you*, Mama. When you lost your cell phone, I could have been wondering if you were hurt, you know."

Beatrice's mind was whirling. So Daisy *hadn't* been at home the night that Judith was murdered. And what about Felicity's cell phone being missing? Miss Sissy had insisted that greed was the motive behind the murder. Felicity didn't seem a bit greedy to Beatrice, but she *was* financially strapped. She was bound and determined to move into Hampstead Columns, too. Determined enough to kill? The quilt was worth a good deal of money, and, with Judith out of the picture, Felicity might be able to persuade Judith's daughter to join her in selling their lots to the developer. Looking at Felicity, it was all hard to believe. But maybe her being so upset was simply a cover. And blaming her own child for a murder she'd committed? It could be that she'd somehow known that Amber had an alibi for Judith's murder.

But *did* Amber really? Yes, she'd been with the doctor that night. She might not have been at his house for very long, though. And it wasn't entirely certain exactly when the murder took place.

Beatrice said, "Posy was up late the night of Judith's murder and saw your car drive by, Felicity. I guess you must have been heading over to Amber's house." It sounded a little bit more like a question than a statement.

Felicity sighed. "I did. I did go past Amber's house. I'd told y'all before that I'd tried to call Amber and she didn't answer. I didn't give up there—I decided to go out and look for her, because I couldn't sleep for worrying. But when I didn't see her car there, I also drove by Judith's house. I thought that Amber might be over there, hashing things out with her. But I didn't see her car there, either. I parked in Judith's driveway, got out and rang the doorbell. She didn't answer, though." Felicity rubbed her forehead. "I guess she was at the park."

"Why did you go over there, Mama?" asked Amber, frowning. "You weren't going to give her that quilt, were you?"

"Don't sell me short, hon," said Felicity sharply. "I could tell how much she wanted that quilt and I was ready to make a deal with her. I was going offer to give her the quilt for free if she'd reconsider selling her property to the developer. It would have been worth it to me. But she wasn't home, so I couldn't ask her. I didn't want to say anything about it after Judith's murder, because I knew it would make me look suspicious, especially after our argument. But nothing happened."

Meadow said, "Felicity, it's a good thing *you* didn't end up getting murdered, wandering around that late at night with a killer on the loose. Did Amber hear what happened to Beatrice after the guild meeting?"

She hadn't. And her face was shocked as Meadow recounted, with as much melodrama as she could muster, Beatrice's scare from the day before.

"Absolutely terrifying," said Felicity somberly. "Amber, now I'm scared to death over you . . . You gave me your phone and you've been wandering around with a murderer on the loose and no way to call for help if you encountered him. I ended up finding mine this afternoon, so you need to have yours back in case you meet up with some attacker."

"You *found* it?"

Felicity looked shamefaced. "Actually, yes. Right before coming over here. I was in the driver's seat and noticed there was an odd lump under the floor mat. It was the phone."

"Well, thank goodness for that. At the very least, you could call for help if you came across whoever is behind these attacks."

"I hate to break this up," said Beatrice with a tight smile, "but I was actually about to climb into bed before Meadow came by. Long day of quilting," she said, ignoring the fact that Meadow was clapping her hands in delight.

Chapter 13

The next morning, Beatrice woke up much later than usual to the aroma of frying bacon and scrambled eggs. She climbed out of bed and padded into the kitchen. Miss Sissy was wielding a spatula with great authority. "Here! Put the bread in the toaster," she said, stirring the eggs.

After breakfast, they spent another quiet morning quilting. They sat in companionable silence most of the time, which was occasionally punctuated by Miss Sissy's grunts of approval as she checked Beatrice's work.

Sometime later, though, Miss Sissy grew restless. She put down the block she was working on. She wandered into the backyard and stared around for a minute before coming back in. She poured herself a glass of tea, but took only a couple of sips before abandoning it. Then she spotted Beatrice's key ring and grasped the keys in her arthritic hand. "Mind if I go for drive?" she asked gruffly.

Mind it? In *her* car, since Miss Sissy's old Lincoln

was still parked outside her house? When Miss Sissy's perception of what qualified as the road was so dramatically skewed? Her answer must have been written all over her face, because Miss Sissy scowled at her, dropping the keys to the counter with a clang and grouchily retreating to the back of the house.

Beatrice guessed their happy idyll was over and the old Miss Sissy was back. To her relief, though, she resurfaced later and asked to go to the Patchwork Cottage. Beatrice drove her there before heading back home for several more quiet hours.

By midafternoon, Beatrice realized that there probably wasn't anything much to cook for supper. And she felt like *she* wanted to cook the next meal. It was all very nice to be cooked for, but sometimes it was nice to show you actually *could* cook.

The weather was beautiful outside, so Beatrice set off on foot toward town. Puffy white clouds drifted across an impossibly blue sky. A playful breeze tickled Beatrice as she walked down the main street. Somewhere in the distance was the chug-chugging sound of someone's aging mower . . . the only sound she could hear besides the birds calling to each other. In Atlanta, the sounds of the city had blended into almost a white noise for Beatrice—so much so that she got to the point where she didn't even hear them anymore. But here, anything interrupting the peaceful quiet was remarkable.

Tweet!

The shrill bleat of a whistle and the various howling,

baying, and barking of dogs that followed made Beatrice's heart lurch in her chest. Finally realizing it must
be Miss Sissy and her whistle, Beatrice relaxed. She
wondered if Miss Sissy were turning into the boy who
cried wolf. If she really *did* need help, would anyone
listen if she blew her whistle? Or would they just figure
it was another false alarm? Miss Sissy was sort of like a
car alarm going off: when they happen enough times,
no one really pays attention to them.

"Beatrice?"

Her heart gave a happy thump this time instead of a
startled one, because the minister, Wyatt Thompson,
was there. He wore a rueful expression. "Do you mind
if I join you? I'm on my way over to the church. Are
you still speaking to me? I have a feeling most of the
town isn't."

"Why? Over Miss Sissy's whistle, you mean? Have
you become a social pariah, minister?"

He nodded with a sheepish smile. "I think so. I've
seen a few eye rolls and head shakes pointed in my
direction."

"But your *intention* was good. You were trying to
protect one of your flock. Or at least make her feel a
little more confident. You didn't know that she was going to turn into a whistle-blowing maniac. And it
worked, didn't it? Miss Sissy doesn't seem like she's
worried about being alone at all." In fact, Miss Sissy
didn't seem worried about *anything.* She was taking a
childish pleasure in scaring the pants off everyone in
town.

"Thanks," said Wyatt. He grimaced at another piercing tweet and series of barks. He quickly changed the subject as they walked along. "Have you settled into town? Gotten everything unpacked?"

"I think I've gotten most of the important things unpacked. I'm starting to think that if I haven't needed or looked for any of the things in the rest of the boxes, I might as well give them away to charity. I don't have enough space in the cottage to keep things that I really don't need."

"I'd love to take the boxes off your hands, if you find that there are things you don't need. There are a few Dappled Hills residents that could use some help—or else we can sell your things at the next yard sale and raise some money for different church activities."

"Makes sense to me. Obviously these are things I don't really need, after all."

"You were on my list of people to check in with today," Wyatt said as they walked along the quiet road.

"What? Oh, because of the attack. It's okay," she said with a shrug. "Thinking back on it, I really shouldn't have gone over there by myself. I guess I just didn't think there'd be somebody in there."

Wyatt shook his head slowly. "Who *would* think that? And you were in there trying to get some things together for Miss Sissy, right? That was thoughtful of you."

Beatrice's heart sang. She tried to keep it out of her voice as she said with careful calm, "I thought she might want her cell phone back."

Wyatt's forehead wrinkled. "Miss Sissy has a cell phone?"

"No, actually, she doesn't. But I'd seen one at her house—and it wasn't there when I went back. I think the person who attacked me was also the person who murdered Judith. She probably went back to get the phone."

"She?"

Beatrice nodded. "The murderer's almost certainly a woman—and most likely someone in the Village Quilters. At our guild meeting the afternoon I was attacked, I mentioned the cell phone. And Posy mentioned that she was worried she'd left Miss Sissy's door unlocked. Next thing I know, the cell phone is gone and I've got a nasty bump on my head."

"This," said Wyatt in a quiet voice, "is one of the most peaceful and beautiful places in the world. I'm so sorry you haven't had a chance to see that side of Dappled Hills since you moved here."

Without thinking, Beatrice reached out and put her hand on the minister's arm. He'd sounded so regretful that she really couldn't help it. "I know you love this town a lot. And I promise that I'm falling in love with it, too. I'm not holding the sins of one person against the whole town. I've never lived anywhere more beautiful or with such friendly people."

"That's a relief. I'd hate for you to have a negative first impression of the town. It really is a special place." He smiled that slow, spreading smile of his that made Beatrice feel warm.

"But I do feel like the sooner this murder is solved, the better it is for everybody in this community. Right now everyone is suspicious of everyone else," said Beatrice.

Wyatt said, "Exactly. I checked with Ramsay yesterday, and he said there hadn't been any breaks in the case yet. It's still early, though."

"Was there anything you saw that night, Wyatt? After you left the bee?"

"Actually, I spent a long time at the church after I greeted the quilters. Our church custodian wasn't available that night, so I stayed behind—working in the office—to lock up after everyone left."

"So, you were actually the *last* to leave. I thought you'd left right after the bee started. You must have been out around the time of Judith's murder, then. Did you happen to notice anything?"

"Well, I did see Meadow out near the park, but that's not exactly unusual. She's frequently on the hunt for Boris. One funny thing I saw," said Wyatt slowly, "was on the *other* side of the park, as I kept on driving. I saw Judith *leaving* the park."

"Leaving it? What time was it?"

"By this time, it must have been eleven thirty—pretty late."

As Wyatt made his departure and entered the church, Beatrice wondered over the new information. It was indeed perplexing. Had Judith finished up her walk, started heading home, then met up with someone who persuaded her to go back into the park? Was it Meadow? Had Judith left and then gone back to the park for something she'd forgotten?

When Beatrice returned home, she saw that Miss Sissy was taking a very thorough nap in the backyard hammock. It seemed like a good time to try out the tomato pie recipe. With a little salad on the side and some fresh watermelon, it would make a light supper for them.

This time Beatrice really focused on the recipe—and, luckily, the recipe was detailed—even down to squeezing some of the juice out of the tomato to keep the pie from being too soggy.

When the timer went off, Beatrice opened the oven door and looked hopefully inside. The pie was golden brown and perfect—not sunken at all.

There was no way even Miss Sissy could take exception to that pie, thought Beatrice as she sliced up the watermelon and rinsed some spinach for the salad. Things were definitely looking up. The quilting was starting to click. The cooking was coming along. Maybe she could even keep a houseplant alive now.

There was a thumping and a "Hello?" outside Beatrice's front door, and she peered out a little anxiously. Surely murderers don't announce themselves at the front door, she told herself sternly.

It was Meadow, trying to juggle a bag, a cake and a bowl and simultaneously reach out for Beatrice's doorbell,.

"Thank goodness you're here!" said Meadow a bit

breathlessly. "I guess I'd have had to go tripping back home, dropping everything as I went."

Meadow barreled in with her bags and laid everything down on the kitchen table. She saw the food and exclaimed loudly, hands on her hips, "Would you look at that! Isn't that the prettiest little pie you've ever laid your eyes on? I should have called ahead—it looks like you won't be needing my cake after all."

Beatrice said quickly, because Meadow was, she reminded herself, an extraordinary cook, "It's a tomato pie, so I still need a dessert."

"Perfect! I've got a bowl of salad, some homemade bread and a cake. It'll be the perfect meal."

Beatrice was so happy to see the food that she was just opening her mouth to invite Meadow to stay for a little while when Meadow plopped down on her sofa and put her feet up on the coffee table. "I'm so worn out!" she exclaimed. "For some reason, this group quilt has been the devil to keep straight."

"But we're all doing our own thing, aren't we?" She was doing *her* own thing, anyway.

"We are. But the idea is to keep *some* kind of continuity in there with the background and some of the patches. I guess it'll turn out fine. It seems like everybody has been calling me up to consult with me about it this time." Meadow shrugged. "Maybe everyone just is feeling a little scared with a killer running around— and they're wanting to connect a little more than usual. But enough of that. You look so intense, Beatrice! You

remind me of Ramsay when he's getting all interroga-
tional. What *is* it?"

"I was talking with Wyatt a little while ago . . ."

Meadow clapped her hands in delight and Beatrice
impatiently shook her head. "Meadow! We both happened to be walking into town at the same time."

"He's something special, though, isn't he? Those
eyes. That smile." Meadow beamed.

"*Anyway*, he mentioned that he had seen you, Meadow,
the night of Judith's murder. Very near the park."

"Ohhhh . . . that. Yes, I might have gone farther than
I thought looking for that naughty Boris. Always causing trouble. He took it into his head this morning to
pull all the clothes off the clothesline. They plopped
right into the mud. Now tell me: does your Noo-noo
ever do things like that?"

Noo-noo looked appalled at the very idea. Or maybe
she was just appalled by Meadow in general, and the
loudness of her. It seemed almost like Meadow was trying to change the subject. Meadow *did* have a disjointed
train of thought, but this seemed even worse than
usual. They looked absently through the back window.
A bee that was flying from one azalea bush to the next
took a sudden detour and lit on Miss Sissy, who leaped
up with alarm, nearly capsizing the hammock and
blowing her whistle. As if on cue, Meadow shoved herself up from the sofa. "Well, I've got to be going now.
Otherwise I'll start feeling guilty again that you're sad-
dled with Miss Sissy."

Miss Sissy pushed open the back door. The startling finale of her nap had evidently put her in a crabby mood.

"Hi there, Miss Sissy!" said Meadow cheerily.

She got a suspicious scowl in return. "It isn't time to turn in the quilt blocks!" said Miss Sissy in a defensive tone.

With determined patience, Meadow said, "No, ma'am! I'm just bringing some goodies for you to have alongside your supper."

Miss Sissy perked up a bit at the mention of supper.

"Meadow and I were discussing Judith's murder again," said Beatrice, hoping to catch Miss Sissy off guard.

Her wizened face darkened. "Liar! She's not part of the DAR!"

Meadow seemed to take this all in stride. "But, Miss Sissy, I never claimed to be a member of the Daughters of the American Revolution. My grandparents stowed away on a boat from Ireland."

Miss Sissy scowled.

"I think Miss Sissy was thinking about someone else," said Beatrice. She reached out for the old lady's hand. "Were you out the night that Judith died?" Miss Sissy looked startled. "I know you didn't have anything to do with it, but did you *see* or hear anything? The entire town was wandering around at the park after the quilting bee."

Miss Sissy's other hand gripped tightly at the whistle around her neck, as if she were hanging on for dear life.

Meadow said kindly, "Did you see Posy? I know Posy is a great friend of yours. I saw her, too, but it wasn't anything—I know she was out to check on her shop or something. Can you imagine Posy killing anyone? I sure can't."

A look of great relief passed over the old woman's face as she nodded.

"Did you notice anybody else?" pressed Beatrice.

Miss Sissy grunted. In a hard-to-hear voice, she said, "Georgia. I saw Georgia out, too. On her bicycle."

Really, no one in Dappled Hills seemed to sleep. Including Miss Sissy.

"What were *you* doing out that late?" asked Meadow, tilting her head curiously to one side. "Wasn't it a little late for you to be out?"

"Not for Miss Sissy," said Beatrice drily. The old lady was practically nocturnal. "I think you probably saw Georgia on her way home from dropping off a note on my front porch. She was worried that I was stirring up trouble because I told Felicity what her quilt was worth."

"Georgia doesn't like any trouble, that's for sure," said Meadow. "She's much more likely to steer clear of it or warn people off."

Miss Sissy looked even more relieved. Could Georgia have dropped a note by Judith's house, too, to make sure she wouldn't blab about Savannah? That little warning could have turned into something more . . .

Chapter 14

Beatrice seemed to have caught Miss Sissy's insomnia. The old woman was snoring emphatically from Beatrice's guest room as Beatrice lay awake and tried counting sheep, cows, chickens—whatever country creatures came to mind.

Finally, she got up for the day at four o'clock. The only *nice* thing about getting up that early was the peacefulness of it all. The birds were still sleeping, too. She worked on her new quilt block a little in the quiet.

She'd thought that Miss Sissy might have gotten up by five thirty and they might have had an early breakfast, but she was still determinedly asleep. The pots and pans were a disaster in the cabinet, so she didn't dare to try to pull one out. She could only imagine the clanging cacophony that would result.

Noo-noo had been watching her hopefully for some time, occasionally looking at her leash and collar with innocent brown eyes. Why not?

The air was crisp and foggy as Beatrice and Noo-noo set out on their walk, and it was still overwhelmingly quiet. The quiet after the constant white noise of omnipresent sound in Atlanta had been a hard adjustment, but it was growing on her now. And she found that it really wasn't as silent as she'd thought it was; there was the chirping and tweeting of birds, the breeze rustling the leaves and buzzing bees visiting flowers.

Noo-noo's ears lay back before popping back up as she trotted ahead at a brisk clip as though she'd seen or heard someone.

Coming out of the fog ahead was a small figure walking an equally small dog. Beatrice felt a little chill up her spine at the remarkable similarity between this morning and the one when she'd discovered Judith's body.

But despite the foreboding feeling, she couldn't really see anything but a gentle kindness as Posy joined her with a smile. Duchess, the beagle, happily greeted Noo-noo. Clearly, the *dogs* didn't act spooked, and dogs were always more intuitive than people were. She straightened up and sternly squashed her jitters.

"It's my fellow early riser!" exclaimed Posy. "I was just thinking yesterday that I should call you and set up an official walk. How nice to happen on you and Noo-noo this way!"

Beatrice smiled. Once again Posy had referred to an animal as if she were talking to a person. Noo-noo grinned at Posy with delight.

"I felt a little guilty that poor Noo-noo hadn't gone

out walking lately. Besides, I've been up forever—practically all night!"

Posy said, "You, too? I think I'm driving Cork a little crazy with my nocturnal wanderings. I'll do a little laundry, put away some dishes, type in some shop accounting, putter around the house. I do believe he even misses Miss Sissy—at least if she were there, then I'd have someone to sit up and quilt with in the middle of the night. This whole tragedy with Judith—it's been so sad. I don't think I've slept a full night since it all started." Her robin's-egg blue eyes were full of sad curiosity. "What kept you up last night, Beatrice?"

Beatrice took a deep breath as they walked slowly to the park, retracing their steps from that morning as if subconsciously drawn there.

Later, Posy came by Beatrice's house to pick up Miss Sissy and take her to the Patchwork Cottage. Beatrice spent a quiet day nursing a bit of a headache left over from her attack. Toward the end of the afternoon, she headed off to the Patchwork Cottage to shop for a little fabric and to take Miss Sissy back home. Meadow and Felicity were in the shop and Felicity, thankfully, seemed back to normal.

"I've got some great news to tell y'all!" she said, chin held high. "Amber, the clever girl, contacted an appraiser who specializes in quilts. He confirmed what Beatrice told us—that the quilt I've got is very rare and valuable and, he thought, in excellent condition!"

"That's great news, Felicity!" Meadow hugged her.

"He thought that, at auction, a collector would pay top dollar. I think it's going to bring in the extra money that I need as a rainy-day fund for Hampstead Columns!" She took a deep breath. "Not only that, but Judith's daughter decided to divest herself of her mom's house, too. The developer called her up and made her an offer she couldn't refuse. I was scared to mention it in case I jinxed it before. But the developer jumped on the deal, and now I'll have even more stashed in my savings. And it's perfect timing, because Hampstead Columns called me and said my name had just come up on the waiting list!"

Meadow's eyes grew misty. "I'm really going to miss you, Felicity. And what will become of the Village Quilters if both you and Amber leave the group?" She rummaged around in her patchwork pocketbook and consoled herself with a pack of crackers.

"I can still participate in some of the group quilts," said Felicity in a reasonable tone. "You can pop the kit in the mail to me and I can make a block. Lots of quilters are participating in guilds from long distance. Besides, Hampstead Columns isn't much of a drive. I'll be a frequent visitor."

A few minutes later, the shop bell rang and Daisy Butler came in.

Daisy meandered around some fat quarter displays, peering over at the sofas, absently rubbing the poison ivy rash on her arm. "I'm glad you're here, Daisy," said Posy warmly. "I'd just gotten some new fabric in off the truck this morning, and I thought of you as soon as I saw it." Daisy followed Posy behind the counter, where Posy dug in a cardboard packing box for the new fabric.

Beatrice couldn't keep her eyes off of Daisy's figure. Something just wasn't right there. She'd noticed something about Daisy, but now she couldn't put her finger on what it was she'd noticed.

"Do you smell something funny?" asked Meadow, wrinkling her nose.

"Hmm?" asked Felicity. She sniffed the air. "Oh, that's just calamine lotion. Remember? Daisy has poison ivy."

Calamine lotion. Beatrice's heart felt like it had skipped a couple of beats. That was the familiar smell that she hadn't been able to place the afternoon she'd been attacked.

A funny thing about Miss Sissy's house, thought Beatrice—it was almost surrounded by poison ivy. There were lots of other vines—thorny vines, Virginia creepers, wisteria, honeysuckle—but poison ivy was what was really taking over the front of her house. Thinking back, Beatrice recalled how Daisy made quite a point at the guild meeting that she'd gotten poison ivy in her own backyard. She made it an opportunity to brag about how Harrison set her up with a yard service. But Beatrice was sure that Daisy hadn't gotten her rash from her own immaculate yard.

A flood of other realizations hit her. Daisy's resemblance to Judith—could it have been *Daisy* that Wyatt had seen leaving the park the night Judith was mur-

dered? That placed Daisy at the scene of the crime,
even though she'd said at the dinner party that she'd
decided not to take a walk that night. And Miss Sissy
had such a strong reaction when Daisy dropped by to
check on Beatrice after the attack. She'd been more
riled up than usual, fussing about liars and deceivers—
and Russians. Did *Miss Sissy* know something about
Daisy?

Beatrice raised her eyes from Daisy's arm, feeling
like she wanted to think things through and maybe figure out what Miss Sissy had been getting at.

Daisy was already checking out. "Sorry I don't have
more time to shop your new fabrics, Posy, but I'm running late for my dentist appointment. I'll try to pop by
later this afternoon, but it'll probably be tomorrow.
Two fillings. My face will be a puffy mess." She quickly
left the shop.

"I should go, too," Beatrice announced. "Miss Sissy,
are you ready? Noo-noo needs a walk before he gets
fed, and I could use one, too."

"Could you?" asked Meadow doubtfully. "Somehow it seems like it would be a better idea to go home
and take a nap. Weren't you just saying you've had an
off-and-on headache?"

"I'm fine," Beatrice said firmly, picking up her pocketbook and pulling her keys out of the bag. "It'll be a
short walk."

Felicity looked sad. "I used to have a favorite walk.
Right off downtown here. The pathways are tidy, the
view is beautiful and my dogs could always handle the

walk, even when they got old. Now *I'm* too old to walk it. The incline is just a little too steep. But the rhododendrons are gorgeous there this time of year."

"Right off downtown?" asked Beatrice. "I've seen that turn but didn't know where it led. Noo-noo is probably getting tired of the park and the same old smells. Thanks for the tip, Felicity—I'll give the trail a try."

Meadow said, "Noo-noo will have a real smorgasbord of smells—deer, squirrels, foxes. Maybe the occasional bobcat. He'll be in olfactory heaven." Meadow's pocketbook suddenly started blaring a folk song. She pulled out her phone. "What? Not again! But I *did* make sure he didn't get out! He's probably out to nip over and visit with Beatrice, Ramsay. All right, all right." She hung up. "Beatrice, if you could, please keep an eye out for Boris. He seems to think you're buddies now. Ramsay went home for lunch—and didn't wait for me to make the tomato sandwiches!—and says that Boris is AWOL again. Heaven knows how long he's been out."

Probably the beast has broken into the house and is snarfing up all my food, thought Beatrice gloomily.

As soon as Beatrice and Miss Sissy walked in the door, Noo-noo grabbed her leash and ran circles around Beatrice, with the leash trailing behind her suggestively. Beatrice leaned down to rub her and she flopped over onto her back for a tummy scratch, leash still clamped in her teeth. "We'll have a little walk. You've had a rough time lately, haven't you? Boris wants to be friends with both of us, but I guess we're both a little standoffish. Aren't we?"

There was a tugging at her sleeve and she looked down a bit at Miss Sissy's wizened face. "I have something for you," she said gruffly, opening her hand and holding out her silver whistle with the red cord. "Wear this while you're gone. To keep you safe," she said in a tone that brooked no disagreement.

Beatrice took it from her gnarled fist. "Thanks, Miss Sissy." She opened her purse to drop it in, but Miss Sissy snatched the cord back. "No! Around your neck." Beatrice sighed and bent her head down obediently so that Miss Sissy could slip the cord around her neck. Miss Sissy emphatically nodded at the sight of the whistle in place, then wandered off into the back of the house again, presumably to take another nap.

She smiled. Miss Sissy couldn't have paid her a bigger compliment.

Beatrice decided to drive to the trail. Downtown and back was a walk in itself, and adding a mountain trail to it was more than Beatrice thought she should handle—especially after she'd gotten such a bump on the head recently. She laced up her walking shoes and she and Noo-noo headed out to the car.

As Noo-noo happily stuck her head out the car window, Beatrice thought again about Daisy. She could easily have been the person behind Miss Sissy's attack. And why would she have done it if she hadn't killed Judith? It wasn't as if Daisy was trying to protect anyone . . . All she really seemed to care about was herself and her status in Dappled Hills as the doctor's wife.

Daisy had probably lurked in the vines while looking for a way into Miss Sissy's house. The house wasn't exactly Fort Knox—there were probably all kinds of unlatched windows and unbolted doors. Miss Sissy was crazy, but she was clever. She'd never have let Daisy in if she thought she was any kind of a threat. Daisy likely had a scuffle with Miss Sissy and lost her cell phone in the process. Could the poison ivy be the plague of contagion that Miss Sissy had been babbling about?

Daisy had been misleading them all. Beatrice was convinced that *she* was the one who had persuaded Judith to dye her hair until it was similar to Daisy's own. Meadow clearly hadn't made the suggestion, despite what Daisy claimed. Daisy hadn't received the recent threatening letters that she said she'd gotten—Georgia said that she hadn't sent any letters to anyone but Beatrice for at least a year. Why would Daisy lie about something like that? The only reason that Beatrice could come up with was that she wanted to claim that *she* was the intended victim, not Judith.

Beatrice parked the car at the small graveled area at the base of the trail. Noo-noo jumped eagerly out of the car, and they started up the incline. The vegetation on the sides of the trail was gorgeous and lush, just as Felicity had said. She and Noo-noo seemed to be the only ones out on the trail. The way Noo-noo was bounding up the trail, it wouldn't be long before they were at the summit.

A quick rustling behind them from a tree alongside the path made Beatrice jump and Noo-noo spin around. *Daisy*. Beatrice's heart sank as she saw the spiteful expression on her face. The path was narrow, and Beatrice hugged closer to the rocky wall beside her, pulling away from the treachery of the jagged cliff on the other side.

Chapter 15

"You decided to go on your walk after all," said Daisy with a malicious grin. "Mind if I walk with you a little?" She gave a mocking chortle. "What's wrong, Beatrice? You're looking at me as if I had horns on my head."

Beatrice felt a chill run along her spine and hoped for a second that Noo-noo would suddenly turn into a vicious attack dog and save them both. She grimaced as the corgi flopped over on her back for a tummy rub. Daisy smirked.

"I'm guessing you're not here to check out Felicity's favorite trail," said Beatrice briskly. "Particularly wearing those ridiculous shoes." She raised her eyebrows to indicate the heels that Daisy was wearing. "So I suppose you realized at the Patchwork Cottage that I was on to you. You might be morally bankrupt, but you do seem to have a very healthy sense of self-preservation."

Daisy's eyes narrowed until they were mere slits. "What I don't understand is how you figured it out.

And why you figured it out at Posy's shop, of all places."

"That nasty rash of yours," said Beatrice, nodding at Daisy's arm. "You've been putting calamine lotion on it. Which is curious, really," said Beatrice with a sniff, "considering you're married to the good doctor. It's sort of an old-fashioned remedy, isn't it? And I finally was able to place that smell from the night I was attacked at Miss Sissy's house. Forgot your phone there, didn't you? You were probably wondering what had happened to it . . . until I mentioned that I'd seen one in Miss Sissy's house."

"But why," said Daisy, lazily stroking Noo-noo, "would you think that I would want to kill Judith? What possible good would it have done?"

Beatrice cleared her throat quietly. She had no desire to show this woman how shaken she was by her. She raised her chin a little. "You're living quite a lie, aren't you, Daisy? You've built your whole identity around being the doctor's wife. It's more than a status thing, although Miss Sissy had that part nailed. You *are* the doctor's wife—it's not just a *part* of who you are; it's *all* of what you are. You're using your status in town to be part of or run all these different clubs and organizations. It's given you a sense of importance and self-worth. When Amber started having an affair with your husband"—a look of distaste pulled the corners of Daisy's mouth down—"it threatened more than just your marriage. It threatened your whole identity."

"Why, then," asked Daisy in a quiet voice, "wouldn't

I have killed Amber? Why would I have killed Judith?" She sounded almost curious, as if she wanted to hear the answer.

"Because you didn't really mind who your husband slept with," said Beatrice. "That wasn't something that worried you. You knew your husband wasn't going to leave you for a girl like Amber. And, in fact, you were planning on 'helping' Amber move to a large city. Judith must have seen the two of them together, I'm guessing. And she wasn't the kind of person to let things go. At the quilting bee, she said something about you not being what you seemed. And she said that what you *were* was about to change. She knew something, all right. Maybe she saw Amber and your husband together one day. She knew your status was about to change. And, considering the fact that she'd tried blackmailing Meadow, I suppose she probably tried blackmailing you, too—unless she simply enjoyed holding it over your head."

Daisy's eyes were cold. "She was always jealous of me."

Noo-noo stirred restlessly at Beatrice's feet, apparently concerned over the angry tone of the conversation.

"You spent a little time thinking about how to get rid of her. Public humiliation wasn't something you'd tolerate. You set up the crime in advance, telling Judith she'd look great with red hair like yours. Then you followed her out to the park that night and took the opportunity to murder her. What did you use as a weapon? Something portable—maybe something you could keep in a handbag. A hammer?"

"A rubber mallet," said Daisy between gritted teeth.

Beatrice continued. "It must have seemed easy at first. But nothing is really as easy as it seems, is it? Miss Sissy was the first problem. Who'd have thought that she had any rational thoughts in her head at all, with all her crazy talk about Russians and *Little Orphan Annie* radio shows? But she did. Maybe her rational thoughts come and go and maybe they're overshadowed by craziness most of the time, but she still *can* make sense. She mentioned to Posy and me that she'd 'seen them kissing.' I'm thinking she must have seen Amber and your husband together. Maybe she saw you follow Judith out to the park that night. She even had a handle on your motive for murdering Judith: it was all about money and status. Without your husband, you'd lose your comfortable lifestyle and place in society. And you were desperate to hold on to them." Beatrice's disdainful tone made Noo-noo give small growling sounds under her breath. "What was on the papers you took from Miss Sissy's house? When I regained consciousness after you attacked me, they were gone."

Daisy gave her a scornful look. "Crazy ramblings. Her usual thing—wickedness, evil, trespasses. And my name all over the papers."

"Then I was the next problem," said Beatrice. "I was just getting settled in the town, was recently retired, and was looking for something to do. When I mentioned Miss Sissy's cell phone at the guild meeting, you obviously figured out what had happened to your phone and that you were going to have to go back for it. Would you have attacked me that day if I hadn't burst in on you? I'm thinking I wasn't enough of a threat to you at that point. Was I?"

"I guess you'll never know," answered Daisy coolly. "Since you had this *horrible*, tragic accident on your walk today." She lunged at Beatrice as if to hurl her over the side of the mountain.

Beatrice was ready for her, though. She reached around her neck, pulled out Miss Sissy's whistle and blew an extended, piercing blast that made Daisy cower. Noo-noo, after gaping at her mistress, started frantically barking. Beatrice ducked out of the way and grabbed on to Daisy's arms, grappling with her at the cliff's edge. Noo-noo continued barking and darted back and forth at Daisy's legs. Daisy's grip was stronger than it looked, and Beatrice helplessly felt herself being propelled toward the sheer rocky face of the mountainside.

A tremendous crashing noise through the bushes made Daisy freeze, her grip tightening on Beatrice's arms. And suddenly lunging toward them with a determined look on his face was Boris. With a deep-throated bark, he galloped at Daisy, hitting her in the side and making her release her hold on Beatrice. Daisy stumbled as the huge animal charged again at her. She took a lurching step to regain her balance, but tripped over Noo-noo and crashed backward onto the narrow path, hitting her head resoundingly on the rocky surface. Beatrice, shaking, fumbled for her phone to call for help.

She found that Daisy wasn't the only one who needed help getting off the mountain. Beatrice, who never liked asking for help, needed assistance to get back down the mountain. Her legs simply weren't going to support her descent. There she sat on the hard ground, knotty roots poking her in the behind while she was in danger of being licked to death by Boris and Noonoo.

The medical exam that she impatiently submitted to showed she was completely healthy. Fortunately, under the circumstances, the exam was *not* conducted by Dr. Butler, but by physicians in nearby Lenoir. Beatrice breathed a grateful sigh at finally being back in her bungalow, sinking into her overstuffed gingham sofa.

Since it was Dappled Hills, the news of Daisy's accident and arrest and Beatrice's close call rapidly spread through the village. Piper had rushed to her side while she was at the doctor's office and was now bustling around the small cottage, covering Beatrice with unwanted blankets, handing her cups of weak, undrinkable coffee (Piper was a tea drinker), and clucking over everything she did.

Meadow had unfortunately decided that her presence was vitally required—*unfortunately* because she seemed to be one of those people who when the waterworks turn on, you'd have to have a plumber to get them to stop. But she's really the only person in the cottage who can brew a decent cup of coffee, thought Beatrice with a sigh.

"One of the things that touches my heart about today," said Meadow in between sobs, "is that my own, dear Boris played a part. Dear Boris—such a treasure!" She broke down again.

Beatrice, who was ordinarily conflicted over Boris's intentions over *anything* (since food was a likely motive for most of the beast's actions), had to agree. If Boris hadn't been there . . . well, she didn't think she and little Noo-noo would have had a chance against Daisy.

She shivered again, leading Piper to put another cup of watery coffee in her hands. This one, thought Beatrice, peering closely at the brew, had actual grounds floating around it in.

There was a light tap at the door, and Piper peered out before opening up for an apologetic-looking Posy and a fiery-eyed Miss Sissy, who had a blue-veined hand gripping her wooden cane with ferocious strength. "I'm sorry," said Posy to Piper in her gentle voice. "Miss Sissy felt . . . very strongly, actually, that she needed to come by and talk to Beatrice."

This, thought Beatrice, I have to hear.

Miss Sissy flitted across the room. "Wickedness!"

Beatrice frowned. "Daisy, you mean?"

"Death comes to the wicked," said Miss Sissy, nodding smugly. "She lied. Lied!"

"You could," suggested Beatrice in what she thought was a very mild voice, considering, "have given us a hint. I might have been more careful around her." She stopped herself, though. Miss Sissy's lucidity was intermittent and her occasional flashes of brilliance were mostly overshadowed by confusion. She reached out to hug the old woman, who drew back in surprise before fiercely returning the hug. "Did you know, Miss Sissy, your whistle and Meadow's dog saved my life? I blew it just as hard as I could, and that's when Boris came crashing out of nowhere and helped distract Daisy enough for me to escape."

Beatrice watched in surprise as the old woman actually seemed to choke up. She quickly took charge of herself again, though, and said gruffly, "She always acted like she was from a rich family."

Beatrice looked to Posy for some translation. She cleared her throat. "Daisy mentioned in the past that she was from a wealthy Charleston family. Actually, that her family was among the first colonists to settle in the Charleston area. She even dropped once that she was a member, although an inactive one, of the DAR."

"Russians!" hissed Miss Sissy with delight. "They were all Russians! I knew her grandparents. They didn't live in Charleston; they lived only twenty miles from here. Russian immigrants who were dirt-poor. She cared about money because she'd never *had* money. Greedy." Miss Sissy beamed, showing off the fact that she'd forgotten to put her teeth in.

Meadow sobbed again, and Miss Sissy's thin mouth twisted downward in disapproval of the sound. "What a waste! Who cares about money, anyway? It's *life* that's important."

"Love of money is the root of all evil," crowed Miss Sissy.

Posy stood up quickly. "Beatrice is looking a little spent. Shall we continue our visit at the shop and let her have a rest?"

Beatrice watched with relief as they made their good-byes and left. Piper sank into a large armchair, kicked off her shoes and curled her legs underneath her. She started picking at some flaking polish on one nail, which Beatrice knew was a sign that she was anxious about something. "All right, spill it, Piper. You've got something on your mind, don't you?"

Piper blew out a breath. "Well, now that Meadow is gone, I guess I can talk about it. It's horrible timing, that's all, especially considering everything that happened today. But I can't *not* think about it, and if I don't say anything, then I'm going to feel guiltier than ever!"

Looking at Piper's flushed face, Beatrice saw a happy glow underneath the anxiety. It was a glow she'd been seeing for the past week, and she had a feeling she knew who was responsible for it. "Is it something about Ash, Piper?"

Piper looked relieved. "Yes, it sure is, Mama. He's gone back to California, as you know. He had to get back to work, since he'd been here on break. The thing is, well, I think our relationship might have a chance. *We* think the relationship might have a chance. I've got some money saved up, and I bought a plane ticket and made hotel reservations for myself to spend a week in California. Sightseeing and, well, and Ash-seeing, too."

She swallowed and looked at her mother with big eyes. "But with all that's happened . . ."

Beatrice reached out and squeezed Piper's hand. "It's all over now, though. Go on and head on your vacation. You don't have too long before school starts back, so fit it in while you can. I'm absolutely fine."

Piper smiled at Beatrice. "Can I get you something? Maybe some more coffee?"

God forbid. "No, sweetie. I'm fine."

"So, what do you think, Mama? I know it's all crazy. You retired from your dream job in Atlanta to move to a tiny town in the middle of nowhere with nothing to do but get attacked by murderers."

"Actually, only one murderer," demurred Beatrice.

"And I haven't been spending the time with you that I'd planned on! I've brought you to Dappled Hills and proceeded to ignore you," said Piper ruefully.

"I *did* follow you here to Dappled Hills. You were actually the *only* reason I moved here. But since moving here, I've found reasons of my own for wanting to stay. I've made my own connections—to the town, the people, the way of life . . . even the quilting."

Piper looked absolutely thunderstruck. "You don't mind the silly shows at the plaza, and the town's ridiculous newspaper and Bertha's Heart Attack on a Plate? And Meadow always bursting in on you with the huge beast?"

"Well, the huge beast helped save my life today. And I'm learning tolerance," said Beatrice with a bob of her head. "I'm even giving meditation a go—with varying degrees of success. But what I've found here in Dappled Hills is *me*. I've been buried in ancient artifacts for so long in Atlanta that I wasn't even sure I could be excavated. But I have been." She pulled a block from a tote bag next to the coffee table. "Take a look at my block for the group quilt."

Piper gently took the block from her mother. She smiled as she saw the block. It wasn't perfect, but it was a good start: the wooden WELCOME TO DAPPLED HILLS sign with its curlicue letters and honeysuckle vines in the background. Piper blinked at the words on the sign. "You managed to sew the words on."

"Oh, Miss Sissy helped me with the harder parts," said Beatrice. "But I did a lot of it."

Piper left for home, still looking a bit surprised, and Beatrice got up from her sofa and made a pot of real coffee—a little on the strong side. She settled back into the cushions with a steaming cup and pushed aside *Whispers of Summer*. Noo-noo gently snored at her feet as Beatrice studied with great concentration her new book, *Vibrant Quilting—Daring to Thrill*.

Two weeks later, Beatrice hosted her first guild meeting. It was a little on the cramped side in the cottage, but everyone assured her it was just *cozy*.

Meadow made her usual guild announcements, then beamed. "And now for my favorite part, y'all. Wait until you see the group quilt!" Meadow carefully pulled the quilt out of her bag.

Everyone stood up to take a look.

"It's lovely," sighed Georgia with her hands clasped to her chest.

Savannah frowned and opened her mouth as if to criticize some imperfections . . . then she relaxed. "It *is* lovely. And the most beautiful thing about it is that it's *not* perfect."

Beatrice smiled at her. "It just tells a story, like all good art should, about the people who made it." All the personalities were reflected there, from Savannah's sternness in the precise stitching to Meadow's happy-go-lucky serenity. All of the Village Quilters were represented here, stitched together on the quilt, although Daisy's block had never been collected. And Beatrice's own block was there, radiating homecoming and contentment.

Meadow said Beatrice's name, which brought her back to the present of the guild meeting. "Could you organize our quilt auction for us? Maybe we should even plan on having the auction in a bigger town, like Asheville."

The quilters chatted excitedly as Beatrice reflected that Meadow was again putting more things on her to-do list. But for some reason, Beatrice didn't mind as much. It was almost like she was back setting up shows for the museum again, and she quickly jotted down some ideas for staging the auction. Retirement, so far, hadn't been as quiet as envisioned . . . but it was a lot more interesting.

Quilting Tips

Snip off a small triangular section (½-inch or less) from the corners of fabrics before prewashing them. This will help keep the fabric edges from fraying and getting tangled. Washing the snipped fabric inside a pillowcase or lingerie bag will also help.

Put broken and bent needles into old childproof containers to keep your trash from being hazardous.

Old cereal and pizza boxes make handy templates.

Consider using parchment paper and freezer paper for paper piecing, fusible appliqué and tracing, and when designing patterns.

Place shelf liner under your rulers or templates to keep them stationary when working with your rotary cutter. Shelf liner is also handy to have next to your sewing machine to keep your sewing notions from falling on the floor. A nonmoisturizing bar of soap makes a great pin cushion. It also helps needles easily pass through fabric.

Recipes

Cheese Straws

½ lb. sharp Cheddar cheese, softened
½ lb. butter, softened
2½ cups flour
3 Tbsp. cold water
1 tsp. salt
¼ tsp. cayenne

Preheat oven to 350 degrees. Cream together cheese and butter. Add remaining ingredients, mixing until smooth. Roll mixture on a lightly floured surface until thin. Cut into narrow strips with a pastry wheel. Place strips on an ungreased cookie sheet. Bake at 350 for 8–10 minutes.

Pineapple Cheese Dip

16 oz. softened cream cheese
1 cup crushed pineapple
12–14 Maraschino cherries
1 round loaf Hawaiian bread

Process the cream cheese, pineapple, and cherries in a food processor. Scoop out the Hawaiian bread to form a bowl and place the dip inside the bowl to serve.

Ham Rolls

1 tray of 1-inch dinner rolls
½ lb. thinly sliced Swiss cheese
1 lb. shaved ham
1 stick of butter
1½ Tbsp. prepared mustard
1½ Tbsp. dried onion flakes
¾ Tbsp. poppy seeds
½ tsp. Worcestershire sauce

Preheat oven to 350 degrees. Cut the dinner rolls in half. Lay the ham and cheese on the bottom half, then cover with the top half of the rolls. Melt the butter and add the remaining ingredients to the butter. Pour the mixture on top of the rolls. Cover with foil and bake for 15 minutes at 350 degrees.

Cheese and Bacon Puffs

1 cup mayonnaise
½ cup grated Cheddar cheese
2 tsp. drained horseradish
1 Tbsp. sherry
½ cup cooked, crumbled bacon
30 crackers or 1 sleeve of party-sized bread slices

Combine all ingredients, spread on party-sized bread slices or crackers, and broil bread on a cookie sheet until golden brown and bubbling, about 5 minutes. Serve hot.

Read on for a sneak peek at the next
Southern Quilting Mystery by
Elizabeth Craig
Coming in early 2013 from Obsidian

"It's dying, Beatrice. A ghastly, gasping, tragic death. And it's up to us to *save* it!"

Beatrice studied her neighbor, Meadow Downey. To the casual eye, she didn't *look* fanatical. But, when it came to the Village Quilters guild, Meadow was nothing less than fanatic. "I hardly think the guild is dying, Meadow. We're just hitting a little membership snag. More like a hiccup, really. It's the kind of thing that happens in all groups from time to time."

"A membership *crisis*, you mean! We must infuse new life into the Village Quilters!" Meadow's eyes gleamed maniacally behind the red frames of her glasses.

"Clearly, you have someone in mind. Considering your unexpected visit and your carefully practiced speech," said Beatrice drily. "Who's your intended victim . . . erm . . . your candidate?"

"Jo Paxton would be the perfect new member," said Meadow, sitting up straight and confident in one of

Beatrice's armchairs. "She's smart, capable, reliable and a fabulous quilter. She also judges quilting competitions throughout the Southeast. She's ideal."

"Jo Paxton? Isn't she our postal carrier?" asked Beatrice.

"The very one," said Meadow, beaming.

"*Capable* and *reliable*? Those are words you'd use to describe her? Really?"

"You wouldn't?" asked Meadow, her sunny face clouding up just a little.

"Not if she's to be judged based on her mail-delivery aptitude, I wouldn't. I've never been able to figure out when exactly the mail is supposed to be in my mailbox. And frequently, I get your mail and you've been getting mine. I get Piper's mail almost every day." Not that her daughter really got anything but catalogs.

Now Meadow's broad face creased with a frown. "I can't imagine where you got this impression of Jo. She seems like an incredibly efficient carrier to me. Always prompt and accurate."

"If the mail in your mailbox is correctly addressed, that's because I'm switching them out. They've already been corrected by the time you get your mail. I've seen you checking your mail the next morning, when you're out getting your paper. It looks like you don't know when your mail is actually delivered. I promise it's frequently late," said Beatrice.

"Of course I know when the mail is delivered! And I'm very impressed that Jo delivers it so early in the morning. She must be at my house by five a.m. to get it in the box by the time I check it! And those Sunday deliveries . . . remarkable!"

Beatrice sat back and studied Meadow. She looked a little clueless, placidly sitting there with her mismatched clothes, red spectacles and a messy gray braid that fell to her waist. "Meadow, she *doesn't* deliver the mail at five in the morning. Or on Sundays. She delivers it the day *before*. You're just *checking* it that early in the morning. You're getting the mail from the previous day."

Meadow waved her hands dismissively. "I don't even care. All I ever get in the mail is bills, anyway. Besides the delivery problems, do you have any other issues with Jo?"

Beatrice thought carefully. "Well—"

"Exactly! Me either. That's why she's going to be such a great member of the group. I've gone ahead and asked her and she said she'd love to join up with us!"

Beatrice gritted her teeth. "Then why did you ask me about it, if you'd already invited Jo to join the Village Quilters?"

"I needed to be validated. We all need validation, Beatrice."

"But . . . isn't she in another quilting guild? I remember her being with another group at that last quilting bee."

"She *was* with the Cut-Ups, but she had a misunderstanding with them, so she ended up leaving the group. Or maybe they asked her to leave. Anyway, she's free to join our guild," said Meadow.

"That should be a red flag right there. Why was she asked to leave? Who did she upset? Why would we want someone like that in our group?"

"To make life interesting, of course!" Meadow slapped her hands on her thighs to loudly emphasize her point and her huge beast, Boris, sprang up and started excitedly galloping around Beatrice's sofa.

Beatrice's head hurt. Her cottage living room was tiny enough without Meadow's larger-than-life presence. The fact that Meadow brought Boris along for her breakfast-time visit didn't help matters, either. Beatrice's corgi, Noo-noo, looked on with concern. Meadow claimed that Boris was a mixture of Great Dane, Newfoundland . . . and corgi. If there *was* any corgi in Boris, it had gotten the short end of the genetic stick. And Noo-noo certainly didn't see evidence of it at all.

"Beatrice, I don't think it was any major disagreement. It was probably just a matter of creative differences. As I mentioned, Jo is a quilt show judge, too, and seems to be thought very highly of. She probably just wanted the guild to be more competitive or something."

"Is that the direction that *we* want to go in, though? Is that what she wants for the Village Quilters? Most of our quilters are only quilting for the sheer love of it." Beatrice absently rubbed Boris's massive head as he laid it in her lap. For a moment she thought the beast might start purring.

Meadow shrugged. "We could probably handle a

little more competition, Beatrice. I don't see it as a bad thing. Even you said that we could kick it up a notch. Remember? You have ideas for some interesting designs that might help us in juried shows."

"I do have some design ideas. But I was thinking we'd start out really slow with submitting our quilts for juried shows. Otherwise we could burn out—then it's not fun anymore," said Beatrice.

But Meadow had that stubborn look now. There was no getting around her when she dug her heels in. For some reason she'd gotten a real bee in her bonnet with this membership drive. "I guess including Jo in the group is fine, Meadow," said Beatrice with a sigh. "After all, I don't really know the woman. Maybe she'll grow on me . . . It's not fair of me to judge her solely on her mail-delivery capability."

Meadow beamed. "It'll work out great. You'll see. And I happen to know that Jo mentioned dropping by the Patchwork Cottage right before lunch today for some fat quarters," said Meadow, reaching out to rub Boris. "It would give you a chance to know her better before the first guild meeting. I do want it to go off without a hitch. Can you help me make the meeting go smoothly?"

"Okay. I'll see what I can do during the guild meeting." Beatrice rubbed her eyes. "What time will she be at the shop?"

"She said she'd be there at eleven, so let's meet then. I think you'll really love Jo, once you get to know her!"

* * *

Apparently, every quilter in Dappled Hills had needed quilting supplies at once because the Patchwork Cottage was bustling with shoppers. Beatrice walked into the welcoming environment of the quilt shop.

The Patchwork Cottage, even full of quilters, was a peaceful oasis. Posy always played soft music in the background, frequently featuring local musicians. Visually, it was a feast for the eyes with bolts of fabric and beautiful quilts on display everywhere—draped over antique washstands and an old sewing machine, and hanging on the walls and ceiling to make the space as cozy and welcoming and homey as possible. Posy had also stocked the shop with every imaginable type of notion.

Jo was there, all right. And she was already actively engaged in what looked like an argument with Karen Taylor—a young and very competitive quilter. Wasn't Karen in the Cut-Ups guild? No wonder Jo needed to find another guild. Karen, arms crossed and fire in her eyes, looked as if she might have single-handedly thrown Jo out herself.

"All I'm saying," said Jo, wagging her finger at Karen, "is that you might want to reconsider that pattern combination. It's tacky."

Posy, the gentle and kindhearted shop owner, looked on anxiously.

Karen's eyes narrowed. "Jo, you don't even know what I'm working on. It's an experimental quilt. I'm combining patterns and techniques to—"

"I don't need to know what you're working on to

know it's going to look hideous," said Jo, hands on her hips. "Considering I'm probably going to end up judging it, I thought you'd want the heads-up."

Karen snorted. "I doubt you'll judge it. People talk, Jo, and you have a tendency to stir the pot wherever you judge. Making trouble won't win you friends and it sure won't get you invited to judge quilt shows."

"Then why do I already have three shows on my calendar?" asked Jo.

Karen's response was to turn her back on Jo to closely study Posy's new selection of fat quarters. Jo slapped down her purchases by the cash register and fumed as Posy fumbled through the checkout. Beatrice muttered to Meadow, "This isn't promising. I thought you said I'd *like* Jo once I got to know her."

Meadow shrugged. "Everyone's entitled to a bad day, Beatrice." She squinted as the bell on the shop door rang, pushing her red glasses higher on her nose. "Uh-oh. This isn't going to make things better. It's Opal Woosley. Now, just keep in mind, Beatrice, that these are just a couple of people who don't coexist well. Everyone else just *loves* Jo! Really!"

Opal was an elfish woman with a sharp chin and frizzy brown hair that made her look like she had a fuzzy halo. Her genial expression transformed when she saw Jo. Jo's did, too, and became even grouchier.

"Why the long face, Jo?" The little woman was fairly bristling. "Disappointed that there are no small dogs for you to mow over?"

Jo didn't deign to look at her. Instead, she grabbed

her bag of supplies and shouldered her way through the gawking customers and out the shop's door.

Opal burst into tears and several of the customers patted her as Posy hurried around the sales counter to give her a hug.

Beatrice muttered to Meadow, "Sorry, Meadow. I was wrong. Jo's obviously the perfect choice for our guild."

"So she's had a couple of misunderstandings," said Meadow with a shrug. "Haven't we all?"

Beatrice could see Jo stomping across the narrow main street. She raised her eyebrows when she saw a couple of different women scurry to the opposite side of the street when they caught sight of Jo. Clearly other members of the Jo Paxton fan club.

Beatrice turned back around to listen to Opal, who was still quivering with indignation. "I don't know how she dares to show her face around town after what she's done!"

Beatrice raised a questioning eyebrow at Meadow, who shook her head, making her long braid bob around. "Too long a story," she whispered. "I'll tell you later."